THE
BULLY

WALL STREET JOURNAL & USA TODAY BESTSELLING AUTHOR

DEVNEY PERRY

THE BULLY

ISBN: 978-1-957376-00-4

Editing & Proofreading:

Marion Archer, Making Manuscripts

www.makingmanuscripts.com

Julie Deaton, Deaton Author Services

www.facebook.com/jdproofs

Karen Lawson, The Proof is in the Reading

Judy Zweifel, Judy's Proofreading

www.judysproofreading.com

Cover:

Sarah Hansen © Okay Creations

www.okaycreations.com

OTHER TITLES

Calamity Montana Series

The Bribe

The Bluff

The Brazen

The Bully

The Brawl

The Brood

The Edens Series

Christmas in Quincy - Prequel

Indigo Ridge

Juniper Hill

Garnet Flats

Jasper Vale

Crimson River

Sable Peak

Treasure State Wildcats Series

Coach

Blitz

Clifton Forge Series

Steel King

Riven Knight

Stone Princess

Noble Prince

Fallen Jester

Tin Queen

Jamison Valley Series

The Coppersmith Farmhouse

The Clover Chapel

The Lucky Heart

The Outpost

The Bitterroot Inn

The Candle Palace

Maysen Jar Series

The Birthday List

Letters to Molly

The Dandelion Diary

A Little Too Wild

PROLOGUE

CAL

THE NEW GUY on SportsCenter was annoying as fuck.

I grumbled at the screen, the remote clutched in my hand, as he attempted to crack jokes with the other announcer. "Can we just get to the leading story?" *Me.*

My retirement had been breaking news today, but for the most part, I'd avoided the media. Maybe because I still wasn't sure if I'd made the right decision. Maybe because if I didn't hear it reported on ESPN, then it wasn't real.

"All right, let's get to the news." The camera zeroed in on the new guy and in the upper left corner of the screen, there was my face. "Cal Stark is leaving the NFL as a champion. Big announcement today from the Titans. Three weeks after winning his second Super Bowl with the franchise, the star quarterback announced his retirement, ending his ten-year career with Tennessee."

The camera swung to the other announcer. "Stark has made quite the reputation for himself in the past decade, not only on the field but often with his, uh . . . colorful sideline and post-game antics."

The new guy snickered when the screen cut his way again. "Colorful is one way to put it."

Dickhead.

The other announcer came on screen again and started reciting my stats, but the numbers—passing yards, touchdowns throws, sack percentage—faded to a murmur behind the rush of blood in my ears.

Retired.

I was retired.

I'd quit a winner before injury or age could taint my career. But without football, what the hell was I going to do with my life?

No idea. But I wasn't staying in Nashville, and I wasn't moving home to Denver either.

My phone rang on the coffee table. The damn thing had been ringing all day since my announcement had hit the wire. I'd declined a dozen calls from my agent. Five from my manager. Two from my mother. And a handful from reporters.

Pierce's name flashed on the screen.

I didn't want to talk to anyone but I'd make an exception for my friend. "Hey."

"How are you doing?"

"Truth?" My voice cracked. "Not great."

"Give it time to sink in."

"Yeah," I muttered. "What's new with you? How are Kerrigan and Elias?"

"Everyone's great. Kerr had a checkup today. She's

healthy. The baby's healthy. Elias is ready to be a big brother."

"Good. That's good. I'm excited for you guys."

"Have you given any thought to Calamity?" Since Pierce had moved to Montana, he'd been pushing for me to consider his small town after my retirement.

So far, I'd resisted because the retirement concept hadn't been real, just an idea shared with him and only him. Pierce had been my best friend since high school, and I'd told him about retiring before I'd told my agent and my manager. But as of today, the entire world knew I was done with football.

Retired.

But retirement in Calamity? Sure, it would be great to be closer to Pierce. His family was my family. I'd walk through fire for him and take a bullet for his kid. And today, when my entire world had turned upside down, he was the friend—my only friend—who'd called.

Maybe Calamity was the obvious choice, except unlike me, Pierce had other friends. And he'd already convinced *her* to move there.

Nellie.

The woman who lived to toss those *colorful antics* in my face as retribution for the wrongs I'd done as a teenaged bully. She'd be moving in the spring to work at Pierce's new office. Living that close to Nellie was destined for disaster. But where else was I going to go?

"I'll think about it," I said.

Calamity, Montana.

Could it be my next play?

I didn't hate the idea.

CHAPTER ONE

CAL

"WELCOME HOME." Pierce parked in a space on First Street and clapped me on the shoulder.

"Thanks." I grinned and hopped out of his SUV, breathing in the clean Montana air.

The sidewalks were teeming with tourists out exploring and shopping. Red, white and blue flags decorated store-fronts and lampposts for Memorial Day weekend. Nearly every parking space was taken, and traffic rolled at a leisurely pace on the street.

I'd visited Calamity a few times since Pierce had moved here, but we'd usually escape to his cabin in the mountains. Those vacations hadn't been about the town itself. Today was different. Today, I captured every detail of my new hometown.

The buildings along First had a rustic charm. The grocery store was shaped like a barn, complete with a gable roof and crimson paint. Most of the storefronts had square faces sided with graying barnwood. Others were built from brick, the red blocks faded from decades beneath the sun.

Yeah, this would work. This town was where I'd play the next quarter in my retirement game.

"Sure you don't want to stay with us?" Pierce asked as he joined me on the sidewalk.

"Nah. You guys have enough going on. You don't need a houseguest."

"No, but I do have a guesthouse."

I chuckled. "If the motel is a bust, then I'll take you up on it."

The last thing I wanted was to wear out my welcome before I even had a Montana address. Besides, hotel rooms had become a constant over the years. Before games. After games. I'd spent countless nights sleeping on borrowed pillows.

"Kerrigan's on her way to meet us," Pierce said. "She took Elias to the park while we were on the road."

"'Kay." I did another sweep of downtown, capturing names of stores and restaurants.

Pierce had picked me up from the airport in Bozeman earlier, and we'd spent the two-hour trip to Calamity catching up. Next time, I'd have my charter fly me directly here like I had on my other trips, but I'd wanted to scope out the larger airport today and get a feel for the surrounding area.

If I was going to live here, I wanted to recognize streets and neighborhoods. I wanted to find the best spot for breakfast and join Kerrigan's fitness studio. I turned around and faced The Refinery. Kerrigan had designed it with a modern vibe, a hint of new in this old town with large, gleaming windows that overlooked the street.

"I'm going to pop in to The Refinery. Grab a class schedule," I told Pierce.

He nodded. "I'll wait out here."

I weaved past people and ducked inside the studio, dragging in the scent of eucalyptus. This past year, my lower back had been bothering me, and my trainer had recommended yoga. According to Pierce, The Refinery was the only place in town with classes, so I'd be their newest member.

"Hi." The receptionist greeted me with a smile. "Can I help you?"

"Just looking." I scanned the space, taking in the mirrors on the longest wall and the metal cage jammed with exercise balls. I'd spent a good chunk of my life in gyms, and while this one was smaller than most, it was clean and airy. Perfect for a weekly yoga class. "Do you have a schedule?"

"Sure." She plucked a business card from a holder on the counter, handing it over. "If you scan that with your phone, it will take you to the updated schedule on our website."

"Thanks." I tucked the card away, took one last look around the space, then walked outside, ready to rejoin my friends.

But my footsteps halted on the sidewalk.

Kerrigan stood beside Pierce. Her pregnant belly stretched her sundress. Next to her was Elias's empty stroller. The two-year-old bounced around his parents' feet as Pierce and Kerrigan crowded over a phone.

Neither of them noticed me as they smiled at the screen. And neither did the other woman in their huddle.

Nellie.

Damn. She was the one person I'd hoped to avoid for a while. Either karma was a bitch or Calamity was just that small because not five minutes into my life here and there she was.

My nemesis since high school. The perpetual thorn in my side. The woman who could crawl beneath my skin with a single, contemptuous word.

The most infuriatingly beautiful woman in the world.

Kerrigan laughed at whatever it was they were watching on the phone.

Elias wrapped his arms around her leg. "Mommy, where's Unka Cal?"

"Um . . ." She shook her head, glancing away from the screen and straight to Nellie.

"Uncle *Cal*?" Nellie's smile disappeared. "Please tell me he's in Tennessee where he belongs."

And just like that, our familiar game kicked off again. I unglued my feet and strode their way. "Oh, look. It's my favorite bottle blonde."

Nellie's face turned to ice as she faced me. "Well, if there's anyone in the world who should understand fake, it's you. Fake it till you make it. That's like the model for your career, right? Oh, sorry. Former career. I heard you got fired. Ouch."

This woman. "I was a free agent and retired."

"Sure," she deadpanned.

"Can you two save it for another day?" Pierce asked. "We need to celebrate my wife."

Celebrating? What were we celebrating?

Before I could ask, Elias raced my way. "Unka Cal!"

I picked him up and tickled his side, letting the sound of his giggles soothe any worries that this move was a mistake. This kid, with his mop of dark, wavy hair, had a piece of my heart. "Hey, buddy."

"How about we all go to the brew—" A stream of water trickled down Kerrigan's leg as I settled Elias on my side.

"What the fuck is that?" I asked, eyes locked on the growing puddle. *Gross.*

"Language," Kerrigan snapped. "And that would be my water breaking."

For a second, no one moved. Then Pierce flew into action, taking her arm and steering her to his SUV. "Nellie—"

"I've got Elias," she said. "We'll walk to my place."

"He hasn't had lunch," Kerrigan hollered as Pierce helped her into the passenger seat.

Oh, shit. This was happening. She was having a baby. And someone needed to watch Elias.

"We've got him," I called.

The color drained from Kerrigan's face. Contraction, maybe? Or maybe she didn't trust me to babysit. I'd never babysat before but I could keep Elias alive for a few hours. How long did it take to have a baby?

"Maybe you should just let Nel—" Pierce closed the door on Kerrigan before she could finish her sentence.

"I've got him," Nellie called loud enough for them to hear.

Pierce gave her a nod, then climbed behind the wheel. He waited for a break in traffic, then reversed out of his spot and tore through town.

Elias clung to my shoulders, tightening his arms around my neck. "Where dit Mommy go?"

"It's okay." I patted his leg. "Your sister is coming. Cool, right?"

The scared look on his face broke my heart.

"How about we have some fun?" Nellie asked, stealing him from my arms. "We'll go to my house and play games and get snacks. Okay?"

He nodded as she kissed his cheek. Then she settled him into the stroller, unlocked the brake and took off for the end of the block, leaving me behind.

"Wait up." I jogged to catch them.

"What are you doing?" she asked as I fell into step beside her.

"Babysitting."

"No." She stopped walking and held up a hand. "You're not coming to my house."

"Oh, I'm coming." I'd be damned if I let Nellie come to the rescue now that I lived here. Pierce was my best friend. If he needed someone to watch his son while his wife birthed their baby girl, it would be me.

"Absolutely not." The color rose in her cheeks. Her soft lips pursed. Those sparkling green eyes narrowed as she stood taller.

God, she was gorgeous when she was angry. Maybe that was why I'd always loved making her mad.

"Lead the way, Blondie."

———

SNAP. *Snap. Snap.*

I'd snapped my fingers more times in the past three hours than I had in a year. "What the fuck is taking so long?"

"For the last time. Stop. Cursing." Nellie's nostrils flared from her stool beside Elias at the island. She lifted her hands, tickling his cheeks before cupping her palms over his ears. "If you keep saying *f-u-c-k*, he will too."

"No, he won't." Okay, maybe he would.

Elias was two and repeated a lot of shit. Like the word shit, which I'd slipped and muttered twenty minutes ago.

Nellie let go of his ears, smiling down at the boy. "Should we put blue on the picture next?"

"Yeah." Elias wrapped a fist around the pen she handed him. The moment he began scribbling, his eyes narrowed in concentration, his tongue poked out from the corner of his mouth.

"Good job." Nellie gave him her undivided attention and had since the moment we'd walked through her front door.

She'd made him a grilled cheese sandwich for lunch. She'd played hide and seek for what had felt like an eternity. She'd turned three plastic storage containers and two wooden spoons into his own personal drum set. She'd even scrounged up enough different colored pens and pencils to make him an art set.

Meanwhile, I was an afterthought. An annoyance.

With Nellie, well . . . our history was complicated at best.

Over the years we'd learned to avoid each other. Somehow we'd have to figure out how to do that in this small town. I had my sights set on living here and giving up on goals wasn't exactly my style.

The sound of children playing echoed down the quaint,

neighborhood streets. A minivan rolled by with a *Baby On Board* sign in the rear window. There'd be a parade along First Street on Monday for Memorial Day.

It was so . . . rural. Different than Nashville or Denver. And this small Montana town was now my home.

Or it would be.

Before Kerrigan had gone into labor, Pierce and I had talked about my plans to move here. They were loose, at best. Buy some land. Build a house. Find something to fill the time I'd once dedicated to football.

Today, it was babysitting. Tomorrow was a mystery.

When was the last time I'd looked into the future and not seen a football in my hand? Ten years? Twenty? Longer? I'd been playing since first grade. Who was Cal Stark without the game?

This wasn't the time for those questions, so I shoved them aside. There were other things to fixate on at the moment, like why hadn't we heard from Pierce. Was Kerrigan okay? Was the baby?

I paced the length of Nellie's kitchen, my footsteps a steady beat on the rich hardwood floors. We'd been in here so long that I'd memorized the space, from the glass-door cabinets to the wooden island to the teal backsplash.

It was charming and homey. "This is the smallest kitchen I've ever seen."

"Then leave." Nellie seethed. "You're not needed."

Story of my damn life. Unless I was on the football field, I was not needed. Especially where Nellie was concerned.

Snap. Snap. Snap.

"Cal," Nellie barked.

"What?"

"Stop. Snapping."

I shot her a scowl but shook my fingers loose.

The snap was a habit I'd developed years ago. The first time I remembered doing it had been at a high school football game my junior year. There'd been scouts in the bleachers. The stadium lights had been shining on me, expecting greatness.

My nerves had started to show and, according to my father, a decent quarterback couldn't have shaking hands. So I'd snapped my fingers three times before every play, and somehow, it had sharpened my focus. I'd been doing it ever since.

"How long does it take to have a baby?"

"A while," she muttered. "Listen . . . we're fine here. You can go."

"No." I cracked my neck.

"Cal!" Nellie winced at her own volume.

Elias dropped his pen.

"Sorry, buddy." She gave him a soft smile and picked up a red Sharpie. "How about red?"

"Yeah." He took it and went to town on his piece of paper.

She closed her eyes and drew in a deep breath, like she was trying to suck patience from the air. "Go. Away. Cal. The cursing and pacing and snapping and cracking of your neck. I don't want Elias to see me strangle you today. Just go away."

"No, thanks, sugar."

"Don't call me sugar."

I planted my hands on the island. "Seriously, what's taking so long?"

"It's only been three hours. It's going to take a while."

"Like how long?"

"I don't know." She tossed up her hands. "Kerrigan could be in labor for hours. And even then, they'll keep her and the baby at the hospital overnight. So would you chill? Once they get settled, Pierce will call us."

"Fine," I mumbled, walking to the kitchen window. My thumb and middle finger touched, ready to snap, but I stopped myself as Nellie cleared her throat.

"Should we take a break from coloring?" she asked Elias. "We could go play outside."

"Yay!" He catapulted off the stool, stumbling as he landed, but he recovered quickly and beat it out of the kitchen.

I hurried to follow as he streaked into the living room.

Nellie rushed to catch him too, and as we both passed through the arched opening, her arm brushed mine.

My feet stopped instantly as sparks shot up my arm. Touching Nellie was as dangerous as catching a live grenade.

She'd felt that electric jolt too. Sometimes it made her melt. Others, like today, it earned me a snarl. "Why are you here?"

"In your house? Or Calamity?"

"Both." She navigated the maze of boxes, making it to the door just as Elias tugged it open. Then she whisked him outside and left me behind.

Why was I here?

Because I didn't have any other place to go.

Maybe I could have pushed for a few more years in the league, but my contract with Tennessee had expired. I'd helped win them two Super Bowl championships but the general manager had wanted someone younger. Someone cheaper.

Instead of renewing my 39-million-dollar-per-year contract, the second highest in the league, they'd let me walk. Their first-round draft pick was a hotshot quarterback from Michigan.

I could have gone to another team, but another team meant new coaches, new players and new bullshit. More press and more politics for less pay. My agent had warned me that no GM would likely match my former contract given my age, even if my name was Cal Stark.

At thirty-three, I still had years of play left in my bones. I loved football. But I was just so damn tired of the bullshit.

I had enough money to last ten lifetimes, and though I already missed the game, it had been time to walk away. And Calamity sounded like a decent place to start fresh.

"Unka Cal!" Elias waved as I stepped outside. "Watch me."

"I'm watching, bud."

He furrowed his brows and raced across Nellie's lawn, his legs pumping as fast as he could muster.

I jogged to catch him, sweeping him up and tossing him in the air. "When did you get so fast?"

His giggle was the reason I was here. I loved this kid. I was his *Unka Cal*. Elias, Pierce and Kerrigan were family.

Mom was in Denver, living in the same house with the same, ruthless bastard. Until she divorced Dad, there would always be tension between us. An unspoken choice —him or me. She always picked him. So I always picked me.

And if I was giving up football, I might as well live close

to my best friend. He was the only person who didn't expect anything from me.

Not a performance. Not a handout. Not an attitude.

"Nellieeeee." Elias squirmed to be set down. "I'm hungwee."

"Okay, let's get a snack." She held out a hand, taking his, and retreated into her red brick house.

"So much for outside playtime," I muttered.

The last place I wanted to be was inside. There wasn't enough space to put between Nellie and me within those walls. Distance was the key to our survival.

But I followed them through the door anyway, catching the scent of her perfume. Oranges and orchids clung to the air. Habit made me draw it in and hold it. Necessity made me blow it out. On my exhale, I marched to the nearest window. "It's stuffy in here. I'm opening this."

"Fine." She dismissed me with a flick of her wrist, taking Elias to the kitchen.

In nearly two decades, we'd perfected our hate-hate relationship. The reasons for our mutual disdain were as plentiful as the dust particles floating in the air, catching the afternoon glow.

Birds chirped from the oak tree beside Nellie's single-car garage. A breeze blew in the smell of fresh-cut grass and summer sunshine. That scent reminded me of Nellie too. Of memories tainted by angry words and betrayal.

Her voice carried from the kitchen where she bustled around, opening the fridge and cupboard doors. "Do you want crackers? Or a banana?"

"Cwackas," Elias answered.

"Okay. Here's your apple juice."

I hovered in the living room, keeping a wall between us. She didn't need me here. Elias was in good hands because like me, she adored him.

Technically, Nellie was Pierce's employee, his assistant, but that was simply a label. If he had to choose, I wasn't sure if he'd pick my friendship over hers. Which was probably why I'd never pushed him to choose sides.

Snap. Snap. Snap.

She growled from the kitchen, and I could practically hear her eyes roll.

I walked to the other window in the living room, yanking it open too. Boxes were stacked against every wall. The room wasn't large to begin with, but with the cardboard, it was claustrophobic. And there was nowhere to sit. The couch was stacked with boxes too.

"Where's your TV?" I asked, striding into the kitchen.

"I don't have one." She cast me a dismissive glance, then focused on Elias, sweeping crumbs off his shirt as he munched on wheat crackers.

"You don't have a TV."

"I don't have a TV."

I blinked. "Why?"

"Because I just moved here. Because I sold the one I had in Denver. Because I rarely watch TV, and unlike you, I don't need SportsCenter to feel good about myself."

"No, you just need a bottle of hair bleach and a crop top."

If looks could kill, Nellie would have flayed the skin from my bones nineteen years ago. I guess you could say by now, I was used to that murderous, green glare.

"Can't we go somewhere else?" I planted my hands on my hips. "Where there are more than two seats?"

After Kerrigan's water had broken, Nellie and I had walked to her house with Elias in tow. We were only a couple of blocks off First. There had to be places for both kids and adults in Calamity. Pierce and Kerrigan had just opened up a brewery downtown. I hadn't been there yet but maybe they'd put in a kids' play area.

"*We* are staying here." Nellie nodded to Elias. "If you want to sit, the couch is all yours."

"It's full of boxes."

"Then move them. They go in the office upstairs. First door on the left." She pointed at the ceiling, a smirk on her pink lips. "Unless you're afraid to lift anything heavy and hurt your back. Oh, wait. You don't have to worry about silly injuries anymore. Because you got fired."

"I didn't get fired," I gritted out. "I retired."

"Did you though?" She tapped her chin. "Because they didn't rehire you. So it's sort of like they showed you to the door."

This woman.

My blood began to boil.

She was goading me into an argument because usually a fight would send both of us storming away in opposite directions. Except I wasn't leaving. Not until we heard from Pierce. Not until we knew that Kerrigan and the baby were okay.

Nellie wanted me to move boxes? Fine, I'd move boxes. A floor between us seemed like a damn good idea.

I stalked out of the kitchen and hefted the first box from

her couch. The label taunted me, a blinding neon yellow. *Books.* Of course, she'd have me hauling books.

The staircase was steep and the treads nowhere near deep enough for my size-twelve shoes. The wooden handrail was scratched and dinged from years of use. The hallway upstairs felt too narrow for my broad shoulders. But at least the ceilings were tall, and I didn't have to duck to pass through a doorway.

The first room on the right was Nellie's bedroom. Apparently, she'd already unpacked the boxes for that space. A velvet, olive quilt covered the mattress. A mountain of white pillows rested against the oatmeal tufted headboard. The walls were the same startling white as they were in the rest of the house, and not a single box could be found.

Pierce was setting up a satellite office in Calamity for his investment company. He'd mentioned earlier that Nellie had moved here two weeks ago.

Clearly, she'd made getting settled a priority. If all that remained of her boxes were those in the living room, she'd be fully unpacked soon.

She had a head start on life in Montana. I didn't like that she was ahead.

Across the hall from her bedroom was the office. Three empty bookshelves hugged the longest wall. I dropped the box beside her desk, then jogged downstairs to collect the last two.

Except there weren't two on the couch. There were three.

"Did you just put another box on the couch?" I asked her.

"It goes upstairs too." Nellie sauntered into the living room, her hips swaying with each step.

Her jeans molded to her slight curves. The cropped tank showed a sliver of her flat, toned stomach. Her hair was down, the white-blond strands hanging in sleek panels to her waist. And those pretty eyes were always full of fire.

She was maddeningly attractive.

"I'm not moving this shit for you."

She glanced over her shoulder to Elias who was too busy gulping apple juice to hear that I'd cussed. "Because you're so busy at the moment? It's a few boxes. And they're heavy."

"Then don't buy books. Or, follow my lead, and hire a moving company. I'm not going to move my own stuff, let alone yours."

"I—Wait. You're moving here? From Nashville?"

A slow grin spread across my face. "Pierce didn't tell you."

"Tell me what?"

Earlier today, on the sidewalk outside The Refinery, Nellie had been genuinely shocked to see me. Which meant she had no idea. She probably thought I was here on vacation.

Oh, this was going to be fun.

"Do you think that house across the street is for sale?"

She gulped. "You're moving here?"

"I'm moving here."

"No. Absolutely not."

I leaned in closer. "Tell you what. I'll do you a favor. I'll cart one more box upstairs. Since it's the neighborly thing to do."

"You cannot move to Calamity."

"Watch me."

Her hands balled into fists. "You're such an asshole."

"Watch that foul language." I tsked my tongue, then grabbed the closest box and hauled it upstairs.

Taunting her was like trash-talking the best lineman on a fourth-down conversion attempt. Either I'd find a way to get the ball down field, or I'd get my ass sacked. Regardless, the game was a rush.

Nellie Rivera was my most formidable opponent.

The sound of the front door opening and closing rang through the house. I stepped toward the office's window, spotting Nellie and Elias in the yard again. She'd found a ball for him to toss.

She had a smile on her face but there was a tension in her shoulders. A tightness to her moves. I'd known her long enough to know the difference between riling her up and truly getting beneath her skin.

And today, I was in there deep. Nellie did not want me moving to Calamity.

A better man would have walked away. A better man would have given her this town to claim as her own.

But, like she'd said, I was an asshole.

I plopped the box beside my feet. The top hadn't been taped shut like the others, and as it landed, the flaps popped loose, revealing rows of books inside. One with an orange spine caught my eye, so I picked it up, inspecting the cover. It was a compilation of articles from the Harvard Business Review.

I flipped it open, skimming through the pages. A few of the articles I recognized, having read them myself. Most people, Nellie included, probably thought I'd spent the past decade reading only playbooks.

But I'd read and researched and put my money to work. I used the Harvard degree I'd worked my ass off to earn. They'd needed a star quarterback, and I'd wanted an Ivy League education. It had been a win-win. My father had paid my tuition, but after graduation, I hadn't taken a cent from that man. Not even a birthday or Christmas gift. I'd sworn never to be indebted to him again.

It was bad enough knowing his blood ran through my veins.

I returned the book to the box, rifling through the pile. Maybe there'd be one I hadn't read yet. Except the educational texts stopped midway through the box. Beneath them were leather journals. My fingers skimmed a suede cover, and I pulled it out, unwrapping the strap that bound it together. One glance inside and I knew exactly what I held.

Nellie's diary.

A better man would have left it at peace.

My fingers began flipping, stopping on a page filled with Nellie's precise, clean handwriting. A familiar name jumped out from the paper. Phoebe McAdams, the head cheerleader. And a bitch, according to Nellie's entry—which wasn't wrong.

The date in the upper right-hand corner put this journal nineteen years ago. We'd been fourteen. This diary was from our freshman year at Benton. A lot had happened that year. A lot had changed.

Flipping to the next page, I found Pierce's name. Nellie was on a rant about how he'd scored higher on an algebra exam and how all she'd wanted was to beat him for valedictorian. In one of these other diaries, the one from senior year, I'd likely find the gloating entry where she'd won.

I should have expected what came next. I should have expected to see my name in this book. Still, my hands tightened on the diary as I read. My heart thumped hard against my sternum.

I hate Cal Stark.

That was it. Four words, written so many times on the page that my eyes began to cross.

On the next entry, there was a different date in the corner, but those same four words sat alone on the top line.

I hate Cal Stark.

Damn. Maybe deep down, I'd hoped . . .

Who was I kidding? There was no hope.

The sound of the door opening jolted my gaze away from the book, and I slammed the cover closed.

"Unka Cal!" Elias called from downstairs.

"Coming!" I hollered back, bending to right the books and resecure the box's flaps. Then I jogged downstairs, ruffling Elias's dark hair when he hugged me at the knee.

"Pierce just called," Nellie said.

"Okay." I tried not to let it bother me that he'd called her instead of me. I tried not to see those written words but they were burned into my mind. Nellie hated me. No surprise. So why couldn't I look at her face?

"Everything is well, albeit slowly," she said. "Kerrigan and the baby are both doing fine. Kerrigan's mom is going to come by in a while and pick up Elias. She'll take him home with her."

"Great." That was what I'd needed to hear. Now I was

clear to leave. I crouched in front of Elias, holding up a hand for a high five. "Bye, champ. I'll see you soon, okay?"

He smacked my hand. "Bye."

I strode past Nellie, still unable to meet her eyes, but she stopped me before I could escape.

"Cal?"

"Yeah?" I felt her gaze on my profile. I sensed her scrutiny. She knew how to read me as well as I knew how to read her.

"What's wro—never mind."

I was out the door before she could blink, putting blocks between that house and that woman. The sidewalks downtown were crowded with tourists. Country music blared through the open door as I passed Calamity Jane's bar.

A man with a beer belly and tie-dyed fanny pack slowed as I walked by. "Hey, you're Cal Stark."

I lifted a hand and kept on going, but his voice had carried. Other men and a few women stopped and stared. *Shit.*

Why hadn't I taken the side streets to the motel? Calamity was going to be my home, and I was sick of hiding when I ventured out in public. But I should have known better. Why wasn't I wearing a hat and shades?

"Could I get an autograph?" A guy ran up, blocking my path and thrusting his baseball cap in my face.

"Got a pen?"

"Uh . . ." That was a no. I shoved past him and didn't slow, not even when I heard him say, "Guess he really is a dick."

He could hate me. They could all hate me. Because maybe if they hated me, they'd leave me the fuck alone.

With my chin down, I continued to the motel, without another interruption. Pierce had my bags. They were in the back of his Land Rover from when he'd picked me up at the airport. He'd drop them later when he had time. For tonight, I could sleep naked and wear the same thing tomorrow. At least I had my wallet and phone.

The bell above the motel's office door jingled as I stepped inside.

"Hi." The woman behind the reception counter had a wide smile that brought out the laugh lines at her eyes and mouth. "How can I help you?"

"Yeah, I've got a reservation. Cal Stark."

Recognition dawned and she sat a little straighter. "Oh, yes. Welcome. Let me get you checked in."

"Thanks," I said as she went to work.

Pierce and Kerrigan had offered to let me stay at their house, but they had enough going on, preparing for the baby. They didn't need a houseguest. So I'd asked Kerrigan if she could get me a reservation at the motel. When my assistant had called, they'd been booked solid through August.

Kerrigan had scored me the room. My assistant had been fired—not because of the motel but because he'd stolen one of my jerseys and hawked it online. The world was full of liars and thieves, and a fair share always seemed to gravitate in my direction.

"You'll be in room seven." The woman handed me a room key. "My name is Marcy. I'm the owner here. Please let me know if you need anything."

"A toothbrush?"

"Sure." She disappeared to a back room and came out

with not just a toothbrush, but a travel-sized tube of tooth-paste and mini bottle of Listerine.

"Appreciate it." With a nod, I left the office, weaving past cars in the crowded parking lot.

The moment I stepped inside my room, I locked the door and tossed the key on the dresser, taking a minute to assess the place. It wasn't a five-star resort, but Pierce had stayed here a few times. If it was good enough for him, it was good enough for me.

And they had a TV.

But I didn't pick up the remote. I reached behind my back, lifting the hem of my white button-down shirt, and pulled Nellie's diary from where I'd stuffed it in the waist-band of my jeans.

A better man would have left it behind.

But I wasn't a better man.

Just ask Nellie.

CHAPTER TWO

NELLIE

THE SOUNDS of a coffee shop were as comforting to me as a warm blanket on a winter day. The sputter of a steam wand in milk. The banging of a barista emptying a portafilter. The drip of espresso into a shot glass.

Years ago, I'd been in between jobs and struggling to decide my next step. At the time, I'd been living in Charlotte, and four blocks from my apartment, there'd been this moody little coffee shop in search of a waitress. I'd contemplated taking the minimum-wage job for the scents and sounds alone. If it wouldn't have sent my mother into a tizzy about wasting my education, I might have applied.

Instead, I'd moved back to Denver and had randomly bumped into Pierce. He'd offered me a job at his company, Grays Peak Investments, and Mom would never know that for a brief moment, I'd nearly followed in her footsteps.

It was for the best. Mom hated coffee. If I'd taken that waitress job, I'd probably hate coffee too, and then I would have missed out on the charm of the Calamity Coffee Co.

A man with a mustache joined the line for the counter, smiling politely as he took his place behind me. "Morning."

"Good morning."

He wore the signature brown uniform of a delivery driver. Maybe my neighborhood was on his route.

My neighborhood. Two weeks in Montana and I still couldn't believe I lived here. That this was home.

This was *my* coffee shop. The tourists taking up every table were visiting *my* town. The Memorial Day parade later this morning would honor the fallen in *my* community.

Mine. Calamity was mine.

From the charming shops along First, to the welcoming neighborhoods, to the rugged countryside, there was a lot to love.

Pierce had moved here two years ago, even though Grays Peak had its headquarters in Denver. After about a year of working remotely, he'd decided it was time to establish a satellite office. When he'd asked me if I'd consider a move, I'd immediately agreed.

Twenty of us would be making Calamity home. Construction on the office building had just finished, and the keys were safely tucked in my purse. I'd be working in the space alone for a while until the others arrived.

Everyone else moving to Montana had kids. They'd wait until the school year was finished before making the trip. But there'd been nothing keeping me in Denver.

My parents had left the city three years ago, relocating to Arizona for milder winters. After too many years working in the dirt, hunched over flower beds, Dad's knees bothered him in the cold.

There'd been no friends begging me to stay. Certainly no

love interests. When was the last time I'd gone on a date? A year ago? I made a mental note to delete my dating profile.

I hadn't missed Denver for a minute. The only blemish on my first two weeks in Calamity was Cal. I'd chastise Kerrigan and Pierce later for failing to mention that he was moving here too.

"Nellie," a woman called my name.

I spun around, seeing Larke breeze through the coffee shop's doors. The UPS guy was the only one behind me, so I shifted aside. "You can go in front of me."

"Are you sure?"

"Yep." I motioned him forward, then hugged Larke as she joined me in line. "Hey!"

"Hi! How are you?"

"Good. Congratulations, Aunt Larke."

"Thanks." Her smile widened, making her look more like Kerrigan. The sisters had the same chestnut hair and pretty brown eyes. "She's so cute and tiny."

Pierce and Kerrigan had a beautiful baby girl. Constance Sullivan had joined the world in the early hours yesterday morning. They'd been released from the hospital already and had decided to get out of town for a few days, retreating to their cabin in the mountains. Though *cabin* wasn't exactly the right term. More like a mountain ski lodge.

"What are you up to?" Larke asked.

"Oh, nothing much. I came down for coffee before the parade and to do a little wandering."

"Smart. It will be crazy busy in about an hour."

"I was thinking of taking an adventure to the hardware store. I've dug through every remaining box in my house, and I can't find my Swiffer wand or my can opener."

"Well, after the excitement of the hardware store, I doubt I'll be able to compete," she teased. "But a few of us are meeting at Jane's this afternoon. You should join us."

"Oh, um . . . sure."

"It's just a small group of girlfriends. There aren't a lot of women our age in Calamity, so we tend to stick together."

"Sounds fantastic." My voice was too bright. My stomach began to knot. I wasn't good at joining girl groups. Not that I didn't like them, I just didn't have much experience.

The line inched forward, the two of us shuffling along with it.

"I'll warn you that we mostly gossip," Larke said. "Most of us grew up here, so we know everyone in town. If we talk about other people the whole time, it's not to leave you out. It's just . . . that's what we know."

"Got it." At least I had been warned instead of showing up and feeling like the outsider.

Maybe she could sense my unease because she put a hand on my forearm and gave it a squeeze. "It's a fun group. Everyone will love having you there."

I hoped so. I didn't have a lot of close friends, especially given this was a new town. Pierce and Kerrigan were at the top of my list, but they were busy growing their family.

My one and only female friend from high school had gone to college in Florida and the two of us had grown apart. I hadn't spoken to Sareena in years.

Girls in college had been more interested in partying than their studies. I'd had a scholarship to maintain, so slacking off to attend keggers and chase boys hadn't been an option. My Friday nights had been spent at the library.

Or maybe those were just the excuses I'd made for myself. I hadn't made friends in Charlotte or Denver either.

"What time?" I asked Larke.

"Three or four?"

"I'll be there." And maybe it was just that easy.

Meet for a drink. See new faces. Engage in a bit of harmless gossip.

Make friends.

The barista, a pretty young woman with a honey-blond ponytail and silver nose ring, greeted us when we reached the counter. "Hey, Larke. Want your usual?"

"Yes, please." She gestured between us as she did introductions. "Kristen, this is Nellie. Nellie, Kristen."

"Hi." I waved.

"Hey. Nice to meet you."

"Nellie's going to meet us at Jane's later," Larke said.

"Oh, sweet." Kristen nodded. "Do you want a coffee?"

"Please. Iced vanilla latte. Double."

"Coming right up." Kristen plucked two plastic cups from the stack, writing our orders on the sides with a green marker.

Larke and I shifted out of the way to make room for the next customer, sharing pictures of baby Constance as we waited. Then, with our drinks in hand, walked outside together.

"Good luck shopping. I'll see you in a bit." Larke took a step away, but I stopped her before she could leave.

"Hey, Larke? Thanks for inviting me. I don't, um . . . I don't have a lot of friends."

Maybe admitting it was unnecessary. But Mom had always told me that part of friendship was letting your vulnerabilities show. Dropping my guard was never going to get easier if I didn't get more practice.

"This is a small town." Larke laughed. "You're going to have more friends than you know how to deal with. That's a blessing and a curse, by the way."

I smiled. "Noted."

"See ya soon." She set off in one direction, while I turned in the opposite.

The sky was a cloudless blue, the morning air crisp. The sun shone brightly, warming my face as I set out on a leisurely stroll.

Calamity was tucked into a mountain valley in south-west Montana. Sweeping, green meadows sprawled toward the towering, indigo peaks in the distance. The new Grays Peak building was located in the outskirts of town, and from my corner office, I'd have an unobstructed view of the breathtaking landscape.

Cars and trucks rolled down the street, their pace not much faster than my own. The absence of noise was notice-able. No honking. No sirens. No beeping crosswalk alarms.

People meandered the sidewalks. No one was in a hurry to get from one end of town to the other. The tourists were here to explore and soak in every detail. So I joined them, window-shopping as I sipped my coffee.

Calamity had history and character. Once upon a time, maybe one of these buildings had been called the General Store. Jane's might have been the saloon, complete with swinging doors and a hitching post. Instead of cars parked in diagonal spaces, horse-drawn buggies would have traversed this street.

Part of the reason I'd bought a home built in 1953 was

because I wanted to soak in the old stories. I wanted to live in a place where memories had been made. My house reminded me of my childhood home in Denver. That two-bedroom house, albeit small, had been happy.

No more high-rise apartments where I had a better relationship with the doorman than my neighbors. No more lonely weekends working because I had nothing else to do but focus on my career. No more Friday nights alone with a sudoku puzzle and a pint of ice cream.

I wasn't just in Calamity for a job and change of location. I was here to banish my solitary life. To create a home.

Why was Cal moving to Calamity? *Why did he pop into my mind so often?*

This sleepy town was not his scene. He was all about loud stadiums and ruckus fans. He craved the spotlight and attention, even if it was negative. He'd be miserable here.

And that misery would be contagious.

There wasn't a person on earth who set me on edge like Cal Stark. A single glare from his hazel eyes and my blood pressure would spike. He always had a rude comment. His favorite pastime outside of football was making fun of my hair or clothes. Rarely an encounter passed when he didn't deliver at least one insult.

Granted, he could say the same about me. Neither of us held back when it came to the censure.

The constant tension between us would ruin everything. Cal couldn't move here. He had to leave.

My entire adult life—and most of my teenage years—I'd worked to prove myself to the world. And to Cal. I was honest enough with myself to admit that part of what drove me was a desire to show him I was good enough. To show him that I wasn't . . . less.

The doubts and insecurities he'd helped create in my years at Benton still existed deep beneath the surface. Maybe they always would.

God bless high school.

If Cal lived here, I'd be tiptoeing around Calamity, constantly on guard. I didn't want to go to the grocery store and fear my cart would bump into his in the frozen food aisle. I didn't want to walk into Jane's for a girls' night and see him sitting at the bar.

I didn't want to walk down First Street on Memorial Day weekend and spot him at the other end of the block.

Speak of the devil. "Are you freaking kidding me?"

There was a crowd surrounding him. It was mostly men and teenage boys but a few women were mixed in with the huddle. A brunette was in the process of hiking up the hem of her skirt. And in the center of the cluster, Cal stood head and shoulders above the rest.

His chocolate-brown hair had grown out this spring, the ends curling at the nape. His chiseled jaw was dusted with stubble. His biceps strained at the sleeves of his T-shirt.

The man hadn't just been given exceptional athletic talent, he'd also been gifted with an extraordinarily handsome face. It was unfair. Utterly unfair.

Cal wore a tight, fake smile on his smooth lips as he scribbled his name on caps and napkins and whatever else the mob was thrusting his way. His knuckles were white as they gripped the marker. His shoulders were tense. His eyes narrowed. Even irritated, he was devastatingly good-looking.

For a split second, I felt bad for him. For just a moment, I wished those people would leave him be. Constantly being hounded for an autograph or a photo had to be exhausting.

My empathy was short-lived. Every time I felt compassion toward Cal, a memory from high school would pop into my head.

Like the time he'd *accidentally* thrown water on me my freshman year. I'd been wearing a white shirt and a thin bra. To this day I could hear the jeers from the football players who'd been in the hallway.

No, I refused to pity Cal.

"Not after he made me self-conscious about my nipples," I mumbled.

An older woman gave me a sideways look as she passed by.

Whoops.

No, Cal could not live here too. He needed to be in Tennessee or Tallahassee or Timbuktu for all I cared. Somewhere far, far away from Montana.

But God, that man was stubborn. He'd stay here just because I wanted him to leave. Unless . . .

What if I made his life agony? Yes, he was pig headed, but if he was unhappy, maybe he'd reconsider. An evil grin tugged at the corners of my mouth. I doubted it would work, but it was worth a try.

Calamity was mine.

"I got here first."

The ice in my coffee rattled as it melted. The sound sparked an idea. With a smirk on my lips, I marched toward the group. The woman with the skirt looked me up and down as I approached, probably thinking I'd be a threat to her chances at scoring a famous, wealthy man.

I didn't spare her a glance. My eyes stayed locked on Cal.

He shifted, taking another paper to sign, when he spotted me. For the briefest moment, there was relief in his gaze. Did he think I was coming to his rescue? That was Pierce's job, not mine.

But I used his assumption to my advantage, and when he started nudging through the crush, pushing my way, I let him use that strong, muscled body to clear a path.

"Excuse me," he told one guy.

Cal usually started off polite. It was when people didn't budge that he'd snap a *get the fuck out of my way*. And those moments were typically the ones caught on camera, then posted to YouTube and Twitter.

I steeled my spine as he pushed past the edge of the gathering. My hand threatened to tremble, but I kept my grip on my coffee cup tight. So tight the lid popped free.

Perfect.

"Hey." Cal jerked up his chin. "Can we go some—"

His question was cut short when my hand shot out for the waistband of his jeans. I gripped it, tugged, and poured the remainder of my vanilla latte down his pants. He gasped, jumping back with a yelp. Ice cubes traveled down his legs, escaping the hem and clattering to the sidewalk, breaking beside his feet. The creamy liquid darkened the denim of his crotch as it spread.

God, that is satisfying.

"What the hell, Nellie?" Cal swept at his pants, his palm coming away wet. Droplets went flying as he shook it out.

He glared down the straight line of his nose. The sharp corners of his jaw flexed. His gray T-shirt molded to the broad planes of his chest and accentuated the hard lines of his pecs as he seethed.

"That's for sending a dick pic to my mom!" I lied.

A chorus of gasps filled the air. Men inched away. The woman with the short skirt turned on a heel and vanished. One of the younger teens looked Cal up and down and muttered, "Dude. Gross."

My pulse raced. My hands shook. But I stood still, fighting to keep a straight face as I faced the man who'd been my archnemesis for nearly twenty years.

Damn, that had been satisfying. Almost orgasmic.

"The. Fuck?" Cal's nostrils flared as he planted his hands on his narrow hips.

I stood on my toes, leaning in closer. "You threw water on me once. Remember? Consider this leveling the score."

His eyes widened, the sun catching the flecks of gold and caramel in his irises.

Maybe I shouldn't have reminded him. Maybe I should have let him wonder why I'd doused him with espresso and milk.

But I remembered everything from high school. Every time he'd bullied me. Every time he'd made me cry. Every time I'd cursed his name.

It had taken me a long time to feel comfortable in my own skin. Maybe that was normal for all women. The only treatment for our insecurities was time and age—even then, there wasn't a cure. Some days, I was sure the self-conscious thoughts about my hair or my career or my success or my body were gone for good. Others, those familiar doubts would creep out from their depths and ruin a beautiful day.

Behind each of my insecurities was a face. Cal's

teenaged face. Intentionally and unintentionally, his high school antics had given me flaws. He'd shined a light on my imperfections, ripping away my youthful rose-colored glasses.

He made me vulnerable. He made me weak. No one could tear through my defenses quite like Cal.

I wanted to live here without the fear of him lurking behind every corner. So I'd use my memories, I'd steal the plays from his book and do my best to run Cal out of town.

This was my home now.

And Calamity wasn't big enough for us both.

―

Dear Diary,

Cal threw water on me today. He did it on purpose too. When Mr. Gregsmith confronted him about it, Cal lied and said he tripped. It was his word against mine. I think maybe Mr. Gregsmith believed me, but I'm just a scholarship kid so Cal got off with a warning not to walk around with an open water bottle. I was talking to John at my locker when Cal did it. Maybe John was flirting with me? I don't know. Cal came walking down the hallway with his horrible jock friends. Why couldn't he just keep on walking? Why can't he just leave me alone? He didn't even pretend to trip. He just flung out his wrist and I got freaking soaked. And you know those stupid white uniform shirts are really thin. Everyone in the hallway started laughing. Some guy cracked a joke about my nipples and then John started laughing too. Do you think maybe he was in on Cal's joke? That maybe he was flirting with me to help Cal? Whatever. John's not even that cute. His bottom teeth are crooked. Are my nipples big? I don't know what size is normal. Is there a way to shrink them? Like a cream or something? Maybe Mom will let me buy a padded bra the next time we go shopping. I still have some birthday money left over, and Mrs. Murphy would probably pay me to mow her lawn next week. I was going to use my savings for a new backpack, but I'd rather Cal tease me for the duct tape holding the strap together than because I have weird nipples. I hate Cal Stark. Like, a lot.

Nellie

CHAPTER THREE

CAL

THE DIARY GAVE a *thump* as I slammed it closed.

"Fuck." I tossed it on the bed beside me and dragged a hand over my face.

I'd read that journal cover to cover. Twice.

About half of Nellie's entries were about school, fretting over test scores and worrying about homework assignments. If I would have put in a fraction of her effort, I might have aced more exams. But school had been her obsession while football had been mine. And my B-plus average had been good enough.

I hadn't realized until reading her journal just how much pressure Nellie had been dealing with in high school. Whether she'd put it on herself or not, having a perfect 4.0 GPA had been her sole focus. She'd dedicated morning, noon and night to studies. Anything to ensure her scholarship hadn't been at risk. And this book was just for freshman year. Classes had only gotten harder as we'd aged.

Benton was the most sought-after private high school in

Denver. My admission had been guaranteed. So had my graduation. I could have failed every course and they still would have handed me a cap and gown, simply because I was Colter Stark's son.

Amassing money was Benton's favorite sport.

They balanced their elitist reputation by offering scholarships to five kids in each grade level. Nellie had been one of the five in our class. Girls like Phoebe, whose parents wrote tuition checks, made sure to remind Nellie that her parents could not.

Interlaced in the diary were a few other accounts of nasty run-ins with the cheerleaders. But otherwise, the rest of that damn book was about me.

She hated me.

Hell, after reading that diary, I hated me too.

The jeans and T-shirt I'd been wearing earlier were in a pile on the floor. My motel room reeked of stale coffee. I'd had to take another shower because my skin had been sticky with sweetened milk.

Never in a million years would I have expected Nellie to throw her coffee on me. She preferred insults to injury. Considering my jeans had definitely suffered physical injury, this was a new tactic.

All I'd wanted this morning was a quick breakfast. I'd thought if I could make it to First before the parade started at ten, I'd have a shot at a peaceful meal at the White Oak. I'd been one block away from the café when a group of kids had recognized me. People had appeared out of thin air, surrounding me for selfies and autographs. I'd had nowhere to run and nowhere to hide.

My Land Rover was currently in transit from Nashville

to Montana, and it couldn't get here fast enough. At least with a car, I wouldn't be limited to restaurants within walking distance to the motel.

My stomach growled. Thanks to Nellie's spectacle earlier, all I'd had to eat was a granola bar from the motel's vending machine.

You threw water on me once. Remember?

Oh, I remembered. Even if I hadn't just read her diary entry, I would have remembered.

That motherfucker John Flickerman had been bragging in the locker room after gym class, gloating that he'd be the guy to score Nellie's virginity. She'd kept to herself at Benton, especially when it had come to guys, but she'd clearly had a crush on him.

I'd known that John would laugh if I threw water on her. I'd known she'd never talk to the douchebag again if he laughed. So I'd doused her.

I hadn't meant to give her a goddamn nipple complex.

She had perfect nipples.

The coffee smell was getting old, so I snagged the stained clothes from the floor, grabbed my wallet and room key, then headed out the door. The jeans were tossed in the nearest trash can—I'd have to figure out my laundry situation later. The shirt was probably salvageable, there was only coffee on its hem, but I had a spare, so it was dumped too. Then I paced the length of the motel as I waited for my realtor to arrive.

Flower baskets hung from the second floor's exterior walkway. Pots had been planted beside each room, their blooms a riot of color against the red-painted doors. The parking lot was full, like it had been all weekend, but it was quiet. Most of the guests were probably downtown for the parade.

Beside the office's door was an old wagon wheel with *LOBBY* stenciled in white across a spoke. The motel's dark wooden exterior soaked in the heat from the morning sun. As I walked, whichever shoulder was closest to the wall absorbed the radiating warmth.

Did these rooms have air-conditioning? It would get hot as the summer progressed. Though I guess it didn't matter. My stay at the motel would be short-lived.

A black Toyota SUV eased into the parking lot. The woman behind the wheel waved, then eased to a stop as I approached.

"Hi, Mr. Stark," she greeted as I slid into the passenger seat. "I'm Jessa Nickels."

"Cal," I corrected, like I had when she'd called me Mr. Stark on the phone last week. My father was *Mr. Stark*.

"Nice to officially meet you." She reached over to shake my hand. "Would you like to grab a coffee before we head out? Chat a bit?"

"No." Absolutely not. I had no interest in coffee or making small talk.

There weren't many realtors in Calamity, and when I'd asked Kerrigan for a recommendation, she'd given me Jessa's name. She'd also warned that Jessa wasn't always the epitome of discreet. But of my limited options, apparently Jessa was the best, so before I'd arranged this meeting, my attorney had sent her a nondisclosure agreement and stern email reinforcing my need for privacy.

"Okay, then I guess we can just head out." She handed

me a manila folder filled with property spec sheets. "We'll start at the top and work our way down the line."

"All right." I nodded toward the exit. "Let's go."

"We'll be going to a few places currently occupied. With the parade, it worked out well for the owners to be gone for an hour or two."

"'Kay." I flipped the folder and scanned the first property sheet as Jessa drove.

Maybe it was rude to ask that Jessa meet with me today, but I didn't care that it was a holiday weekend. The sooner I had a house, the better. I needed a temporary place to live while building a permanent home. And I also needed land for that permanent home.

I'd left nearly everything in Nashville. When it was time, I'd have my house packed and my belongings shipped. But for now, I'd hired a property management company to make sure the place didn't burn down.

The next four hours were spent traipsing across Calamity.

Every house she showed me was lacking. Either it was too close to a neighbor or it was too close to the school. I stared at the rancher we'd just toured and scrunched my nose. This one was too close to a pasture of cows.

"I'm not waking up to that smell every day."

"Okay." Jessa forced a tight smile. "Well, this was the last viewing. Unfortunately, there isn't a lot of inventory in Calamity."

Kerrigan and Pierce had warned me that was the case. I walked to her SUV, climbed inside and slammed the door behind me.

Jessa scurried to catch up. "I can make some calls. See if anyone who's been on the fence might consider a sale."

"Sure," I muttered. I wasn't going to hold my breath she'd find anything appealing. "What about vacant land?"

I had a meeting with a contractor tomorrow, the same guy who'd built Pierce and Kerrigan's place. He was a friend of Kerrigan's from the area and came highly recommended. Maybe I could pay him an exorbitant amount and escalate the construction timeline. That was if I found some property.

Jessa stretched to the backseat and pulled out another folder, this one green. She clutched it, hesitant to pass it over. "There's only one property for sale in the area that has the acreage you're looking for."

I held out my hand for the folder. "Then let's hope I like it."

———

IT WAS NEARLY six by the time I returned to my hotel room. Jessa had earned her commission today.

We'd driven out to a property in the mountain foothills, and I'd known the moment my foot had hit the dirt it was mine.

There were plenty of massive evergreens to hide a house. I'd have space to install gates and security. It wasn't on a main road, so I didn't have to worry about traffic. Best of all? My nearest neighbor would be three miles away.

I pulled my phone from my pocket, hitting Pierce's name.

He answered on a yawn. "Hey."

"How's it going?"

"Fine. Tired."

"How's Kerrigan and Constance?"

"Good." There was a softness in his voice. He probably had a dreamy smile on his face, the same one he'd had yesterday when he'd taken me to the hospital to meet his daughter. "I'm glad we came up to the cabin. It's been easier to relax here."

"How long are you staying?"

"We'll probably head back tomorrow. Maybe the next day. We've got a checkup with Constance's doctor coming."

"Elias doing okay?"

Pierce chuckled. "He's pretty enamored with his baby sister."

"As he should be. Need anything?"

"No, but thanks. Nellie's got us covered."

Of course, she did. Nellie always beat me to the rescue.

"What's happening with you?" Pierce asked.

"I just put an offer in on a ranch." A thrill raced through my veins. I was offering cash and pushing for a short close. I wanted that place in my name within a month.

"Is it that three-hundred-acre property about fifteen minutes out of town?"

"Yeah. How'd you know?"

"Kerrigan and I had a bet that you'd buy that one."

I grinned. "Who won?"

"She did. I thought you'd pick something that was less maintenance."

"Yeah, it'll take some work." I'd do what I wanted myself and hire out the rest. "But what the hell else do I have to do?"

"You could take that job at ESPN. It would keep you connected to the game."

I sighed. "I don't know. But I don't want to talk about me. You sure everything is going okay?"

"It's great." There was that dreamy smile again. "Thanks for checking in."

"Holler when you're back. Or if you need anything." As soon as my car showed up, Nellie wouldn't be the only one to help out.

"Will do. Bye."

I ended the call and tucked my phone away as a hunger pang struck.

Jessa had stopped by a sandwich spot today and grabbed a couple of subs to eat between showings. But that had been hours ago, and I was starved. I'd have to brave downtown for dinner again. Except before I could eat, I had another stop to make.

I left my room for the motel's lobby, finding Marcy inside.

"Hi, Mr. Stark." She braced as I came through the door, like she was expecting me to complain. Either that was typical at a motel—that guests only came to visit when they were checking in, checking out or bitching—or Marcy knew about my reputation. Maybe she and her husband were football fans.

I didn't take offense. Maintaining my reputation as an asshole kept some people away. Not many, but some.

"You can call me Cal. And I'd like a room."

She blinked. "A different room? Oh, um . . . is something wrong with yours? It's the biggest one we have and—"

"It's fine." I held up a hand. "I want a room, that room, for as long as I need it."

"Huh? I'm sorry, Mr. Stark. I'm not following."

"Cal," I corrected. "I'd like to stay here, live here, while my house is being built."

"In the hotel?"

I drummed my fingers on the counter. Patience had never been my forte, especially when I was hungry. "Yes."

"Oh." She shook her head. "I'm sorry. We don't do long-term stays."

"Make an exception. It's guaranteed income through the summer and fall." Maybe even the winter if I couldn't get a jump on construction.

"But we're fully booked. I'm sure Kerrigan told you that. I was only able to get you that room because of a last-minute cancelation. Summer in Calamity is our busiest time of year."

Well, shit. A growl came from my throat.

I guess I could settle for one of the properties I'd viewed today. Or, I could live in Bozeman. They had more real estate offerings and plenty of new construction. But it was two hours away, and Nellie would just love that, wouldn't she? She'd dumped one iced latte down my pants and think she'd chased me from Calamity.

No. I wasn't giving her that satisfaction.

"Marcy, work with me here." I liked this motel. It was clean. Relatively quiet. The bed was comfortable. After so many years of away games, hotels had become a regular part of my life.

"I'm sorry. The only spot I'd have for you to stay is . . ." She trailed off, then held up a finger. "Give me a minute."

She disappeared into the back room, the same one where she'd gotten my toothbrush. The murmur of her voice carried into the lobby, but I couldn't make out the words.

My fingers continued their drumming on the counter, the muted taps growing louder as the minutes passed, until finally Marcy returned and breezed past me for the door.

"I have an idea," she said. "You'll need to keep an open mind."

"Okay," I drawled, following her outside. People only told you to keep an open mind when they knew you weren't going to like what they had to say.

She rounded the corner of the L-shaped building and walked its length along a gravel path. Behind the motel was a white brick, single-story house with a sage-green door. Parked beside a small fenced yard, in a gravel space, was a gleaming silver and black Winnebago bus.

"This is my mom's house," she said. "She lets us park our RV here."

Yeah, my mind was not open enough for this.

"We go camping in the fall and early spring, before tourist season gets into full swing." Marcy stopped beside the camper, taking out a key from her pocket and slipping it into the lock. "But we're so busy, we can't get away in the summer."

The door popped open and she let me take the metal stairs first.

I had to crouch through the doorway, but inside, I was able to stand tall. Unexpected considering my six-foot-four frame. My feet would hang off the end of the bed, but that was true for most places I slept.

Marcy followed me inside, pulling up a shade to let in

more light. "There isn't a washer and dryer, but you can use the motel's, free of charge of course. You'd have your own kitchen. And you wouldn't be sharing a wall with other hotel guests."

Straight for the kill, this one. Maybe she knew I wanted a quiet place to eat and had no desire to hear noises from whoever was staying in the room beside mine.

I strode the length of the bus, taking in the taupe couches and dove-gray walls. The kitchen wasn't big but it would be enough to make myself meals. Eating out was already getting old.

Was I really considering this? Maybe I should have just bought a house today. Or I could buy my own Winnebago. But where would I park it?

"How much?" I asked.

"Um . . . the same price as a room?" She laughed. "I honestly didn't think I'd even get you through the door."

"I might need it through the fall. And winter. If I get comfortable here, I don't want you kicking me out so you can road-trip to wherever it is you camp."

"No problem." She held up her hands. "We can make different travel plans this year."

"You have to clean, just like you would if I was staying at the motel."

"Deal."

I held out my hand. "Deal."

"I'll get it all ready." Her eyes sparkled as she shook my hand. "You can move in tomorrow."

Without another word, I left her in the camper and strode outside. I stopped by my room to grab a hat and a pair of sunglasses. Then I headed downtown for some food.

I'd eaten at Pierce and Kerrigan's brewery the past two nights. As much as I wanted to support my friends, I was ready for a change. When I heard the music from Calamity Jane's, I jogged across the street and stepped into the dark bar.

My trips to Montana had mostly been spent at Pierce's cabin, so I hadn't been to many places in town, including Jane's. But as I took off my sunglasses and glanced around, it was exactly as I'd expected. Not quite a dive, but it leaned heavily toward that end of the spectrum.

Beneath the dim lights, tables filled the center of the room. Booths hugged the forest-green walls. At least, they looked green. It was hard to tell beneath the abundance of tin and aluminum beer signs. And was that a buffalo? Yep, sure was. The taxidermic bust hung beside the stage.

The bar itself stretched across the far wall. Behind it were mirrored shelves teeming with liquor bottles. I took an empty stool, leaning on the glossy surface, and nodded to the bartender.

She held up a finger, then plucked a beer can from a cooler. The top popped with a hiss.

That sound, combined with the smell of burgers and fries, made my mouth water. A couple at one of the tables was inhaling a basket of onion rings. I spotted mozzarella sticks and an overflowing plate of nachos.

I'd have to extend my workout tomorrow, but I was hungry enough to order everything on the damn menu.

A waitress strode from the door that led to the kitchen, her tray stacked with boats of hot wings. I was drooling over the wings when a swish of white-blond hair caught my eye.

Nellie's gaze locked with mine, and for the briefest

moment, the rest of the bar vanished as she glared at me from over the rim of a martini glass.

Would she throw that drink on me too? I hoped not. I hated vodka and olives. She had three of the latter skewered on a toothpick.

Larke Hale was sitting beside her. I didn't know Kerrigan's sister well, but from the scowl on her face, it didn't take much to know that Nellie had been sharing stories. The two other women cast similar looks over their shoulders.

Whatever. They could bash me all they wanted as long as I got some food.

"What can I get for you?" The bartender appeared, setting a cardboard coaster on the bar top.

"Beer, whatever you've got on tap. Cheeseburger. Onion rings. Fries."

"You're Cal Stark."

Not a question. "Yes."

"Jane Fulson. This is my bar." She nodded to the television mounted on the wall beside the pool table. "That TV only plays Broncos games."

"Okay." Could a man just get some food? "I like football. I'll be happy if you have a game on, period."

Jane was probably in her fifties, close to Mom's age. Her hair was white. Her skin leathery and tan. She was thin and average height, but I squirmed a bit as she looked me up and down with those shrewd, brown eyes. I was guessing most people didn't mess with Jane.

She reminded me of Nellie in that way.

With one last inspection, Jane shoved away from the bar and filled a pint glass with an amber. She set it on my coaster, then left me in peace.

I chugged half my beer, feeling eyes on my spine. When I dared a glance to Nellie's table, sure enough, every woman seated had her eyes locked my way.

That was a lot of angry faces. Maybe I should have requested my meal to go.

The door opened and a blast of light flashed from outside as two women entered, a blonde and a brunette. I turned back to my beer, ready to finish, then did a double take.

"You've got to be kidding me." I cast my eyes to the tall, wooden ceiling. Definitely should have gone to the brewery.

It was a small world. Whoever said otherwise hadn't been to Calamity.

Years ago, in Nashville, I'd dated the brunette. Everly Christian was beautiful, but it hadn't taken long to realize there'd been no spark. Maybe I hadn't been the nicest guy at the time. I might have ghosted her. Or maybe she'd ghosted me? Regardless, we'd gone our separate ways.

Until the weekend I'd shown up to stand as Pierce's best man. Everly not only lived in Montana, but was married to some local artist and was tight with Kerrigan.

The blonde was Lucy Ross, a famous country singer who'd performed the national anthem before a few games. Apparently she was married to the sheriff.

Everly didn't like me. Neither did Lucy.

No surprise, they joined Nellie's table.

The heat from their glares intensified, like flames licking my skin. I drained my beer, then studied my coaster. Eyes down. Hat pulled low.

Maybe Calamity was a mistake, after all. Maybe I should have tallied the number of people who liked me and compared it to the number of those who didn't. Though I wasn't sure there was a town in America where the final score would be in my favor.

So what if the entire female population in this county hated me? I'd just bought a ranch. I'd rented a Winnebago. There was no going back. Somehow, we'd all have to coexist.

I risked another glance. The other women had turned away, but Nellie's green eyes were waiting.

She looked stunning. She looked pissed. She looked determined.

She looked like I was about to suffer.

Fuck my life.

CHAPTER FOUR

NELLIE

"WHY ARE the hot ones always jerks?" Larke asked.

"Great question." I scoffed, my eyes glued to Cal's spine as he tried to blend in with the bar. But he was too tall, too broad and too . . . *Cal* to blend. He stood out like a blob of white bird poop on a car's otherwise clean windshield.

"For the record, not *all* the hot ones are jerks." Lucy held up a finger. "I caught a sweet hottie."

"I caught a grumpy hottie," Everly said. "But he's sweet to me, so that's all that counts."

"Okay, fine," Larke said. "I stand corrected. But most of the hot ones are assholes."

"Yep." Melody, another one of Larke's friends I'd met tonight, clinked her wineglass with Kristen's.

"Total assholes." I took another sip of my vodka martini.

It was my second tonight, and I was rocking a lovely buzz. It tempered the guilt that had plagued me since throwing coffee on Cal this morning.

Sure, it had been impulsive. In the moment, it had felt

great. Better than great. It had felt like justice. But by the time I'd made it home from the hardware store, I'd had a knot in my stomach.

Cal was staying at the motel, so it wasn't like he could just toss his shirt in the laundry. There'd been a lot of people standing by and someone might have videoed the exchange to post on social media. He was my sworn enemy, but I didn't want rumors flying that he was a dick pics fanatic.

Fuck you, guilt. If I wouldn't have committed to meeting Larke and the girls for drinks, I probably would have gone to the motel with an apology note and offered to wash his shirt.

There was something wrong with me.

I had this exasperating habit of feeling bad for Cal.

"I heard you dumped coffee in Cal's pants today." Everly laughed. "I really wish I would have been there to see it."

"Me too." Lucy giggled. "I bet the look on his face was priceless."

My jaw dropped. "I've made the gossip mill already?"

"It doesn't take much," Larke said.

"Did he really send a dick pic to your mom?" Lucy asked, lowering her voice.

"No." I shrugged. "It was just the first thought that popped into my head."

"Brilliant." Everly raised her glass. "To Nellie. Welcome to Calamity. You're going to fit right in."

"Thanks." I leaned in and joined the cheers.

Kristen finished the last of her chardonnay and sighed. "This has been so fun, but I'd better get going. I'm opening the coffee shop tomorrow, and if I have one more glass of wine, I'll want two and then I won't get home until late and be hungover in the morning."

"I'll go with you." Melody stood from her chair, tucking a lock of her dark hair behind an ear. "I need to finish my lesson plan."

"Ugh. I need to do mine too," Larke said. They were both teachers at the elementary school. Larke taught fifth grade and Melody third. "Later."

"Great to meet you, Nellie," Melody said.

"You too."

"Come by for coffee tomorrow," Kristen said. "Friends and family discount."

"Thank you. I will." I'd learned tonight that Kristen wasn't just a barista but the shop's owner.

So far, girls' night had been a success. There'd been no awkward silences. No moments of feeling like the odd woman out. No forced smiles or conversation. Maybe making friends wasn't as hard as I'd made it out to be.

"So where are your husbands?" Larke asked Lucy and Everly as we all shifted closer around the table.

"They're on daddy duty," Everly said, checking the time on her phone. "And I'll warn you that I can't stay long. Hux is scrambling to finish a commission piece and breastfeeding means I don't get to stray far from the baby."

"I'm just glad you came by," I said.

Lucy put her hand over mine. "We're glad you're here."

We spent the next thirty minutes catching up. I'd gotten to know Lucy and Everly these past couple of years thanks to Kerrigan. During my visits to Calamity, Kerrigan had made it a point to introduce us all.

They were at a different stage in their lives than I was in mine, both married with young kids. Everly's daughter was a toddler and her son just two months old. Lucy's baby girl was five months and her son nearly three. Kerrigan had Elias and now a newborn.

Meanwhile, I was married to my career with no relationship prospects. Thirty-three wasn't old. There was time to meet the right guy. Why rush?

"Want to see pictures?" Lucy unlocked her phone and began swiping through photos. Everly joined in to do the same.

With every picture, my biological clock ticked louder. *Tick. Tock. Tick. Tock.* It was so loud by the time they put their phones away, the noise had drowned out the country music playing over the bar's sound system.

That clock needed to shut the hell up.

I loved kids. I wanted kids. But I wanted what my parents had too. Love. Passion. Friendship.

Maybe I'd find a nice guy in Calamity. Maybe not. For tonight, I'd simply be grateful for friends. That seemed like enough of a hurdle to leap for one day.

"Do you guys want to order some dinner?" Larke asked, picking up the menu Jane had brought us earlier. "Or a snack? I'm hungry."

"I wish. But I'd better head home and relieve Hux." Everly nodded to her breasts. "And some of this pressure."

Since they'd ridden downtown together, Lucy stood too.

"Come and see me at the gallery." Everly hugged me goodbye.

"I do need some art for my house."

"I'm singing with the band here next weekend if you want to come watch," Lucy said. "It's usually a fun time."

I smiled wider. "I'll be here."

With one last wave, they headed for the door, casting a glare in Cal's direction before walking outside.

He was hunched over his space, his fingers clasped around his pint glass, still trying to blend. Every time the waitress pushed through the swinging door that led to the kitchen, Cal perked up, but the food on her tray was never for him.

He'd clearly come for dinner. The bar was packed, but it wasn't exactly quiet either. I suspected that as soon as he inhaled his meal, he'd retreat to the safety of his motel room.

"This has been so much fun," I told Larke as we sat back down to finish our drinks. "Thank you for inviting me."

"Of course. I'm so glad you're—oh, no." She ducked her chin, shifting so her back was to the door as a man strode inside.

"What?"

"Oh, it's this new salesman who works at Dad's dealership. His name is Peter. I went in last month to take my brother this book I thought he'd like. Zach got busy with a customer, so I was just hanging at the sales desk. Peter started hitting on me and not in the smooth, subtle way. More in the overly aggressive, you know he's going to be horrible in bed, kind of way."

I cringed.

"Exactly. He's asked me out twice since and still hasn't caught on that I'm very, very not interested."

"Ah." I watched as Peter walked to the bar, surveying the room.

Luckily for Larke, she wasn't the person who caught his attention. No, he had already zeroed in on Cal. Peter took the stool directly beside Cal's and held out a hand.

Cal only spared him a flat look.

But did Peter get the hint? Nope. He nudged Cal's elbow with his own, then started talking like they were long-lost friends. His nasal laugh carried across the room and he spoke with his hands flailing.

Cal's shoulders curled in tighter. He adjusted the brim of his hat, pulling it lower. I'd give this situation three minutes. Either Cal would tell Peter to scram, or he'd give up on his meal and walk.

Poor Cal.

No. Damn it. He'd never earned my pity, so when would I stop giving it freely?

"Can I ask you something?" Larke nodded to the bar. "Kerrigan is torn about Cal. Don't get me wrong, she's on your side. She adores you. But she says he's . . . nice. Especially around Pierce. And she says he's really good with Elias."

"He is," I admitted. Cal was undeniably sweet with Elias. They loved each other. And the same was true with Pierce. "Cal is different around Pierce. He always has been. They are fiercely loyal to one another."

"Does that bug you?" she asked.

"No. Pierce is a good friend. He's loyal to me too." And I'd never ask him to take sides.

Somehow Pierce had managed to maintain friendships with both Cal and me, while respecting the fact that Cal and I couldn't play nice in the sandbox.

"Well, I'm on your side," she said. "Even if Cal is insanely gorgeous."

I stiffened and took another gulp of my martini.

There was no desire or sexual undertone to Larke's statement. It was simply factual. Cal was insanely gorgeous. She could add that to his Wikipedia page and no one would contest it. Larke hadn't said it to bother me, yet a twinge crawled beneath my skin, making me shift uncomfortably in my seat.

Freaking Cal.

I wasn't going to let him ruin my night, so I brushed off the feeling and took another drink.

"I haven't been on a decent date in a year." Larke groaned. "I miss sex. Good, toe-curling, can't-get-enough-of-each-other sex. And my prospects in Calamity are slim. I might die a spinster with my vibrator clutched to my hand."

I laughed. "I'm giving up on dating, much to my mother's dismay. The last guy I went out with was a year ago. He was this suave, sexy attorney who took me to flashy restaurants and ordered expensive bottles of wine. I found out after two weeks that he wasn't an attorney but a suit salesman. He lived on his sister's couch and he was looking to score my apartment, not me."

"Asshole."

"Pretty much."

Apparently, he'd been scoping out my building, searching for prey. I'd only found out the truth because he'd dated a woman three floors down. After she'd spotted us together, she'd caught me in the elevator to give me a warning. I'd dumped him and thanked her.

Part of me thought she and I would have shared a comradery after dealing with such a creep. But the few times I'd seen her in the building's on-site gym afterward, she'd barely spared me a glance.

My apartment in Denver had been in the Grays Peak

building. The company offices occupied the top floors while the lower levels were residential. Staff members had first pick whenever vacancies came open.

The views of the city were stellar. I'd woken up many mornings to watch the sun rise over the mountains in the distance. The location was close to the best restaurants and boutique shops. The apartments themselves were top-of-the-line.

But I hadn't known my neighbors. I hadn't felt part of a community. And those restaurants? I'd usually eaten at them alone.

No, I'd take my little house on my simple street in Calamity. Because after only two weeks, it already felt more like home.

Even if Cal was a temporary thorn in my side.

Peter was still talking to him, blathering on like Cal was actually participating in the conversation.

"Can I ask you something else?" Larke asked, following my gaze. "Have you and Cal ever . . ."

"Oh. Uh . . ." I didn't even get the chance to lie. My face gave away the truth. *Damn it.*

"Sorry." She held up her hands. "That was none of my business. I didn't mean to pry."

"It's fine." This was part of friendship, right? Confiding in each other? Did that even count as a confession?

"No, that was rude," she said. "It's just that earlier, when he looked at you, it was like the rest of the room disappeared. And the two of you seem to—"

"Hate each other," I finished.

"Yeah. Of course." She smiled and straightened. "I was thinking about ordering food, but it looks like the kitchen is backed up. I don't know if I can wait an hour. Maybe we should call it a night?"

"Yeah, I think I'd better head home too. Tomorrow is the first day at the new Grays Peak building, and I have a feeling it will be hectic trying to work and get my office set up."

"This was so fun." She stood, pulling me into her arms when I was on my feet. "Call me. I was going to come watch Lucy sing too. Let's go together."

Yes, please. The worst part about being single was constantly going places alone.

"I'd love to." I picked up my purse and dug out my wallet while she did the same, each of us leaving cash on the table for Jane. "I'm going to use the restroom before I walk home."

"Okay. Bye."

I waited until Larke walked out the door before crossing the bar, not for the restroom, but Cal's stool.

Peter was yammering on about cars and how he could give friends a great deal on the newest model Ford half-ton.

Cal's hands were balled into fists. His jaw was clenched. To steal Larke's phrase, he was insanely gorgeous, even when he was angry. Fury gave his features an edge. But Cal was never more attractive than when he smiled. And that side of Cal was as rare as his championship rings.

Frustration simmered beneath the bulging muscles of his shoulders. His traps were bunched and pulled close to his ears. Peter was about to get tossed off that damn stool if he didn't shut up soon.

"Hi." I slid onto the stool on Cal's other side.

He glanced over, then slid his beer glass away. "You can throw another drink on me, but it won't run me out of town."

"But it would be fun."

He frowned.

"Why are you here, Stark?"

"Because I was hungry. But if I'd known it was going to take a fucking year to get my food, I would have gone somewhere else."

"Not the bar. Calamity. Why are you in Calamity?"

"I live here. Thought I'd better get to know my local bartender."

On cue, Jane appeared with a cheeseburger, fries and a basket of onion rings. "Another beer?"

He shook his head. "Water."

"Say please, Cal," I ordered.

The corner of Jane's lip turned up as she waited.

"Please," he gritted out.

"Nellie, can I get you anything?" she asked.

"No, thanks."

Larke had introduced us earlier. When I'd asked Jane if she could make me a martini, she'd informed me that it would be with vodka and it would be dirty. I'd liked her immediately.

Jane filled a glass with ice water for Cal, then brought him a bottle of ketchup before helping a customer at the opposite end of the bar.

Cal tore into his burger, his eyes closing on the first bite. A deep, throaty moan came from his chest. The last time I'd heard that moan it had not been over food.

A pulse bloomed between my legs. I crossed them, shoving forbidden memories aside, and focused on my task at hand.

Cal had to leave. He couldn't live here. My window of opportunity to convince him of such was short. As soon as he had a home, it would be much harder to run him out of town. So I had to push and push hard.

"Looks like you've made a new friend." I leaned in closer, my shoulder brushing his. The heat from his skin seeped through his thin T-shirt.

He stopped chewing, his gaze dropping to where we touched.

The air around us crackled. The world blurred. The little voice in the back of my mind whispered. *More.*

I shied away and blinked reality back into focus.

That voice got me in trouble, especially where Cal was concerned.

"Is this really how you want to spend your evenings?" I glanced past him to Peter who was doing his best to eavesdrop. "Have your ear talked off? Have your neighbor tell you how you botched the AFC Championship when you threw that pick six in the third quarter?"

Cal's nostrils flared as he growled a warning, "Nellie."

Razzing him about football was always a guaranteed way to make his temper spike.

"You don't fit in here," I said.

"Who says?"

"Me."

"And you're the expert on Montana?"

I'd known him for nearly twenty years. No, I wasn't an expert on Montana. But I had figured out Cal a long, long time ago. "There's no place for you to hide here, Cal. Everyone in town will see your true colors."

He tensed.

Bullseye.

We both knew I was right. There would be no blending

into crowds, no matter how hard he tried. Cal would always stand apart. And though he loved being the center of attention on the football field, he was oddly private in his personal life.

Someone would eventually intrude and piss him off. Then he'd explode. A town this size, people would talk.

Maybe I didn't have to run him out of town. Maybe he'd do that all on his own.

"You'd be happier in a bigger city. There, you'd fit."

"Maybe I don't fit anywhere," he murmured, toying with a french fry. "You're being particularly harsh today."

Now it was my turn to tense.

Harsh had never been my style. That was Cal's specialty.

I opened my mouth to apologize, but before I could speak, Cal glanced over with his signature smirk.

"Maybe the one who needs to leave town is you, Blondie? Maybe if I make your life miserable enough, you'll head back to Denver. Isn't that what you're trying to do to me? Make me leave?"

My nostrils flared. "So what if I am?"

"Two can play that game. But don't worry, I'm sure Pierce will still let you be his secretary, even if you lived in Colorado."

Any guilt vanished. Now all I wanted was to sprinkle arsenic over his onion rings.

"First of all, I'm not a secretary." I'd given up telling him to stop calling me Blondie ages ago, but the secretary comment always struck a nerve. "Second, you will never run me out of this town."

It was ironic that we'd both jumped to that conclusion.

That instead of trying to find an amicable peace, our instincts were to drive the other away.

But that was the world of Nellie Rivera and Cal Stark.

We drew battle lines.

We'd been drawing them since we were fourteen.

"I bet you could find an old house in Denver," he said. "Something with a lawn that your dad could mow."

This son of a bitch. There were a few buttons Cal knew were risky to press. The subject of my father was one of them.

"I hate you," I seethed.

"Then go away."

I slid off my stool.

Cal chomped another bite of his burger, grinning as he chewed.

If he thought I'd just walk away, if he thought he'd won this round, he was about to be disappointed.

Instead of leaving the stool, I climbed up again, this time on my knees. My fingers went to my lips and I let out an ear-splitting whistle.

Jane, bless her heart, killed the background music.

"Ladies and gentlemen, Mr. Cal Stark, *the* Cal Stark, former NFL quarterback"—I pointed down at him as he gaped up at me—"has been so overwhelmed with the welcome Calamity has given him that he's covering every-one's tab tonight. Food. Drinks. Everything."

A round of cheers broke out. The crowd applauded.

And I clapped right along with them, a sugar-sweet smile on my face as I picked up his beer, draining the glass dry. "Bottoms up!"

The whoops and whistles were deafening as glasses were raised in the air.

This scheme could backfire and endear Cal to the community. But it could also set expectations that every time he came into the bar, he'd cover the bill. If I knew Cal, which I did, this would give him pause each time he stepped into a restaurant. Especially if I was in the room.

His glare was razor-sharp as a rush of people scrambled to the bar, ordering another round of drinks. The waitress was being flagged by nearly every table. Peter clapped a hand on Cal's shoulder—which Cal instantly brushed off.

The bar was so loud that after I set down Cal's empty glass, I had to lean in close and speak into his ear. "Spend a little of that money. Let everyone in town know that you're rich. That's what you're good at, right?"

His shoulders slumped. For a split second, he looked miserable.

The room was a riot of rowdy, happy people. And Cal looked hurt.

Hurt by me.

I hopped off the stool, slung my purse over a shoulder and marched out the door. As I stormed the blocks home, I couldn't tell who I was angry at. Cal? Or myself? That wounded look of his was stuck in my head for the rest of the night.

Damn him. Damn this guilt.

Maintaining my guard was nearly impossible when I felt bad for that man.

I really hated Cal Stark.

Dear Diary,

*Cal told the whole school that my dad was his gardener today
so every time one of his dumb friends walked by me in the
hall, they made this lawnmower sound. A bunch of them
started doing it in the cafeteria at lunch and it was so loud
and it was so annoying and it was horrible. I cried in the bathroom. Dad came to pick me up today and he could tell I was
upset but I lied and told him it was because I didn't score a
hundred percent on my math quiz. He's going to help me
study later even though I did get a hundred. I hate this stupid
school. I just want to quit. I know Mom wants me to have this
opportunity and that Benton means I can get into a good
college and probably get a scholarship for my tuition. But
what's wrong with community college? What's wrong with
managing the Coffee Cup or being a gardener? I just want to
go to a regular school and be a regular kid. And forget Cal
Stark ever existed.*

N

CHAPTER FIVE

CAL

THE CALAMITY HARDWARE store had exactly two camping chairs. Red and green. I picked the green one because it had cupholders in each armrest. Part of me had been tempted to order a chair online and have it shipped to the motel, but if I was going to live in Calamity, I might as well spend my money at the local businesses. Even if that meant I had to go out in public.

The hardware store wasn't huge, but after breezing through the aisles, there wasn't much they didn't have. Building supplies. Camping and outdoor gear. Clothing and shoes. Even a toy section.

I'd picked up a foam sword for Elias.

"This all for you today, Cal?" the clerk asked as I carried my haul to the register.

"Yeah." I didn't ask how he knew my name. I didn't ask if he'd been one of the many I'd met at Jane's on Monday. I just dug the wallet from my pocket and shoved my credit card into the reader.

"Sure was generous of you to cover the tab at Jane's the other night."

"Yep." Not only had I been swarmed with people who'd wanted to shake my hand, I'd also had the pleasure of paying Jane over eleven hundred dollars, plus a twenty percent tip. All thanks to the *generous* Nellie Rivera.

"Anything else for you today?" he asked.

"Nope." I took the receipt from his hand, tucked my chair and the sword under an arm, then strode out the door. I'd managed to make my morning stops without seeing many people. With any luck, I'd be back in the Winnebago before I spotted another soul.

Marcy had come through like a champ with the RV. She'd stocked it with essentials, food included. She'd cleaned it top to bottom. And she'd made sure I had Wi-Fi and a streaming stick for the small television in the bedroom.

I'd been holed up inside for the past four days. It felt like an epic waste of time to have spent days watching movies, but what the hell else did I have to do?

Going anywhere in public was a risk, but this morning, I'd had no choice but to brave the grocery store or face starvation. I'd gone there first, loading up on enough food to last me the week. And then I'd gone to the hardware store, walking through the door a minute after they'd opened at seven. If shopping this early meant I didn't have to interact with many people, I'd gladly wake up an hour earlier than normal.

The only productive thing I'd done this week was exercise. Every morning I'd go for a run at dawn, then do calisthenics on the floor of the RV. Eventually, I'd have to find a weight room. I'd probably try yoga at The Refinery and hope it would loosen the strain in my lower back. But for now, I'd pop a few pain pills each morning and avoid human interaction whenever possible.

I was hiding.

Just like Nellie had predicted.

My Land Rover was parked on the street, the black paint gleaming compared to the dusty Chevy truck parked three spaces down. My car had arrived yesterday from Nashville, and being behind the wheel gave me a sense of freedom I'd missed over the past week.

If Nellie did chase me out of town, at least I'd have wheels.

The motel's parking lot was full as I drove past. Guests had streamed in last night for the first weekend in June, and as Marcy had promised, the place was packed. Luckily, I bypassed it all and eased down the alley to park beside the Winnebago.

It didn't take long to haul everything inside and unload my groceries. While I brewed another pot of coffee, I unpacked my chair, taking it out of the case and ripping off the tag. Then I set it up outside next to the camper's door.

My makeshift patio.

Montana had a lot of positives from the sprawling mountains to the big, blue sky. There were a hell of a lot fewer people in the state than anywhere else I'd lived. And the lazy summer mornings with birds chirping, the sun shining and a fresh breeze were hard to beat.

I settled into my seat, coffee mug in one hand, and Nellie's diary in the other. If I hadn't been watching TV these past four days, I'd been rereading her journal. This was the sixth—or seventh?—pass.

She'd had more diaries in that box. What did the other years say about me? Too bad I hadn't thought to snag those too.

Reading her thoughts, her struggles, had become an obsession. It had taken football's place. Instead of overthinking practices or replaying mistakes I'd made in a game, I'd fixated on this little book.

Sipping my coffee, I flipped it open to the page I'd read last night. The entry was from the lawnmower day. I'd long forgotten about that day, but after reading this entry, I could practically hear the noise from the cafeteria.

There was a lot in this journal that irritated me, but this entry pissed me right the fuck off. Because I hadn't done anything wrong. Nellie had blamed me, like I'd done something malicious. When all I'd done was tell the truth.

There'd been a girl in Spanish class who'd been gossiping about Nellie. She'd been snickering that Nellie's dad was unemployed, so I'd corrected her. Told her that Nellie's dad was a gardener and that he worked at our place.

Just me sharing facts. Except Nellie had assumed I'd done it to spite her.

How could I have known it would become this thing through the school? Maybe my crime hadn't been telling everyone to shut up.

"What are you reading?"

I flinched at the voice and my coffee sloshed over the rim of the mug. My glare flew to the woman at my side who was staring over my shoulder in an attempt to read Nellie's diary.

I slammed the book closed and shook out my wet hand. "Who are you?"

"Harry. Short for Harriet." She put her hands on her

hips. Her gray hair was cut into a short pixie style. Her thick-framed glasses were the same color brown as her eyes. "Who are you?"

"Cal Stark. Though you already knew that, didn't you?"

"Finally emerged from your cave." She motioned to the bus. "About time."

I frowned. "You must be Marcy's mother."

"I am." She gave me a single nod, turned on the heel of her cowboy boot and walked away.

I leaned forward in the chair, waiting to see if she'd come back, but then a door slammed shut.

"Okay," I drawled and swallowed the rest of my coffee. I was about to head in for a refill when Harry appeared, rounding the side of the RV with her own camp chair in tow.

Well, fuck.

So much for hiding.

She set up her chair beside mine, close enough that our arm rests were touching. Then she plopped down in the seat and let out a sigh.

I stared at her profile, waiting for her to speak, but she sat there, her eyes aimed at the grassy field that stretched behind the motel. "Did you need something?"

"Did I ask you for something?"

"No."

"Then I guess you answered your own question."

I blinked.

"My chair is better than yours," she declared. It had a sturdy metal frame and folded in half rather than collapsed into a column. The material was a thick, gray mesh instead of my green canvas.

"So it is."

"People tell me I'm blunt."

I chuckled. "People tell me the same."

"Small talk annoys me."

"Same here."

"If you give me any bullshit about the weather, I'll walk."

"Is that all it will take? Because today is beautiful. It's supposed to get into the seventies. Ten percent chance of rain around five."

"Smart-ass," she muttered. "I like to sleep in, so don't get too loud in the mornings."

"Have I been loud?"

"Not yet. Let's keep it that way."

"Fair enough."

She sank deeper into her seat, stretching out her legs and crossing one ankle over the other. Her Wrangler jeans were rolled into a cuff at the hem. "I don't like visitors."

I arched an eyebrow and nodded to her chair. "Neither do I."

"We're neighbors. That's different."

"Is it?"

"Entirely." She said it was different, therefore, it was different. This was a woman who didn't argue. Harry was a boss. "My daughter is busy."

"Marcy?"

"Yes." She nodded. "She takes care of a lot of things on her own. From time to time, I do some housekeeping to help her out. Summers are busy."

"She mentioned that the other day."

"You're paying her to clean?"

"Yes." I sat up straighter, unsure where this was going

but sure I wasn't going to like it. "She rented me the bus, like a motel room."

"Ah." Harry nodded. "Well, I volunteered to clean the Winnebago for her. Like a motel room."

"You?" This woman had to be over seventy years old. There was no way I'd be able to sit back and let her scrub my toilet or mop the floors.

"Me."

Fuck. I blew out a long breath. "Forget it. I'll clean it myself."

A smile ghosted her lips. Guess that was what she'd wanted to hear. And that was the reason for her visit. One moment she was lounging in her superior chair, the next she was on her feet, gone without another word.

"Nice chat, Harry," I called as she disappeared around the RV's corner.

"See you around, Cal," she called back.

I shook my head and stood, leaving both chairs in place as I went inside for more coffee. The moment I stepped through the door, my phone rang. Pierce's name flashed on the screen.

"Hey," I answered.

"Hi," he said. "You busy?"

"No. What's up?"

"Nellie just called. Something's wrong with her car. She was on her way to the office and it broke down. She called for a tow but I guess the driver's out on another call. It's going to be a while."

And there probably weren't a lot of other garages with tow trucks in Calamity.

"I don't want her sitting on the side of the road for

hours," Pierce said. "I'd pick her up myself, but we just got to the hospital for Constance's checkup. I'll be a bit. I get that you two have . . . issues. But can you set them aside and go get her?"

The baby was crying in the background. Pierce had called me when they'd gotten home from the cabin but I hadn't seen him since before they'd left. He sounded exhausted. "Yeah. I got her. No problem."

"Thanks. I'll text you directions."

"'Kay." I ended the call and dragged a hand through my hair. *Damn.* I wasn't ready to face Nellie yet, but when Pierce asked for help, I helped.

So I grabbed my keys, forgetting the coffee. I shot Nellie's diary a glare, leaving it on the counter, then headed for my car.

My phone dinged as I climbed behind the wheel. Then I followed the directions in Pierce's text down First Street and to the highway, taking a few turns until I was headed down a narrow road bordered by a barbed wire fence.

Nellie's silver sedan glinted beneath the sky. The woman herself was leaning against the driver's side door with her arms crossed over her chest. Her hair was nearly a perfect white under the sun, like untouched snow. She'd curled the silky strands today and the waves spiraled down her shoulders and spine. Her lips were painted a sinful shade of red.

She pushed off the car and stood tall as I eased off the road and parked behind her. Her lips flattened when I stepped outside.

Guess she wouldn't be greeting me with a smile today.

"Hey." I jerked up my chin.

"I see that Pierce didn't listen when I told him I'd be fine to just wait for the tow truck."

"So I can go?" I hooked a thumb over my shoulder.

"No," she muttered. "Could you give me a ride to the office?"

"That's why I'm here. But you have to say please."

She was constantly telling me to say please. To mind my manners. It was refreshing to throw that her direction for a change.

"Please."

"Better."

She rolled her eyes and turned, opening her door before bending inside. Her slacks molded to the curve of her ass. Her blouse rode up, revealing the dimples at her lower back.

My cock jerked. My hands inched for a touch. Just one. To grab those hips and palm that ass. This was not a safe direction for my thoughts, so I spun away and kicked a pebble across the pavement. "What's up with your car?"

"I have no idea." She hauled a tote bag from the car and slammed the door closed. The keys she tucked beside the gas cap. "The check engine light came on and then the engine revved before there was this nasty burning smell. I didn't know what else to do, so I just pulled over."

"It's probably your transmission."

"Awesome." She pinched the bridge of her nose. "That sounds like I won't have a working car today."

"Doubtful."

"Great," she deadpanned as she walked past me for my car.

I let myself take a single look of her ass in those slacks

and the sway of her hips. Then I got behind the wheel and slammed a pair of shades over my eyes. "Which direction?"

"Straight for about two miles. Then the road curves. Just follow it."

The scent of her perfume filled the cab as I pulled onto the road. It was the smell of beauty and temptation. I hit the button to roll down the window.

Nellie did the same to hers.

We rode in silence, the air whipping through the cab until a building came into view. It was a single story with sparkly windows and rustic, wooden siding. Clearly new. Clearly expensive. But it complemented the natural landscape and the mountain foothills in the backdrop.

Nellie rifled through her bag, snatching a different set of keys as I eased into the empty parking lot.

"Is anyone here?"

"No, it's just me right now until the others move. Thanks for the ride."

"Welcome." How was she supposed to get home?

She moved to open the door but stopped when her fingertips grazed the handle. "About the other night, at Jane's. I'm sorry."

"For what? Making me spend a bunch of money?"

"No." She shook her head. "When I said I hated you."

"Don't you?"

The apology was clear on her face. But the answer to my question was not. She lifted a shoulder. Not a yes. Not a no.

Did she hate me? According to her diary, she'd hated me at fourteen. She'd probably hated me since. And maybe she'd apologized for voicing it on Monday. But that didn't necessarily make it untrue.

"Thanks again." She opened the door and stepped outside.

"I'll pick you up at five." The sentence flew out of my mouth before I could stop it.

"Don't worry about it. I'll find a ride. They might even have my car fixed by then."

We both knew the chances of that were slim. "It's just a ride, Nellie. And I've got nothing else to do."

"Fine." Her shoulders sagged. "Five."

"Hey, Nell?" I stopped her before she could shut the door.

"Yeah?"

"Do you? Hate me?"

There was no mistaking the vulnerability in my voice. This was her chance to shove the dagger in deep. To shred me to ribbons. To go for the kill.

The corner of her mouth turned up. "Not today."

CHAPTER SIX

NELLIE

THE LONGER THIS phone call with my mechanic continued, the further my heart sank.

"I can probably have it ready for you Monday afternoon," he said. "I think I've got the parts to fix it. We got lucky there."

"Okay." Except I didn't feel lucky. That car was less than a year old and there was a very real chance I'd bought a lemon. At least it was under warranty. "Will you call me when it's ready?"

"Yep. We've got some loaners if you need a car."

"No, that's all right." I had nowhere to go this weekend that wasn't within walking distance to my house. Hopefully Larke could give me a lift to the office on Monday morning. Worst case, I'd call a cab. "Thank you."

"No problem. Talk to you soon."

I ended the call and slumped into my chair. As Cal had suspected, my transmission was busted. But at least my lemon had gotten me to Montana. Being stranded on a highway between Denver and Calamity would have been much worse than a few days without a vehicle and a couple of shuttle rides from Cal.

It was almost five, so I closed my laptop and loaded it into my bag. I'd spent most of my day on disappointing phone calls, my mechanic's the cherry on top. Along with my broken-down car, I was now minus my assistant, Suzie, and effectively doing two jobs, hers and my own, until I could hire her replacement.

But I'd manage. I'd work longer hours so that Pierce could enjoy his time at home with Kerrigan and the kids.

For years I'd worked as Pierce's assistant. It had started as a temporary gig, something to fill the gap while I'd hunted for my dream job. But about a year after I'd started at Grays Peak, I'd realized that the reason I hadn't applied anywhere else or sent my résumé to corporate recruiters was because I had my dream job.

Stellar boss. Flexible schedule. Daily challenges. Excellent pay. Responsibility and respect. The only thing I'd lacked was a prestigious title, and my ego could have lived without it. Until one day, Pierce had walked into my office with a box of letterpress business cards.

Vice President did look lovely beneath my name.

There were days when I still threatened to quit. Every time Pierce irritated me, I'd threaten to walk. It kept him on his toes. But we both knew I wasn't going anywhere.

After graduating from UNC with my bachelor's degree, I'd stayed in Charlotte. The city had been familiar and comfortable. The tech company where I'd done an internship my senior year had offered me a full-time position as a business analyst.

The work had been fine, but my boss had turned out to be a slimy bastard. He'd taken credit for my ideas and pitched them as his own. He'd downplayed my accomplishments and talked badly about me behind closed doors. I'd endured it for a while, but after three years, when I'd wanted to quit every day, finally . . . I'd quit.

Mom and Dad had been ecstatic when I'd told them I was moving home, even though I'd been unemployed. The week I'd returned to Denver, ready to apply anywhere and everywhere, I'd bumped into Pierce at a restaurant. We'd lost touch after high school, so we'd chatted for a while and caught up over drinks.

He'd been desperate for a decent assistant.

I'd been eager for a salary.

My official title was vice president to the CEO, which basically gave me free rein to make decisions in his stead. I knew when to check with him. I knew when I had the authority to approve proposals and make hiring decisions. He'd granted me a lot of leeway to help run the company.

Our CFO was waiting for me to review next year's fiscal projections, but instead of doing my job, today I'd spent covering for Suzie.

She'd only been working as my assistant for a couple of months. I'd hired her to do Pierce's actual assistant duties, like schedule travel and manage his calendar. As a bonus, she could be in Denver while I was in Calamity. She was supposed to be my eyes and ears at headquarters.

Suzie was supposed to be helping out with the relocation company, getting details coordinated for the employees moving to Montana. Instead, she'd called me before I'd even left the house this morning and quit.

Then my car had died.

Then Cal had shown up.

Normally, a Cal encounter would be the worst part of my day. But today, it had actually been . . . the best. *Strange.*

Well, he'd be here in minutes. And knowing Cal, he'd say something dickish on the drive home, like call me Pierce's secretary, and the world would be back to normal.

Secretary. God, that one irked me. I'd worked my entire life to prove myself. I doubted Cal knew just how deep it cut to have my accomplishments downplayed.

In high school, I had this obsession to beat the rich kids. To prove that I might not have their money, but I had the brains. When I beat Pierce for valedictorian, I was so proud. So smug. Yet as I stood at the podium, getting ready to deliver my speech, all of my arrogance evaporated. Because I was staring at a crowd of people who would never accept me.

Ace every test. Get a full ride to a prestigious university. Be smart. Be kind.

None of it mattered.

To them, I would always be less.

So I gave my speech. I tossed my cap in the air. I let Mom and Dad take a hundred pictures and throw a party in our backyard. And later that night, when I was alone in my room, I cried for an hour.

It had taken me a long time to realize that I wasn't less. That I was comfortable in my skin. That I was just me. That I *liked* me.

But there was one person who had the inherent ability to bring my adolescent doubts out of the shadows.

Cal.

With my bag hooked on my shoulder, I shut off the lights

to my office. I made sure the alarm in the lobby was set. Then I walked out the door, locking the office behind me. I'd just turned the key when the sound of an engine purred through the lot.

Cal had on the same sunglasses he'd worn this morning, but his hair was trapped beneath a baseball hat. It accentuated the definition of his jaw. It highlighted the stubble on his tapered chin.

My breath caught as he came to a stop. Damn him for being so handsome. Damn this attraction. Whether he was in a three-piece suit, a football uniform, or jeans and a T-shirt like he was today, it was always difficult to tear my eyes away from Cal.

"Hi." I gave him a tight smile as I opened the passenger door and climbed inside.

The windows were already down. *Good.* Cal smelled as good as he looked, and that heady scent of leather and spice and male was hard to ignore. This morning, when I'd caught myself breathing in his intoxicating cologne, I'd practically stuck my head out the window.

"Hey." His voice had this delicious, deep rumble. How many women had fallen into his bed because of that baritone whisper? *At least one.*

I stuffed my bag between my feet and buckled my seat belt. "Thanks for the ride."

"Sure." He pulled away from the building and headed into town, driving with one wrist casually draped over the steering wheel. The ends of his hair stuck out from beneath the hat, the strands curling.

"You need a haircut." I actually loved his hair a little long and messy. Which was why I needed him to cut it.

"You sound like my mother." He chuckled. "She said the same thing when I was on FaceTime with her earlier."

"Is she still in Denver?"

"Yep." He nodded and shifted his hand to the wheel, gripping it too tight. "Still living in the same house."

Probably with his father. Last I'd heard, they were still married. Not that I'd ask. Cal's dad could go fuck himself.

"Your parents are still in Denver too, right?" he asked.

"No, they're in Arizona." Mom and Dad were coming to visit in a couple of weeks. I'd have to make sure they were far, far from Cal because he was not someone either of my parents would want to see.

"Oh." His forehead furrowed. "I didn't realize they'd moved."

"We don't exactly share personal updates, do we?"

"No, we don't." He glanced over, staring for a moment too long.

My heart thrummed harder. Desire curled in my lower belly. I blamed it on his stupid Tennessee Titans hat. It made him look relaxed. Normal. Sexy. "Eyes on the road, Stark."

The corner of his mouth twitched but he obeyed. "Why Arizona?"

"The weather."

He hummed, the soothing sound filling the cab.

I shifted, crossing my legs. The throb in my core was beginning to bloom, but I refused to let Cal—his voice, his smell, his freaking hat—turn me on. Not today.

My bag toppled to the side at my ankles as I twisted, shifting closer to the window as the air rushed past my face. I breathed in the summer air and studied the landscape, from the green meadows to the indigo mountain tips still capped with untouched snow.

Downtown was abuzz for a Friday evening as we eased down First. The parking spaces outside Jane's were full. The bar would be packed later if Lucy was singing. Larke had texted me earlier and asked if I wanted to meet her around eight. That gave me time to make some dinner. Unwind. Then refresh my hair and makeup.

Cal navigated the streets to my house like he'd been there ten times, not once. And when he pulled up to the curb, he didn't bother putting the Land Rover in park.

"Thanks." I opened the door and swept up my bag.

He stayed quiet as I shut the door. Then he was gone, his taillights disappearing down the block.

"Huh." Not exactly a friendly conversation, but then again, no conversations with Cal were ever friendly. But we hadn't fought. The absence of banter and bickering was . . . unsettling.

Was something wrong? Was he upset or angry?

"Not my problem," I muttered as I walked across the sidewalk to unlock my front door.

I set my bag on the table in the entryway, then kicked off my heels.

The living room was finally void of boxes. I'd spent the evenings this week putting the last of my belongings away. The random kitchen gadgets had been stowed in drawers. The knickknacks had been placed on various surfaces. And since my TV cabinet looked empty and sad in the living room, I'd ordered a new flat screen.

The only boxes I hadn't unpacked were those that Cal had hauled to the office upstairs. I needed to sort through my old diaries, business texts and romance novels, but I'd decided to save that job for a snowy winter day. For now, those boxes were stacked in the office's closet.

Little by little, the house was becoming mine. Every time I walked through the door, I felt more at peace.

I unbuttoned my blouse, letting it hang open at the front. A stretchy pair of jeans, a cotton tee and a bra without underwire were calling my name. But before I could head upstairs to change, the doorbell rang.

"Shit." I rebuttoned my shirt, hitting every other hole, then rushed to the door, opening it to see Cal.

His SUV was parked on the street and he'd left his sunglasses behind. His gaze darted to my chest and the buttons I'd missed. Those hazel pools darkened, the gold flecks swirling with chocolate and green. He'd turned his hat backward. Why was that so flipping hot?

"Did you forget something?" My voice was breathy.

He held up a tube of lipstick. *My* lipstick. It must have fallen out of my bag.

"Oh. Thanks." I took it from his hand, waiting for him to turn and leave. But he stepped forward, forcing me out of the way as he came inside. "Cal, what are you—"

He crushed his mouth to mine.

I gasped, clinging to his shoulders as he swept me deeper into the room, kicking the door closed. The slam rattled the walls. The sweep of his tongue shook my bones.

With one hand I gripped his shirt, balling it into a fist to pull him closer. But with the other hand, I shoved his shoulder away.

This was us.

Push and pull. Cold or hot. Off to on.

We were magnets, one flip and we'd repulse each other. But turned the other way, there was no ripping us apart.

The rational part of my brain screamed for me to kick him out. *Make him leave.* But that little voice, the voice that hated reason and craved passion, whispered *yes, yes, yes.*

I tore my mouth away, the two of us panting for breath.

His eyes locked with mine, searching for my decision. Searching for an answer. Anything that might explain this chemistry. "Don't answer the fucking door with your blouse unbuttoned."

I raised my chin, my hand tightening even tighter on his shirt. "What are you going to do about it?"

Cal gripped the collar of my shirt and pulled. *Whoosh.* Buttons went flying as the sound of shredding seams filled the room.

"I liked this blouse, asshole."

"Leveling the score, remember? I had to throw my T-shirt away last week." He reached a hand behind his head and grabbed his tee, yanking it over his head. It dropped to the floor as I shrugged off the tattered remains of my top.

Cal's naked torso was a gift to humankind. From broad pecs to chiseled abs to ripped arms, his body was honed to perfection. Add in that delicious V at his hips and the naughty little voice laughed victoriously. *Yes.* There would be no stopping, not tonight.

I could stare at him for hours, but he never let me. There was no such thing as slow when the clothes began piling on the floor. His shirt was gone and his mouth was on mine again.

I'd regret this tomorrow. History would repeat itself, and

I'd spend hours chastising myself for being so damn weak. Still, I kissed him back, matching him beat for beat.

Some decisions were worth the shame.

His mouth was an addiction. The softness of his lips. The bite of his teeth. The wet heat of his wicked tongue. He kissed the way he played football. He kissed the way he fucked.

Without restraint.

Cal's hands found my ass, squeezing so hard I squealed down his throat. But he didn't let up. He knew I liked it rough and always delivered.

I slid my hands between us, fumbling for the button and zipper of his jeans. While I worked them free, he flipped the hooks on my bra, tugging it off my arms. With a few deft flicks of his long fingers, my slacks were unclasped and pooled at my bare feet.

My hand was poised, ready to dive into his boxers, but before I could wrap a hand around his shaft, my entire body jerked. I teetered on my feet, tearing my lips away from his to glance at my bare hips.

Cal had ripped off the panties.

"Stop tearing my clothes."

He met my glare, then hauled me into his arms, spinning me until my back hit the wall. His frame trapped mine. Where Cal wanted me, Cal pinned me.

I'd never liked being manhandled, but Cal was the exception to every rule. No one compared to his strength. No one could lift me like I weighed nothing. His hands gripped me beneath my thighs, spreading my knees wide as he pushed his hips forward. The roughness of his jeans brushed my sensitive flesh.

"When did you start wearing panties?" he asked as I wrapped my legs around his waist.

Instead of giving him an answer, I leaned forward and latched on to his neck, sucking and nipping so hard I'd leave a mark.

He groaned, the vibration racing straight to my clit. The dusting of coarse hair on his chest caressed my nipples as Cal's arousal hardened against my aching core.

"Fuck me," I whispered against his lips. "Now."

A hand abandoned my leg and dove into his jeans pocket, coming out with a condom.

I didn't ask why he had one at the ready.

There were a lot of questions I didn't ask when it came to Cal.

Either he knew this was going to happen. Or he had it in case it was going to happen with some other woman.

I blocked that thought from my mind as he shoved his jeans down, just a few inches. Enough to free his thick cock and roll on the condom. As he positioned the tip at my entrance, I gave him a warning glare. "Slow."

"Did you forget who gives the orders?" He thrust forward, hard and fast, filling me completely.

I cried out, savoring the stretch as my body adjusted to his size.

He dropped his forehead to mine. "You feel so fucking good."

"Oh, God." My eyes drifted shut. No one moved like Cal. No one made me feel like Cal.

He eased out, his hands sliding to my ass, pulling my cheeks apart just slightly with those long fingers. Then he slid inside again, this time inch by inch. It was only when he was seated as deep as he could go that I let go of the breath I'd been holding.

His eyes locked with mine, his Adam's apple bobbing. "Fuck, Nell."

"More. Harder." I clung to his shoulders, aching for a release.

It had been too long. We hadn't been together in months. Not since his last trip to Denver and one of our spontaneous hookups. The first time had been in Charlotte. Ever since, it had just . . . happened.

Push and pull. Cold or hot. Off to on.

Cal began to move in a punishing rhythm, thrust after thrust. With every stroke I built higher. Hotter. Together, we were an inferno. Sex with Cal was exhilarating and bold. He moved with the same arrogance he did in every other aspect of his life. He knew he could shatter me into pieces. He made sure of it. He worked me up until I was nothing but trembling limbs and hitched breaths.

"Come." He dropped his mouth to my pulse and sucked, the pistoning of his cock never slowing. His shaft dragged against my clit as his hands palmed my ass.

Every cell in my being was on fire. One more thrust and I came undone, crying out as stars broke behind my eyes. I pulsed and clenched, so overwhelmed by sensation that I was lost to anything but the orgasm.

He growled against my neck, then groaned my name and came on a roar.

I forced my eyes open in time to see his handsome face twist in ecstasy. The parted lips. The sharp corners of his jaw. And that damn backward hat.

Even after his release Cal kept me against the wall for a

few heartbeats until the aftershocks stopped. Then he pulled himself free and set me on my unsteady feet.

Regret flooded my mind, like a bucket of iced water being dumped over my head. It happened every time, at the exact moment our bodies were no longer connected. The guilt wasn't only about the sex. It was also because we had nothing to say.

Because when it came to Cal, I was weak.

I could have stopped him. This time. The others. I probably should have stopped him.

Instead, I'd succumbed to this insatiable craving. That devilish little voice who hungered for Cal in a way that I'd never had with another man.

Why him?

That question would get me into trouble, so I pushed the hair out of my face and breezed past Cal, walking straight for the stairs. "Bye, Cal."

I didn't look back. I didn't wait to see if he had anything to say. I doubted I'd want to hear it anyway.

Locked in my bedroom, I immediately went to the shower. My hands were jittery as I cleaned Cal's scent from my body. I dropped the mascara wand twice while I freshened my makeup. The skin between my legs was tender as I pulled on fresh panties.

Dressed in jeans and a tee, I tiptoed downstairs, and as expected, found only my ruined clothes waiting. Cal was long gone.

Because this was what we did. This was who we were.

We fought. We fucked.

We went our separate ways. Until the next time I caved.

Until the next time I listened to that evil little voice.

Dear Diary,

I saw Cal kissing Phoebe McAdams today. He had her pushed up against a locker as they sucked face. I was coming out of the library. Mr. Edwards gave me a pass from study hall because I wanted some new books. I almost dropped my pile when I saw him totally making out with her. I don't think they saw me because I tried to hide. Phoebe was grabbing Cal's butt. He had his hands on her chest. They were like locked together. Like they couldn't get close enough. He didn't kiss me like that. How flipping pathetic am I that I let Cal Stark kiss me yesterday? Yeah. He kissed me yesterday. Sorry for not writing about it. I was sort of in a weird place last night. Like excited and confused and nervous. Dad warned me to stay away from him. He said Cal wasn't like us. I think maybe Dad could tell I liked Cal, so I lied and called Cal a dumb jock. I told Dad that I hated Cal. I don't know why I did that. I don't like lying. Except it's the truth now, isn't it? Cal is a dumb jock. And a jerk. He was my first kiss too. I thought he liked me. I liked him. A lot. How stupid am I to think that a guy like Cal Stark could actually want me? I bet everything he told me yesterday about his dad and football was crap. It was some sick trick. I wish I could take that kiss back. I wish I could have a redo. Is this what it means to be used? Because I never want to feel this way again. Never ever. Boys suck. And I hate Cal Stark.

Nellie

CHAPTER SEVEN

CAL

THE FIRST ENTRY in Nellie's diary was the hardest one to read. So I'd made myself read it a hundred times.

The book rested on my chest as I stared at the Winnebago's ceiling. My bedroom was cast in a dim gray. The lights from the motel and Harry's porch seeped through the RV's windows and thin shades.

In the past three days, I'd had a hell of a time sleeping. Not only from the light—I preferred pitch-black—but from the noise in my head. It was four in the morning and I'd popped awake like I'd been asleep for eight hours, not five.

Boredom was a fickle bastard. Retirement had given me too much free time and now my brain wouldn't shut the fuck up. My workouts got a little longer each day. I'd spent more time cooking and cleaning in the past three days than I had in three years. Marcy had let me do laundry in the motel's utility room and as of this afternoon, besides the clothes on my back, not one article in the closet was dirty.

Straying far from the camper wasn't appealing, so I'd done my best to stick close and stay busy. Except there'd been too many empty minutes. And when the temptation was overpowering, I'd reach for Nellie's journal. Another week and I'd be able to recite the entries from memory.

Maybe I should have stolen another diary. While she'd been in the shower the other day and I'd been standing in her living room, my dick still hard, I'd thought about taking one, maybe two more.

But, coward that I was, I'd walked out the door instead. I didn't need to steal more diaries to know what she'd written. I hadn't exactly gotten nicer to Nellie as our high school years had progressed. Football had become more and more of a focus each year, but I'd been the same callous prick to her for years.

How could she stand to let me touch her? How could she let me inside her body?

How had I been her first kiss?

She deserved better.

That day was as crystal clear in my memory as yesterday.

Nellie's dad was working on my parents' yard, and she'd tagged along that afternoon. It was right after school started our freshman year. Early September. I remembered, not because of the date in her journal, but because football season was going strong and it was the Monday after our first home game.

Dad had bitched at me all weekend because I'd sat on the bench for most of the game. Even though I was better, Coach had played the senior quarterback. It was the guy's last season and everyone knew he wouldn't play college ball.

But did Dad cut me any slack? No. He blamed me for not being a starter.

Work harder.

Show them you're the fucking star.

Make them see that you're the obvious choice.

He'd made me throw two hundred passes that weekend into the net beside the pool. My punishment for not shining bright enough.

I was supposed to do another fifty after I came home from practice. Mom had picked me up from school, and when we got home, I'd gone straight for a football, grabbing it with a wince. My shoulder was dead. She told me that she'd cover with Dad. That she'd lie and tell him I threw for an hour.

Mom lied to Dad a lot on my behalf.

Instead of homework or TV, I went outside and hung beside the pool.

I knew who Nellie was. All of us knew who the scholarship kids were at Benton. They stood out, even with our uniforms. Off-brand shoes. Cheap phones. And they kept their chins down. Mostly they were an afterthought.

Not Nellie.

She was impossible not to notice. There was nothing fake about her. Fresh face. Long, pretty blond hair. Green eyes that saw more than the other fourteen-year-old girls.

She had a book under her arm when she found me beside the pool. She'd been surprised and embarrassed, like she'd been caught trespassing. I probably should have let her walk away, but instead, I told her she could sit with me. She did.

She took the lounge chair beside mine and cracked open her biology textbook.

I was supposed to be studying the same thing, so I leaned in closer. The move hurt the hell out of my shoulder, and I must have cringed or grunted or something.

Nellie asked me what happened.

To this day, I still didn't know why I told her. But I spilled everything. How my father was a dick. How he expected perfection. How he hadn't made it to the pros as a quarterback, so he expected me to make up for his shortcomings. How the pressure made me sick at night.

I told her how I wanted to disappoint him just so he'd leave me the fuck alone.

I admitted that I didn't have the courage to stop.

I confessed that the reason I worked my ass off was not because he wanted me to, but because I was better. Because I was going to show that son of a bitch.

No one knew my truths. Not Mom. Not Pierce. Not my other friends. But I gave them to Nellie.

I dropped my guard and let her in.

To this day I wasn't sure why.

We talked while the sound of her father's lawnmower hummed in the background. It couldn't have been more than thirty minutes, but it had been the most important conversation I'd had in a long, long time.

She listened, without judgment. I had money and talent and status. I was a rich kid who had a bright future. She of all people could have thrown it in my face. Instead, she touched my hand and said she was sorry.

That was when I kissed her.

It was fast. Chaste. Sweet. I kissed her the way a nice girl should be kissed. Just a brush of my lips to hers.

Her first.

Damn.

I never told anyone about that kiss, not even Pierce. He knew the rest, my broken relationship with Dad and the reasons I pushed myself to the extreme. But that had come later in high school, when the two of us would get drunk at a house party and spill our guts. Maybe I'd had the courage to tell Pierce because I'd already told Nellie.

Because she'd seen the real me first.

After the kiss, she blushed and smiled. I remember thinking I wanted to do it again. Over and over again, just for that smile. But then the lawnmower stopped, she swept up her book and raced away.

What would have happened if I'd stayed in my chair?

Maybe I would have asked her out on a date at school the next day. Maybe I would have made her my girlfriend. Maybe I would have ruined her.

Maybe her hate was always destined to be the outcome.

Still, I wished I would have stayed in my chair beside the pool.

I was just about to round the corner of the house when I heard her dad talking. He was giving her a lecture.

Stay away from Cal. He's trouble, honey. These people are not like us. They can be cruel, and you are too good for a kid like that.

I'd never officially met Darius Rivera, just seen him in passing. Guess it didn't matter. He'd formed his opinion. I couldn't exactly blame him. After all, Darius knew my father.

The fucking worst part? He was right. He was so goddamn right.

But it wasn't his words that cut deep. It was Nellie's.

Don't worry, Daddy. He's just a dumb jock. I hate him just like all the other rich kids.

It was hard for me to look at her and not hear those words. Decades later and I could picture them coming from her lips. I could feel the blade plunging into my spine. I'd confided in her and all she saw was *a dumb jock*. Someone to hate.

According to this diary, she'd lied to Darius.

Had she? I wanted those words to be a lie.

I *needed* them to be a lie, even if the damage was done.

The next day, I did what other teenage boys did to girls who bruised their egos—I got even. Phoebe and I were in the library for English class. I watched Nellie walk through the door and disappear into the stacks. About the time she was checking out her books, I grabbed Phoebe's hand and snuck her into the hallway.

Then I kissed her. I knew Nellie saw us. I made sure she saw us.

I made sure I was cruel. I made sure I was a dumb jock. And from that day forward, I kept my distance.

Until that night in Charlotte.

The lines between us had blurred that night. There was a constant hate simmering beneath the surface. Attraction was its constant companion. And fuck, but we were hot together.

We'd sparked, and there was no chance of stopping. Like three days ago in her living room. I blamed that on her lipstick. The tube had been rolling around on the floor of my car, and when I'd stopped to pick it up, the red color had made me hard as a rock.

I'd wanted that red on my skin.

A smile tugged at my mouth. I'd had that red all over my lips when I'd come home. Nellie had even left a mark on my neck. It was nearly faded now but I lifted my hand, still picturing the hickey.

Sex with Nellie was laced with desperation. A fear that it might be the last time. So we never held back. We never went easy.

Picturing her naked and hoisted against that wall, I stiffened. "Fuck it."

With her image in my mind, I set the diary aside and went to the cramped shower in the Winnebago. My release was shallow. There was an edge that only Nellie's tight body would erase. But I'd be damned if I went to her again.

Now it was her turn to initiate the next round.

Would she? We'd spent years going back and forth. It was a game, one we'd played from a distance. How would this work with us in the same town? When there weren't thousands of miles keeping us apart?

Would she come to me?

What if she didn't?

I dressed in a pair of charcoal sweats and matching hoodie. The RV felt too cramped, so I slipped outside, took a seat in my green camp chair and tipped my head back to study the stars.

"Pretty night."

"What the—" I flew out of my chair, my hand slamming against my racing heart. "Jesus, Harry. Make a fucking noise next time. You scared the piss out of me."

She plopped down in her chair.

"Are you going to at least apologize?" I asked, staring down at her.

"Nope."

"Nice," I muttered and resumed my seat. "What are you doing up?"

"You first."

No way I was going to explain the reason for my sleeplessness.

"That's what I thought." Even in the dark I could see the smirk on her face.

I sighed, giving my heart a few minutes to return to its normal pace, then tilted my gaze back to the sky.

Harry did the same, sitting in her superior chair, her legs crossed at the ankles. I hadn't seen her since the day she'd brought that chair over. Every time I left and returned, I wondered if she would have snatched it away. But it had been sitting beside mine for days.

She wore flannel pajamas, the print different blocks of red and black. The top matched the pants and on her feet were a pair of yellow clogs, the kind of shoes you'd leave by the door if you just needed to pop outside for a minute.

"Did I wake you up?" I asked.

"No. Sleep isn't always easy."

She didn't offer an explanation as to why. I didn't ask for one. We simply sat in our chairs, shrouded by the cool night air, and watched the curtain of darkness fade.

By the time the sun broke across the horizon, I decided there wasn't a person in Calamity I wanted to live beside other than Harry. Few could offer quiet company.

"Suppose I'd better get some breakfast," I said, breaking the silence.

"Breakfast sounds good." She shoved to her feet. "You're buying."

"I was going to eat here."

"Because you're cheap or . . ." The corner of her mouth turned up as her sentence trailed off.

"I'm not cheap." I'd bought at Jane's the other night, hadn't I? "I don't like public spaces."

"So you'll just hide out here forever."

"No, I'm building a house. Once it's done, I'll hide out there forever."

She laughed, a throaty, rich sound of a woman who didn't laugh often. "You can hide out tomorrow. Get your wallet."

I huffed but stood and followed orders, grabbing my wallet and a hat from the counter inside. Then together, we walked downtown. Me in sweats. Harry in pajamas.

It was early enough that the shops and offices were closed. There were a few cars outside the coffee shop and a handful in front of the café, but otherwise the sidewalks were quiet. A man walked on the opposite side of First. When he glanced our direction, I pulled my hat lower.

"That's Grayson," Harry said. "He's a deputy at the sheriff's department. Good kid."

I shrugged and kept walking. We were a block from the White Oak where breakfast and the privacy of a booth awaited.

Harry pointed down the block to where a woman was walking her labradoodle our way. "That's Carlee. She's been Marcy's best friend since sixth grade."

"Okay," I drawled and flipped up my hood.

Harry scoffed. "What exactly do you think is going to happen if you show your face?"

"I'll probably get hassled."

"You will." She nodded. "If you keep yourself apart, you'll always be a novelty. Do you think Lucy Ross gets hassled every time she comes downtown?"

"I don't know. Does she?"

"No. Because she's one of us. This is her home."

"What about tourists?"

"I'm sure some ask her for an autograph from time to time. But if I saw Lucy with a crowd of people and she looked uncomfortable, what do you think I'd do? What do you think any of us would do?"

"Come to her rescue."

"You're smarter than you look." Harry tapped her temple. "But I don't know if I'd rescue you."

"Fine." I flipped my hood off and raised the brim of my hat. "Better?"

She answered with a smug grin, then waited for me to open the door to the White Oak.

The scent of bacon and cinnamon rolls made my stomach growl as we stepped inside. Harry didn't stop at the hostess station. She plucked two menus from the stack and set off for a table. Did she pick the booth tucked into the corner? No, she chose the table that was directly in the middle of the restaurant.

I sat in the chair across from hers and buried my face in the menu.

"Morning, Harry." The waitress appeared with a carafe of coffee and two ceramic mugs.

"Morning, Marcy."

The name had me looking up.

"Two Marcys in Calamity. My daughter," Harry explained. "And Marcy Davis."

"Ah."

Harry kicked me under the table.

"What?" I gritted, rubbing my shin.

She jerked her chin to Marcy.

"Oh." I sighed and held out my hand. "Nice to meet you, Marcy. I'm Cal."

"You've been in a few times." She shook my hand. "Welcome."

"Thanks."

"I'll give you guys a few minutes," Marcy said, then disappeared.

Harry poured coffee for us both. "Was that so hard?"

"Yes," I said, lifting my cup. It was nearly scalding, but I sipped it anyway.

The door opened and a woman breezed inside wearing charcoal slacks and a sleeveless black blouse. Her hair was twisted into a knot, showcasing the long line of her neck. A neck I'd kissed just days ago.

Nellie.

Christ, but she was beautiful. My body responded instantly, like it always did. A thump of my heart. A breath I had to force myself to take. A spike of heat.

Would I ever stop craving her?

Harry followed my gaze, twisting to peer over her shoulder. By the time she faced forward, my eyes were already locked on the menu again. She did me a favor by reading hers too.

I risked another glance toward the door and found Nellie's green eyes waiting. They widened, just slightly. Then she squared her shoulders and walked toward a booth.

It wasn't empty.

No, sitting across from her was another man.

He stood and kissed her cheek before she could sit.

That was my fucking cheek.

Except it wasn't. Because Nellie was here on a date.

CHAPTER EIGHT

NELLIE

NORMALLY AFTER A HOOKUP, Cal and I would go months without seeing each other. We'd stay a thousand miles apart. It had only been three days since he'd been at my house. And three days wasn't nearly long enough.

I hadn't had time to forgive myself for being weak. I hadn't had time to compartmentalize the sex. I hadn't had time to remind myself that the only feelings I had for Cal Stark were disdain and annoyance.

I needed more than three days. And I really needed him to be in another state, not sitting two tables over while I attempted to eat my breakfast.

"How are the pancakes?" Zach asked.

"Good." I shoved another bite in my mouth. Whatever appetite I'd come to the White Oak with had vanished the moment I'd stepped through the café's door and spotted Cal. It took all my effort to swallow a bite and force a smile. "Thanks again for helping me yesterday."

"No problem." He nodded, sipping his coffee.

My own mug was getting cold. I'd been gulping ice water instead, hoping it would help me chill. My armpits were sticky. My forehead felt dewy. It took effort not to fan my face. Every time Cal's gaze swept to our table, it was like the desert sun had settled directly over my shoulder.

I risked a glance to the side.

Cal was glowering my direction from beneath the brim of his hat.

"How are you liking Calamity so far?" Zach asked.

I barely registered his words, too focused on a different man than my date.

Wait. Was this a date? It seemed like a date. But maybe I was just reading into it.

I'd bumped into Zach at the grocery store yesterday. I'd walked there with a few empty totes, planning to carry everything home. He'd been behind me in the checkout line and we'd gotten to catching up.

Zach was Kerrigan and Larke's older brother, and we'd met a couple of times on my previous trips to Montana. When he'd offered to give me a lift home, I'd gladly accepted because more items than I'd planned to pick up had worked their way into my cart.

He'd driven me home and had helped haul my groceries inside. When I'd told him about my car woes, he'd volunteered to give me a ride to the office this morning. It had been my idea for breakfast. A *thank you* for his shuttle service.

Except it resembled a date. Did Zach think it was a date? He'd kissed my cheek when I'd come in. Maybe that had just been a friendly peck? *Shit.* I hadn't intended this to be a date.

Date. Date. Date. That word sounded like an emergency

alarm, blaring inside my head, screaming at me to exit the building right fucking now. Was it time to leave?

Not that Zach wasn't a nice guy. He was exactly the man I *should* be dating. Clever. Sweet. Employed. But I couldn't think about the merits of this being an actual date with Cal sitting in the same room. Why was he here so early?

Zach and I had planned to meet at six thirty. That would give us time to eat before he dropped me off at the office. This should have been a safe window. But that was the problem with Calamity. It was too damn small.

"Nellie?" Zach set his fork down.

Right. He'd asked me a question. "Oh, sorry. I was just thinking about my car," I lied.

"I can always get you a loaner from the dealership."

"Thanks." I gave him a soft smile. "My mechanic offered me one too. If they don't have my car fixed by this afternoon, I might take you up on that."

"Just holler. Or I'm happy to give you a ride home."

"Thanks. But to answer your question, yes, Calamity has been great. I really love it here."

"I'm glad. It's a good town." He picked up his fork, diving into his scrambled eggs and hash browns.

I watched him eat, studying the flex of his jaw and curve of his lips as he chewed. Zach had a nice face. He had kind brown eyes and thick, chestnut hair. He worked at the Hale family car dealership and had lived in Calamity his entire life. I doubted anyone requested his autograph while he walked down First.

But there was no chemistry. Zero. Not even the tiniest of sparks.

What would it take for a nice guy to make my pulse race? Why was it always Cal?

I stole another look at his table, and this time, his attention was fixed on his breakfast date. The older woman smirked at him, like she'd just delivered an insult and was waiting to see how he'd respond. Who was she? How'd she know Cal?

"That's Harry." Zach leaned in closer, having read my mind. "Her daughter, Marcy, owns the motel."

"Ah." What kind of a name was Harry?

"I guess Cal's living there."

I blinked. "At the motel?"

"Yeah. He rented Marcy's RV that she parks there."

"Huh." I couldn't picture Cal living in a camper. "How do you know that?"

"Small town." He shrugged.

And Cal was a topic of conversation.

I tore my eyes away and studied my pancakes. If Cal was making friends, that didn't bode well for my plan to chase him out of Calamity.

"Nellie."

My eyes flew to Zach's face. "Yeah?"

"I asked if your breakfast was okay. You haven't really touched it."

"It's good. Really good. My stomach just isn't in a great place this morning. And I went a little heavy on the syrup."

"Oh, sorry. Should we go?"

"No, I'm fine. Finish eating. Please. I think it's mostly nerves. I'm interviewing for a new assistant later, and those things always make me anxious. I hate turning anyone down." It wasn't entirely a lie. I was doing interviews today, and I did hate turning people down. But Cal was the reason my stomach was in knots.

"You're sure?" he asked.

"Positive." I gave him my fullest attention while he finished eating. When he asked me a question, I listened and asked a few in return. I ate a few more bites and did my best to block out Cal. No matter how many times I felt his eyes on me, I looked at Zach and only Zach.

My date. Sort of.

The waitress dropped off the bill, and Zach shifted to dig his wallet from a pocket.

"Don't even think about it, Hale." I dove into my purse. "This is my treat today since you're acting as my chauffeur."

Zach chuckled and pulled out his credit card. "My mother will have a conniption if she finds out I didn't buy my date breakfast."

There was that word again. "Um . . . can I ask you something?"

"Shoot."

"Is this a date?"

He laughed. "If you have to ask, then I think the answer is no."

"Sorry." My shoulders slumped.

"Don't be." Zach leaned his elbows on the table. "To be honest, I didn't think this was a date. I don't make a habit of dating my sisters' friends. Gets complicated. Learned that lesson in high school when I dumped one of Kerrigan's friends and came home to find every single shoe of mine was missing its laces."

I giggled. "That's oddly creative."

"I still don't know if it was Kerrigan or the friend who stole them."

"Well, I promise to leave your shoes untouched. And how about we split the check?"

"You got it."

I placed my card on top of his right before the waitress breezed by, snagging them both. She returned in a flash with two receipts and two pens. We scribbled our names and added a tip, then slid from our booth and started for the exit.

Don't look. Don't look.

Cal was staring at me, of that I had no doubt. But I kept my face forward as I followed Zach out the door and into his truck.

It took the entire drive to the office for my heart rate to settle. I waved goodbye to Zach, then headed inside to start my work day. The building was eerily silent as I stopped in the break room to brew a fresh pot of coffee. The drip seemed to echo through the space.

With Pierce at home with Kerrigan and the baby, I'd be the only employee until I could hire an assistant. I'd made the decision this weekend to find someone local, rather than replace the position in Denver.

With a steaming mug in hand, I retreated to my office. Perks of being the first to move in, I chose a corner suite with my own bathroom. The only office larger was Pierce's.

The view from my windows overlooked the valley. It was like working inside the pages of a National Geographic magazine. Whenever I was sick of staring at my computer screen, I could turn to the glass and get lost in the swaying grasses or trace the mountain peaks as they etched a jagged line in the blue sky.

No honking cabs. No blaring sirens. No humming traffic. Maybe the silence wasn't so bad.

My desk was in disarray from the boxes I'd unpacked late last week. One corner had pictures and my framed degree that needed to be hung on the walls. Most of the business texts that were still at home in a closet would come here to fill the empty bookshelf. Maybe by Friday, if I was caught up on work, I could spend a few hours decorating.

I sipped my coffee and replied to a few emails, waiting until my first interview, scheduled for eight. I'd just sent our general counsel a note when the front door dinged, ten minutes early.

"Prompt. Check." I swept up a notebook and the stack of résumés I'd printed on Friday, then made my way to the lobby.

Except it wasn't my interviewee standing beneath the vaulted ceiling and its roughhewn beams. It was Cal.

A rush of heat made my limbs feel like jelly. Just one look and my pulse raced. Why him? Of all the men in the world, why did the spark come with Cal?

His dark sweats didn't do much to hide the strength of his body. The pants molded to his bulky thighs, and the hoodie wrapped around his broad shoulders. His clothes shouldn't have been sexy, but I'd stripped him out of a similar pair of sweats before. I knew the prize beneath.

He had a hand to his jaw, rubbing at the dusting of stubble. It stilled when he spotted me.

"What are you doing here?" My voice was as harsh as I'd hoped. He had to leave. The office. The county. Montana.

He planted his hands on his hips as I crossed the lobby. His scowl from the White Oak was fixed firmly in place, and instead of answering my question, he asked one of his own. "That was Kerrigan's brother, right?"

"Zach." I nodded. "Yes."

"Are you two dating?"

I crossed my arms over my chest. "That's none of your business."

"Like hell it's not. I fucked you on Friday."

"Do you mind?" I huffed. "This is my place of work." Yes, I was alone. But what if I wasn't?

"Answer the question, Nellie. Are you with him?"

Lie. Say yes. "No."

Damn it. Maybe he could teach me how to be a liar one day.

The tension deflated from his frame.

"Happy now? Please go away. I have work to do." I turned on a heel, but he stopped me cold with the whisper of my name.

"Nellie."

God, that voice. The magnet flipped. Push and pull.

"Tell me what you hate about me."

"Excuse me?" I spun around. Was he joking?

"Tell me what you hate about me," he repeated.

"We don't have that much time." I pointed to the clock on the wall. "I have a meeting in ten minutes."

He growled. "One thing. Tell me one thing."

"Cal—"

"Just tell me." There was a desperation in his voice.

"What is wrong with you today?"

"Nellie, please."

Cal never said please. How many times had I reminded him to use manners? To be polite? Hell, I'd done it just last week at Jane's when he'd ordered a water. "Why?"

"Does it matter? One thing. What's one thing you hate about me? This should be an easy question, so just answer me."

"You're mean," I blurted.

Cal didn't flinch or cringe or jerk. He didn't even blink. But I knew I'd hurt him. The sting showed in his hazel eyes.

I opened my mouth to apologize because I was raised to say sorry when you were unkind.

But before I could speak, Cal crossed his arms over his chest. "Give me an example."

"Watch SportsCenter. I'm done with this little game. Go away."

"Indulge me."

"I've been indulging you." I tossed a hand toward the door. "I need to get to work."

"I'm not leaving until you give me an example of a time when I was mean. And it can't be from high school."

"Fine." I mirrored his stance, my legs planted wide and arms crossed. "After the Super Bowl, your last game, there was a kid who came up to you while you were being interviewed. He was there for the Make-A-Wish Foundation."

Cal swallowed hard, knowing exactly where I was going with this.

"He was in a wheelchair. He had your jersey on and the same hat you're wearing right now."

The kid's cap had covered a head without any hair. Cal had been holding the game ball when the kid had approached. It had been clear to everyone—the reporter, the fans in the stadium and the viewers watching from their homes—that the boy had really wanted that ball. But Cal had kept it securely tucked under his arm.

"You should have given him the ball," I said.

He dropped his gaze, not saying a word.

"You asked for an example. Now you have one. Want another? I've got a hundred postgame interview examples." He was usually a complete dickhead after a loss.

"No." He shook his head, shifting his weight between his feet. When he looked up, I expected him to look guilty. But his eyebrows were pulled together, his forehead furrowed. "You watched my games?"

I blinked. *Oh. Shit.*

"How many?"

"I don't know." I flicked my wrist. "Some." *All.*

I'd watched every one of Cal's professional games over the years. I'd watched most in college too whenever they played on TV.

I knew his next question before it came across his lips.

"Why, Nell?"

Why? Because Cal was magic with a football in his hand. He had a raw talent that was utterly beautiful to behold. And when he was playing, I always saw that boy who'd given me my first kiss.

He was in there somewhere. That nice boy who confided in me with his secrets. Maybe it was foolish of me to believe that there was a kind, honest version of Cal buried beneath the layers of arrogance and insolence.

"Why?" he asked again.

There was no way I'd tell him the truth. I opened my mouth, knowing the lie would come easily this time, when the door pushed open behind him and a ding filled the lobby. My first interview.

"Hi." The brunette smiled as she spotted me.

"Hi. Carrie?"

"That's me." She waved, then her gaze darted to Cal. She did a double take. "Oh my God. You're Cal Stark."

He straightened. The mask I'd seen countless times snapped firmly into place. The asshole was back.

Carrie bounced more than walked to his side, taking a hand he hadn't offered. "I heard a rumor that you moved here but I didn't believe it. I'm Carrie."

He tugged his hand free.

"It's so nice to meet you. I'm a huge fan." She was totally unfazed that he hadn't spoken a word. She tucked her hair behind an ear. She smoothed the sides of her skirt. She licked her lips.

My molars ground together as I watched her preen. This interview was pointless.

"Carrie," I snapped.

Her smile faltered at the scowl on my face.

"You can have a seat in the conference room." I nodded to my left.

"Oh, okay." Her feet moved, but her face stayed stuck to Cal. She nearly collided with the goddamn wall.

I waited until she was seated before taking a step closer to Cal.

He didn't speak.

Neither did I.

The walls we'd built as shields were so thick that it was hard to see where mine ended and his began.

Without another word, he turned and shoved out the door.

I watched as he rolled through the parking lot, then I shook my head and joined Carrie in the conference room.

She prattled on and on during her interview while my mind wandered.

Tell me what you hate about me.

Why did he want to know? And why, of all people, would he come to me for an answer?

—

Diary,

Today was a bad day. Cal told the cheerleaders I was a virgin and they made fun of me in gym. It shouldn't have bothered me. I shouldn't have let them see me cry. I should have called them whores or something. I mean, why would I want to be trashy sluts like they are? They're all screwing the guys on the football and basketball teams. At least I won't end up pregnant by some braindead moron who won't make anything of his life. These rich, horrible girls with their fake tans and fake lives. Do they think I don't hear them puking their lunches up in the bathroom? I overheard one of them talking the other day about how her parents took out a million dollar insurance policy on her legs because she wants to be a model. Who does that? I feel like I'm going to school in this parallel universe or something. At least I'm not a spoiled bitch. I hate them. All of them. But I hate Cal Stark the most. Forever and ever.

N

CHAPTER NINE

CAL

THERE WAS a flaw on the diary's page in the lower right corner. Sunshine streamed through my SUV's windshield as I sat parked in front of The Refinery. It made the ecru pages of Nellie's journal appear flawless. But if I ran my finger across the paper, the texture in that corner was raised, like it had once been wet. Like it was where Nellie's tear had fallen.

I wished I could say that it had been a misunderstanding. That I'd made a comment and it had been taken the wrong way. Or that I'd been trying to help, like the water incident. But there was no excuse.

This had just been me being a teenage prick.

Though, to be accurate, I hadn't called her a virgin. I'd called her a prude. In the eyes of a fourteen-year-old girl, which was worse?

If not for the diary, that day would have been forgotten along with thousands of others. But this book had a way of sweeping me into the past with aggravating clarity. You'd think that a guy who'd spent his career being tackled and having his head slammed into the dirt—helmet or no—could at least be blessed with memory issues.

The day I'd called her a prude had been in the spring, close to the end of freshman year. I'd been on the football field, stretching with a few of the guys before the after-school weight training program.

The cheerleaders flocked, like they always did when there were two or more football players in a cluster. Even as a freshman, I got a lot of attention from the girls. I was good-looking. Ripped. Confident. The acne and awkwardness that plagued so many of the guys my age was never an issue. And as of the previous winter, thanks to Phoebe McAdams at a house party, I wasn't a virgin.

While I was stretching, Nellie walked past the field, passing by the end zone beyond the chain-link fence that wrapped around the area. She walked with her head down, her eyes on the concrete sidewalk.

It was Phoebe who made the first snide comment. She called Nellie a brainiac. Then I called her a prude.

A single comment. *She's a prude.*

Then our coach whistled and waved us into the locker room. Nellie disappeared around the corner of the bleachers, out of sight and forgotten.

The journal entry was from the next day.

And my comment was not so forgotten, after all.

I probably should have known better. Done better. Been better. Anyone with two eyes could have looked at Phoebe's face and seen the envy as green as Nellie's eyes. Of course she'd taken my comment and run with it.

Nellie had everything Phoebe's money couldn't buy. Intelligence. Wit. Beauty.

A beauty that radiated from her pure heart.

I closed the diary and reached behind my seat, placing it on the floor of the Land Rover. Pathetic as it was, that book had become my constant companion. Over the past five days, I'd read it again.

Nellie's adolescent thoughts had consumed me. Retiring this young was clearly fucking with my head. I wasn't sure why I couldn't just leave the damn book alone. Just like I wasn't sure what had come over me at Grays Peak last week. I sure as hell wasn't sure why I'd wanted her to verbalize why she hated me.

Maybe I'd been trying to pick a fight. Or maybe I'd been hoping that if I asked her what she hated about me, she'd come up empty.

Of course she hated me. I had the evidence in a leather-bound book. So why couldn't I just accept her hate and move on? Why couldn't I stop thinking about her?

Why did I care about her opinion?

Christ, I was fucking losing it.

"I really need to stop reading that diary," I mumbled.

A blonde came walking down the block. I grabbed my yoga mat from the passenger seat, climbed out of the car and slammed the door. The sound caught Nellie's attention. Her footsteps stuttered on the sidewalk.

I smirked and walked to the door of The Refinery, lingering outside as she marched my direction. "Morning, Blondie. Your roots are showing. Time for a new bottle of peroxide."

She cringed.

I stifled one of my own. Yeah, okay. I was a prick for constantly making fun of her hair. Especially considering I liked the color.

"Go away, Cal."

I yanked the door to the fitness studio open before she could touch the handle. "After you."

"What?" She looked me up and down, taking in the athletic shorts and sleeveless tee. "What are you doing?"

"Yoga."

"No." She clutched the mat rolled under her arm tighter. "This is *my* yoga class."

"Mine too. I'm the newest member at The Refinery."

Nellie closed her eyes, her hands balling into fists. "You do not do yoga."

"Yes, I do. My trainer thought it would be good for my back. Turns out, he was right."

"Can't you afford a private instructor?"

"And not support Kerrigan's business? What kind of friend would that make me?"

"The Cal Stark kind."

The shitty kind. I gestured for her to go inside first. "Shall we?"

She stomped past me, flicking her ponytail so high and hard it whacked me in the face.

We each checked in at the reception counter and toed off our shoes, stowing them in a cubby along with our keys and phones. Then we entered the studio, me keeping pace with Nellie as she crossed the mats to the far end of the room.

With a fast shake, she unrolled her mat and tossed it on the floor.

I did the same, crowding close. Our hands would probably touch during Shavasana.

"Cal." She seethed through gritted teeth, dropping to her knees.

"You seem stressed, Rivera. Work been rough on you this week?"

She blew out an audible breath, then leaned forward into Child's Pose.

Her tank top molded to her frame. Her leggings left little to the imagination. And God, what I wouldn't give to strip it all away. To forget yoga and work out the tension in my body, and hers, with sex.

My cock jerked as I stared at her ass, so I forced myself to my mat, wishing like hell I'd thought this through.

Yoga was the reason I'd come downtown this morning. My back had been killing me all week. Tormenting Nellie was a bonus. I'd chosen this class specifically because Kerrigan had mentioned this was Nellie's favorite.

Last night, I'd gone to Pierce and Kerrigan's place bearing pizza. I'd played with Elias for a couple of hours. I'd held the baby for a minute until she'd started to cry. Then I'd caught up with my friends after insisting on doing the dishes.

When I'd asked Kerrigan about the yoga lineup, she'd told me this was Nellie's class, probably thinking that I'd avoid it. On the contrary . . . Nellie's class was now my class too.

I relaxed into a similar pose, feeling the stretch in my hips, thighs and ankles. I turned my head to face Nellie. "Tell me another one."

"Please go away," she murmured.

"No."

She lengthened her arms even farther, her eyes closed as

her forehead pressed into the mat. "Then shut up."

"Hurry. Before class starts. Tell me another one."

"Another what?"

"Another thing you hate about me."

She shook her head, her ribs expanding with a deep breath. "This is a very strange, very annoying game."

"It's not a game." I lowered my voice. I wasn't sure what it was. Maybe redemption? I just . . . I needed to hear it. I wanted current examples, not the ones from her old diary. "Tell me what you hate about me."

"I hate that you're still in Calamity. Happy now?"

I frowned. "That's stating the obvious. Try again."

She inhaled another breath, blowing it out in a purpose-ful, steady stream. Then she repeated the calming technique, four more times while I studied her profile and the way her sooty eyelashes formed crescent moons against her cheeks.

Nellie didn't have much makeup on today, just a slight coat of mascara. There were four freckles on the bridge of her nose, so faint that normally they were covered with what-ever crap women used to hide what they considered imper-fections.

The first time I'd seen Nellie's freckles had been in Charlotte. The second, the shower at her apartment in Denver when I'd flown to town during the off-season to visit Mom and Pierce.

Nellie had been living in Pierce's building, and I'd bumped into her waiting for the elevator. When she'd gotten off on her floor, so had I. To this day, Pierce thought the reason I hadn't shown at his penthouse on time was because I'd been outside on an urgent call with my agent. No, Nellie and I had just been fucking on her couch.

"You're living in a camper." Her voice was no more than a whisper. "You're worth millions of dollars and you're living in someone else's RV."

Either she'd asked about me or gossip was spreading. Probably both.

It was only a temporary living situation. My architect was nearly done with the design. The build was already on my contractor's calendar. "Your point?"

"You're acting weird," she said. "I thought you'd act too pretentious for the motel, let alone a Winnebago."

"Apparently not." No surprise she thought I was a snob. I tended to have expensive tastes. "You never answered my question the other day. Why did you watch my games?"

"To see you lose." Her nose twitched.

That was bullshit. "Liar."

She shot me a glare. "Then I watched for the inevitable explosion when something didn't go your way or someone pissed you off."

And she'd probably heckled me along with the rest of the world when that explosion had been caught on camera.

My temper had bested me on more than one occasion. The year after we'd won my first Super Bowl, our team had gone through a rebuilding. Our record had been shit, having lost a bunch of veteran players to retirement.

After a particularly brutal ass-kicking by the Colts, a game when nothing had gone right, I'd had a meltdown coming off the field. A drunk fan had taunted me. *You're a has-been, Stark. You fucking suck. Should have quit while you were ahead.*

He'd thrown each of my insecurities in my face. So I'd tossed him my middle finger and a string of colorful obscenities. There'd been a reporter right on my heels. No doubt Nellie had rolled her eyes when they'd aired the segment later that night and the entire sound bite had been a string of bleeps.

One game I'd been so livid about a horseshit penalty that I'd kicked over a table of water coolers. Another time I'd torn off my helmet and sent it sailing toward the sideline after an interception.

I was no stranger to league fines. Whenever a coach had screamed in my face on the sidelines, the camera had been ready.

Maybe it should have bothered me that Nellie had seen my outbursts. It didn't. She'd seen me at my worst long before the cameras had arrived.

The door to the studio opened and three other women strolled inside. Their smiles dulled when they spotted me.

I pushed up to my knees. "Ladies. Mind if I intrude on your class?"

Two scowled. One blushed.

Those were odds I could work with.

A woman wearing a sports bra and flowy pants came out from the back room. Her dark hair was mostly covered in a head wrap as she walked over. "Hi, Nellie."

"Morning." Nellie gave her a smile.

The instructor turned to me and nodded. "You must be Cal. Kerrigan mentioned you'd be joining one of our classes. Though she didn't think it would be this one."

I shrugged. "What better way to start a Saturday than with a little exercise?"

"I couldn't agree more." The instructor's smile widened

before she waved the other women into the space. "Glad you could all make it today."

The ladies exchanged greetings and small talk as they went about laying out their mats and positioning blocks. Nellie didn't move from her mat to mingle. Maybe she didn't know them yet?

"Let's get started." The instructor took up her place at the front of the room, the mirrors her backdrop.

This was the first actual yoga class I'd been to, not that I'd admit that to Nellie. The instructor went through an introduction, her voice steady and monotone as we began the initial poses.

My muscles strained with every stretch, working to get into a flow. It had been a while and I hadn't been good about stretching after my daily workouts. My hamstrings burned. My shoulders ached. But after the first series of movements, the blood began to flow and my body warmed.

"Good, Cal." The instructor walked around the room and her hands found my lower back, pressing lightly against my hips as I bent in Downward Dog. "You've done this before. Your form is excellent."

It was? My last instructor had told me my form was weak. I had too much bulk to maneuver and contort properly. I'd spent too many years building football muscles designed to keep me on my feet and send the ball sailing downfield.

I glanced at Nellie as the instructor padded away just in time to see an eye roll. Okay, so maybe the teacher was just kissing my ass.

Nellie, on the contrary, had a fine form with her ass

perfectly positioned in the air. The last time I'd seen her like that, there'd been no leggings and I'd been behind her, my hands gripping her hips as I'd slammed inside that tight body.

Blood rushed to my groin. *Fuck.* This yoga idea was backfiring.

I snuck in an adjustment to my dick while we shifted into a new position. Then I spent the next twenty minutes refusing to glance at Nellie through the mirror. I kept my focus on the instructor, watching her move and doing my best to mimic her stances.

She kept smiling at me, coming over whenever possible to help me get the pose just right. "You've got great balance," she said as I rested in Warrior II.

"Thanks." I sucked in some air, letting my feet ground into the mat.

Her hands trailed over my shoulders, pressing me deeper into the lunge.

Nellie's gaze met mine in the mirror when I glanced forward. She looked like she was about to murder someone. Normally that look was reserved for me, but today, it was aimed at the instructor. Was she jealous?

A slow grin stretched across my mouth. Yeah, she was jealous.

We shifted directions, practicing the pose on the other side. And once again the instructor's hands found their way onto my body. She grew bolder, sliding her fingers across my shoulders and biceps, trailing all the way to my fingers.

I didn't like strangers touching me, and I could have stopped her. But when she returned to the front of the class and started eye-fucking me from her mat, the irritation on Nellie's face was worth the hassle.

"Bend at the knee." The instructor spoke as we all folded forward.

And then . . . _Braaap._

The entire room stilled at the noise.

Until Nellie broke the silence. "Eww, Cal! Gross. That stinks."

There was no fucking stink because I hadn't farted. She'd made that sound with her mouth.

I looked over, finding her head tucked against the front of her thighs. Her hands were pressed to the floor, fingers splayed. But she was smiling that shit-eating, smug smile. The same one she'd given me after dumping coffee down my pants.

A woman chortled.

Another made an audible sniff in the air.

"Um . . ." The instructor pointed toward the hallway. "The bathroom is—"

"I'm fine," I clipped.

Nellie's smirk stayed firmly in place through the rest of the class. The instructor didn't so much as take a step my way—not that I cared. It had never been about her. No, it had been about Nellie's attention.

It was always about Nellie.

The moment we were dismissed, she rolled up her mat and bolted for the exit, tugging on her shoes and retrieving her phone.

I hustled to keep pace, staying close as she pushed through the door and into the morning sun. She tried to race down the sidewalk but I caught her elbow before she could run away. "Tell me what you hate about me."

"No." She tugged her arm free. "Stop asking me. Find

someone else to point out your flaws, like your assistant or manager or any random person you encounter on the street."

"I'm not asking random people, and I don't have an assistant. My business manager would never be honest." He'd think I'd fire him like I had my assistant. To be fair, I'd fired a lot of assistants. Seven in the last five years. All but one had been because of a confidentiality breach. The latest because he'd been a thief. "You're the only one who will tell me the truth."

"Pierce would."

"Pierce likes me. You don't."

Her mouth pursed in a thin line as the other women from yoga streamed out of The Refinery. We waited for them to pass, Nellie offering a small smile, then when we were alone again, her scowl returned.

"Tell me," I ordered. "Come on. This should be fun for you."

"You're right." She tapped her chin. "This is fun. Okay. I hate how you play a fool."

"Huh? What does that mean?"

"Remember that charity event we went to last year? At the Denver Art Museum?"

I nodded. "Yeah."

Pierce had asked if I'd go in his place because I'd been home that weekend—a trip to see Mom for her birthday. He'd bought a table for Grays Peak and had planned to fly down from Montana to attend, but Elias had gotten sick, so he'd stayed in Calamity.

Nellie had been none too thrilled when I'd waltzed into the gala wearing a tux and sat in the chair beside hers. God, she'd looked beautiful that night, wearing a slinky golden dress with matching heels. I'd hoped to peel the gown off her later, but before they'd even served dessert, she'd excused herself to the ladies' room and had never returned.

"How did I 'play a fool'?" I asked. She was the only person on earth who could frustrate me enough to use air quotes.

"All night long, the conversation was about business. Who was investing in this and that. It was like a wallet-measuring contest."

"And I should have whipped out my fat wallet and slapped it on the table?"

"No. Actually, I was impressed that you didn't."

"Okay," I drawled.

"We were eating dinner and the guy next to me leaned forward to ask if you'd invested in anything noteworthy in Nashville. Do you remember what you told him? You said you spent your money on hookers and blow."

"It was a joke, Nellie." The whole table had laughed. They'd known it was a joke.

"Yeah, it was a joke. And it was you, acting like the dumb jock."

Fuck, I hated those two words. I'd hated hearing them from her mouth at fourteen and I hated hearing them at thirty-three. They were still her default insult, and damn, if they didn't hit dead on target.

"You have at least ten silent partnerships around the country," she said. "Restaurants. Hotels. Small businesses. And those are just the investments you've made through Grays Peak. I suspect you have more."

Her suspicions were correct. Though most of my portfolio was with Grays Peak. Whenever Pierce had a new opportunity pop up that he thought I might be interested in, he'd send me the details. It almost always ended with me writing a check.

The business manager I employed was responsible for overseeing my involvement. And he oversaw the millions I gave to various charities every year. Nellie wouldn't know about those donations. I gave it all anonymously because I didn't need to be invited to functions and fundraisers. I didn't want thank-you cards and plaques with my name on them.

"I don't want people in my business." Especially rich people who had no qualms about asking me for money. It was easier to blow them off at the start. "Is that a crime?"

"You wouldn't have had to go into the specifics at that dinner. You could have been vague and still showed that table you aren't just good at a game. That you have more than two brain cells to rub together."

"Are you kidding?" I scoffed. "So you hate me because I made a joke, then kept my private business private?"

"No." She raised her chin. "I hate you for pretending. For perpetrating this moronic, playboy image."

I stepped closer. "Are you sure it's an image? Maybe it's exactly who I am." *The dumb jock.*

"Then I guess I've got another reason to hate you." She took a step away, then she was gone, storming down the sidewalk that would take her home.

Fuck. What was wrong with me? I scrubbed a hand over my face, watching as she jogged across First. Then I unglued my feet and climbed into my car, retreating to the safety of my Winnebago.

The diary—that fucking diary—got left in the car.

CHAPTER TEN

NELLIE

THERE WAS something reassuring about watching Dad mow my lawn. Like even if a storm brewed on the horizon, it would pass. The sun would shine again.

"He doesn't need to do that," I told Mom.

She joined me at the living room window, a glass of iced tea in her hand. "You know how he is."

I smiled and leaned my head on her shoulder. "Yeah, I do."

Dad pampered Mom. And he pampered me. It was how he showed his love.

I'd told him no less than ten times since I'd picked them up from the Bozeman airport this morning that he wasn't allowed to work on this vacation. No hanging shelves. No fussing with the doors that squeaked in this old house. And absolutely no yard work.

He'd agreed. He'd promised to relax and soak up our long weekend together.

Then I'd made the mistake of going to pee twenty

minutes ago. Before I'd flushed the toilet, he'd snuck out to the garage. The buzz of the lawnmower had greeted me when I'd emerged from the bathroom.

"I missed you guys," I said, leaving the window to sit on the couch.

"We missed you too." Mom joined me, glancing around the room. "I love, love, love your house."

"Isn't it cute?"

"The cutest. It suits you. Much more than that apartment in Denver."

I felt the same, but hearing Mom confirm it reinforced that this move to Calamity had been the right decision.

"Once he's done outside, maybe we could walk downtown," she said. "I want to explore."

"Sure." We could spend a few hours strolling up and down First. The only risk was Cal.

I hadn't seen him since yoga at The Refinery last Saturday. Six days and I wished I could say he hadn't been on my mind. Maybe I should have called him and asked him to avoid downtown this weekend. But knowing Cal, that would have just enticed him.

With any luck, he'd stay locked in his camper to miss the tourists who'd been flocking to town in droves each weekend on their way to tour Yellowstone National Park.

My parents and I would be joining them on their next visit. We'd hoped to squeeze in a visit to see Old Faithful this trip, but both Mom and Dad had to work on Monday. So this visit was just to say hello and see my new house. This fall, when they could get away again, we'd get out of town.

"You look beautiful, honey." Mom stretched an arm across the couch, tugging a lock of my hair. "My pretty girl."

"Thanks. You look good too. I'm jealous of your tan."

"You'll have to visit us this winter and get some sun."

"I will." I smiled and she smiled. If anyone would have been here to take a photograph, our smiles would have been the same.

Dad used to tease that I was a mini Kylie. Mom's blond hair was a shade darker only because she didn't have it colored as often. We had the same green eyes. The same chin. The same shape of our noses, though she had a few more freckles on hers.

She'd only been seventeen when she'd had me. My biological father was a boy she'd been with in high school. I knew his name. I had an old picture she'd saved from a yearbook. But otherwise, he'd never been a part of my life. Neither had Mom's parents.

They'd shunned her after she'd announced her pregnancy. They'd kicked her out of the house, but thankfully, she'd had a sympathetic aunt who'd taken her in. We'd lived in her aunt's basement until I was two.

That's when Mom married Dad.

She always said the day she met Dad was kismet. A waitress at the diner where she'd worked had asked her to swap shifts, so she'd had a random Friday afternoon off. Mom had taken me to a nearby community park to play on the swing set. It had been Dad's last day working for the landscaping company that had maintained the park. A day later, and it would have been someone else cutting the grass.

Dad proclaimed it was love at first sight.

He adopted me after their wedding. We moved into his house, visiting Mom's aunt until she passed away when I was eight. Mom quit the diner and started working at the coffee shop. And we'd had a happy life, just the three of us.

Dad was my dad, even if we didn't share DNA. We looked nothing alike. He had black hair and coffee-colored eyes. His bushy mustache had a few flecks of gray. His frame was short and stocky.

But in so many ways, we were exactly alike. Mom used to tease us that we were born kindred spirits. We could finish each other's sentences. We usually craved the same foods. And though I loved Mom entirely, whenever I needed life advice, Dad was my first phone call.

When I'd decided to move to Calamity, I'd told him first.

The sound of the mower stopped and both Mom and I shot off the couch, heading out the front door.

Dad wiped a bead of sweat from his brow. "This yard needs help."

I laughed. "I know."

"It needs to be aerated. It wouldn't hurt to throw down some fresh seed to fill these patchy spots. Maybe we could swing by that hardware store."

"Nope." I shook my head. "This is your vacation, Dad. Mowing is all you get to do. I can handle the rest. You taught me how to grow a nice lawn, remember?"

He chuckled and held up his hands. "Okay, fine."

"Are you good to do some exploring?" Mom asked, then checked her watch. "We've got some time before we can check into the motel."

"You could cancel your reservation and stay here." The guest bedroom was all ready for company.

"Next time." Dad shook his head. "This is our vacation too."

And I wouldn't begrudge them a little privacy.

The day I'd announced my move date this past winter, they'd made their reservation at the motel. Luckily, they'd called before the motel had been fully booked for the summer.

Mom drained the rest of her tea. "Okay, let's go."

We set off at a leisurely pace, in no rush as we strolled along First. Dad and I wandered into the coffee shop for an afternoon latte while Mom opted to stay on a bench and people-watch.

Mom pulled us into each retail store to browse, not buy. She rarely splurged and this trip had likely drained their *fun money fund*.

I'd offered to purchase their plane tickets but Mom had insisted. She'd also told me not to even ask Dad—his pride was a beautiful and frustrating quality. Another personality trait we had in common.

"Jane's." Mom nodded to the bar as we stood beneath its sign. "Is this Pierce's place?"

"No, he and Kerrigan own the brewery." I pointed down the road. "Want to go there for dinner and a beer?"

"How about we save that for tomorrow?" Dad took the lead, opening the door to Jane's for us both. "Let's try this place tonight. It looks fun."

"Oh, it's got character." I stepped in first, letting my eyes adjust to the darkened light, then scanned the room.

It smelled of burgers and fries and a good time. The music was cranked loud. Jane was behind the bar, mixing a cocktail. Most of the tables were full as were the stools at the bar itself.

A broad frame and wide shoulders pulled my gaze. I'd know that backward hat anywhere.

Shit. Of course Cal would be here today of all days. Karma was a bitch. Hadn't he learned his lesson the last time he'd visited Jane's?

"What's wrong?" Mom asked, stepping in behind me.

"Nothing." I forced a smile and steered her to an empty table. She didn't notice Cal as we sat down, mostly because her back was to him. I held out the other chair that faced away from the bar. "Here you go, Dad. You can sit here."

"No, I want to sit across from my gorgeous wife so I can stare at her all night." He bent and kissed her cheek before taking his seat. A seat that faced the bar.

I grimaced, then pulled out my chair.

"You weren't lying." Dad laughed as he looked around. "Lots of character. I like it."

"Me too," Mom said as the waitress appeared with menus and took our drink order.

"What's good here?" Dad asked, glancing around the room. I felt it the moment he spotted Cal. His body stiffened. His smile dropped. His eyes shot my way for an explanation.

"Sorry," I whispered.

Dad frowned and gave me the *we'll talk about it later* look.

"I think I'll try a cheeseburger and sweet potato fries." Mom's menu closed with a slap. Her chair's legs scraped on the floor as she stood. "I'm going to find the restroom and wash my hands. If the waitress comes back while I'm gone, order for me."

"Okay." I held my breath as she walked away, hoping she

didn't see Cal. She walked right past him, totally oblivious that he was at the bar. I slumped as I exhaled. *Phew.*

"Tell me that's not who it looks like," Dad said.

"I can't." I sighed. "Sorry. I should have told you."

"What's he doing here?" Dad's eyes were glued to Cal's spine.

"Apparently he's living here too."

"You're joking."

I shrugged. "He's friends with Pierce too, remember?"

"Now I wish you would have stayed in Denver. I don't want you anywhere near that man."

Oh, if he only knew. "It's fine, Dad. I learned to tolerate Cal a long time ago. We avoid each other." Sort of.

He huffed and returned to his menu. "I still don't like it."

"I know."

Cal must have felt my gaze on his back because he twisted, looking over his shoulder. When he spotted me, he spun away from the bar. Then he froze as he spotted Dad. He sat straighter. He squared his shoulders. One foot slid off his stool's rung for the floor and he moved like he was going to walk over.

"No," I mouthed, shaking my head.

Cal wasn't welcome near my father, my rule not Dad's.

His shoulders fell. His chin dropped. Then he turned on his stool once more, facing away. A moment later, his hand dug into his jeans pocket for his wallet. With a wad of cash left on the bar, he slid off his stool and crossed the room, head down as he strode to the door.

I tracked every step, watching those long legs and that natural swagger until he was out the door. It should have made the room feel lighter. It should have made me happy.

But damn that guilt.

Damn that wounded look on his face.

"Did you order?" Mom slid into her seat, a wide smile on her face.

"Not yet, sweetheart." Dad put his hand on her shoulder, his thumb tracing a circle on her shirt. Whatever irritation he'd felt from Cal, he'd hide simply to make sure that Mom was smiling.

He protected her.

Like he protected me.

I pushed Cal out of my mind to enjoy the evening with my parents. We talked about their life in Arizona. We laughed as Mom got buzzed off a single tequila sunrise. We inhaled greasy burgers and each other's company until our plates were empty. Then after I insisted on paying for dinner, we meandered along the quiet streets to my home.

"That was fun." Mom giggled, her arm looped with Dad's.

"Sure was." Dad yawned. "But we'd better get to the motel. I'm afraid if I sit on your couch, I'll fall asleep."

We skipped the house and went straight for the garage and piled into my sedan. Calamity's tiny airport didn't connect to commercial flights, so Mom and Dad had flown into Bozeman this morning, and I'd driven the two hours to pick them up. Their carry-on bags we'd left in the trunk. I was already dreading Sunday morning when we'd load them again and I'd have to drop them off.

"This trip is going by too fast," I said as I pulled into the motel's parking lot.

"We'll be back." Mom squeezed my shoulder from the

passenger seat, then we climbed out to help Dad unload their bags from the trunk.

I hung back as they checked in to their room, studying the motel's office and the overflowing flower pots outside. Where was the camper Cal was renting?

Why does my mind always jump to him?

"Breakfast tomorrow?" Dad asked as I walked them to room number five.

"Sounds good. Do you guys want to sleep in?"

"Yes," they answered in unison. It was rare they could sleep late, so their answer was no surprise.

I laughed. "Let's meet at the White Oak around nine."

"We'll be there." He kissed my cheek, then hauled their luggage into the room while I hugged Mom goodnight.

The moment their door closed, I started for my car but curiosity got the better of me and I glanced around the parking lot once more. Cal's camper must be parked next to the building. I passed the office and rounded the motel's corner, spotting a white brick house tucked beyond the narrow alley.

My shoes crunched on the gravel path as I walked toward the house, and beside it, a Winnebago bus. The lights inside the camper glowed white against the darkness.

Just outside the RV's door, Cal was sitting in a collapsible chair, his legs stretched long. His hands were stuffed into the kangaroo pocket of his hoodie, and his head was tipped toward the night sky.

He looked handsome. He looked peaceful.

He looked lonely.

And in that moment, all I wanted to do was crawl into his lap and hold him in my arms.

"Tell me what you hate about me." He spoke without moving, his eyes still glued to the stars.

"How'd you know it was me?" I asked, taking the empty chair beside his. It was a different style and much nicer.

"What if I didn't?"

"So you're asking everyone in Calamity what they hate about you?"

"No, just you." His voice, low and quiet, was a lure, drawing me in closer. He turned his cheek, his eyes dark pools in the muted light. "You drop your parents here?"

"Yeah."

"How long are they in town?"

"Just the weekend."

He nodded, then faced the heavens once more.

"About what happened at the bar . . ." I couldn't bring myself to apologize. Because I wasn't sorry for keeping him from my parents.

"It's fine, Nellie."

"Is it?"

"Yeah," he muttered. "Tell me."

"No." I mirrored his posture, stretching my legs out to watch new stars pop against the midnight backdrop.

"Please."

A please? He must be desperate. "Why does it matter what I think?"

"Humor me."

Maybe if he would have come over tonight at Jane's despite my silent warning, I would have jumped on his demand. I would have listed things I hated about him. But tonight, it felt . . . wrong. So I stayed quiet.

The minutes passed in silence as we stared at the galaxy.

Then Cal stood, retreating up the metal stairs to the RV. A drawer opened and closed. One of the lights flickered off.

It was late. My home beckoned. I pushed out of my chair, but did I leave? No. When Cal's broad frame filled the doorway of the RV, I was standing at the base of the stairs.

He held out a hand.

If I took it, I'd go inside. He'd kiss me, and our clothes would make puddles on the floor.

"I hate that you're the most handsome man I've ever seen." I hated that the confession escaped my lips. I hated that I couldn't resist him.

"Are you coming in?"

"I shouldn't."

"Nell."

God, that voice.

My hand fell into his.

Cal stretched past me the moment I was up the stairs, grabbing the door to pull it closed. Then it was just the two of us, the world outside swallowed by the night. He crowded close. His fingertips skimmed my forehead, pushing the hair away from my temple before he bent, his mouth hovering over mine.

I waited for his kiss, our eyes locked. Except he made me come to him. That was how it always was, wasn't it? Last time, it had been his turn. This time, it was mine.

So I sealed my lips over his and sucked his tongue into my mouth.

Hesitancy vanished. Lines blurred. The hate was set aside.

We dove into the oblivion.

He swept me into his arms and carried me the length of

the RV to his bedroom. A strong arm kept me pinned against his body, our mouths fused, as the other flipped off the remainder of the lights, casting us in darkness.

Cal made my trip to his Winnebago worth it. Three orgasms later, he'd thoroughly pleasured me with his fingers, tongue and cock. With disheveled hair and swollen lips, he walked me to my car, neither of us saying a word.

There was no kiss goodnight.

-

Dear Diary,

*Something really strange happened today. I had to go with
Dad to work after school. Mom's car broke down. Again. For
like the third time this spring. She's just happy it made it
through the winter. Since she couldn't pick me up, Dad came
and got me in between his jobs. We had to go to the Stark
house. It was his last customer of the day. Cal wasn't there,
thank God. He was probably having sex with Phoebe bitch-
face McAdams. I could tell Dad was tired. He took on seven
new clients this spring and he's been getting up super early
and working on the weekends. He told me that if he can just
keep it up, he can get Mom a new car for her birthday and
then I can have her old one after I get my license. Even if it is
a junker and it breaks down all the time, it's better than nothing. Everyone at school is going to make fun of me for it. Jerks.
They can have their Audis and BMWs. It's just a car. I guess
the sprinklers at the Stark place weren't adjusted right and*

Dad didn't like how they were watering. So while he messed with them and did the edging, I offered to mow. I was in their front yard. I had my headphones in so I couldn't hear, but I turned around and Cal's dad was staring at me. I didn't even hear him drive up. He just stood beside his car in the driveway, staring at me. It gave me the creeps. I was wearing my shorts and tank top from gym. Dad stopped at a gas station so I could change out of my uniform. I wish I would have had some jeans. Cal's dad kept looking at my chest. I wasn't sure what to do so I just kept mowing. On my next pass, he was gone. Maybe he didn't like that a kid was cutting his lawn? I don't know. He looks like Cal. They have the same hair and face. Maybe that's why he bugged me. He reminded me of asshole Cal. Still it was weird that he was staring at me, right? Whatever. I really don't like Cal's dad.

Nellie

CHAPTER ELEVEN

CAL

NELLIE'S JOURNAL entry about my dad was the only one in the book that made me laugh. Because after months of being in the same school and unofficially declaring each other as enemies, her dislike of Dad was something we would have wholeheartedly agreed upon.

I really don't like Cal's dad.

"Well . . ." I slammed her diary closed and chuckled. "That makes two of us."

I hadn't spoken to my father in years. Whenever I went home to Denver, I spent my time with Mom. We'd eat lunch at her favorite bistro. We'd go shopping if she wanted to shop. Once, I'd waited at her salon while she'd gotten her hair colored. Then we'd pick a new restaurant to try for dinner.

I'd pick her up from the house and drop her off at the house. But I never went inside.

The last time I'd entered Mom and Dad's house had to have been exactly ten years ago for her birthday. Dad and I had gotten into a fight when he'd decided that appropriate celebratory dinner conversation was critiquing my plays from the previous season.

The asshole had pulled out his phone and recited how many interceptions I'd thrown. How many passing yards the other league quarterbacks had compared to my own. How many times I'd been sacked. How many games I'd lost.

He'd picked my career apart over their chef's beef Wellington. If it hadn't been Mom's special day, I would have left before dessert. But I'd stuck it out, and after our meal, I'd vowed to avoid the bastard at all costs.

Dad was more critical than any coach or manager. Hell, he was worse than Nellie. Then again, she didn't seem to give a damn about the actual football stats, just how I behaved after the game clock had run to zero.

Mom had simply stopped watching my games years ago. Maybe that was why I loved her so much. Either she didn't care about football or she recognized that Dad cared too much. Her apathy balanced the scales. She was more interested in my personal life, always asking if I'd met someone special or if a future daughter-in-law was on the horizon. My answer was always no.

So in a way, I'd been disappointing both my parents for years.

I returned Nellie's journal to the drawer in the kitchen where I'd hidden it last night when she'd stopped by. I doubted she'd visit again but living in the same town . . . things were different.

She'd be pissed as hell if she found out I'd stolen her diary. I'd deal with her fury if that time came, but mostly, I wasn't ready to give it back. Not yet.

Why this book had become so important I still hadn't pinpointed. Maybe because each time I opened the cover and saw her neat script, I didn't feel quite so alone. Maybe because it was a connection to her, to any person, that ran deeper than the surface.

Maybe because torturing myself with the actions of my past was better than sitting around feeling lost without my football career.

With the journal out of sight, I swept up my phone from the counter and pulled up Mom's name. She answered on the second ring.

"Oh, Cal. I got your flowers this morning. They are stunning. Thank you."

"I'm glad you like them." I smiled. "Happy birthday."

"Thanks. I wish you were here to celebrate it with me."

"Next time."

I'd considered flying to Colorado for a quick visit, and had I known that Darius and Kylie Rivera would be in town, I probably would have gone south. Except I was content in Calamity and wasn't quite ready to leave yet. Probably because leaving, even for just a weekend, felt a lot like losing to Nellie.

"How's your special day going?" I asked Mom.

"Good." There was a smile in her voice. "I just arrived at the spa. It was your father's gift."

My jaw ticked. "Isn't that what he got you last year too?"

"Yes, but—oh, shoot. They're waving me in already. Can I call you later, Cal? We're going out to a fancy dinner later, but I should have some time to catch up on the drive home. I'd like to hear how Montana is treating you."

"Of course. Call me whenever."

"Okay."

"Happy birthday, Mom," I said again. "Love you."

"I love you too."

I hung up and stared at my phone, guilt creeping in. She was spending the day at the spa. Damn. I should have gone to see her. At least then she wouldn't be around strangers on her special day. Though the amount of time she spent at the spa, I supposed those people were hardly strangers.

Dad sent Mom to the spa at least one day a week. Always a gift, so she'd feel indebted. It was his way of keeping her pacified. Because according to him, a spoiled wife didn't ask questions. She was more willing to overlook his discretions.

Like the fact that he was probably spending her birthday with his latest mistress.

Was the reason Mom avoided him so willingly because she knew about the girlfriends?

I knew of five myself. Dad hadn't been shy about parading them around whenever Mom was occupied elsewhere. The first I'd met my freshman year in high school, back when he still introduced them as his *assistants*. One had been his travel agent.

Maybe he'd thought I was too young to realize the truth. But he'd spoken too closely into their ears. He'd touched the smalls of their backs. He'd smiled at them like their secret affair was safe with me.

The son of a bitch.

In one of my first games with the Titans, Dad had decided to fly out and watch. He'd asked for two tickets, saying he was bringing a friend.

That friend had turned out to be a twenty-something

brunette with fake tits, a short skirt and a tight ass. When I'd asked him after the game who the fuck she was, he'd brushed it off. Told me it was just sex. He'd said that I'd understand when I was his age.

The fuck I would.

Our relationship had been strained before that day. After that, it had been over.

Any time Dad had asked me to get him tickets, I'd call Mom and invite her first. No surprise, his attendance had dwindled over the years. They'd missed my last two seasons entirely.

This time of year, I'd be in the thick of spring training. I was going to need more to do with my life than sit in this camper.

Christ, I missed football. I missed the focus it stole from my personal life.

My architect had finished the initial draft of the house plans. He was making some tweaks based on my feedback. Hopefully we'd have them finalized this week so they could be submitted to the county for a building permit approval. But even if I had to pick out flooring and tiles and cabinets and paint colors, I was going to need more activity.

For today, it was laundry. A pile of stripped sheets was on the RV's floor. I had Nellie and her impromptu visit last night to thank for a task to do today. As much as I liked her scent on my sheets, it had to go.

Nothing good would come from holding her too close.

I scooped up the pile and walked outside, about to head for the motel's laundry room.

"Cal," Harry called, opening her front door.

"Morning."

"It's too early for me."

It was almost nine, and I'd been up since dawn.

"Laundry?" She nodded to the bundle in my arms.

"Yeah."

She waved me over. "Use my machine. Marcy's swamped today."

And if I went to the laundry room, I would be in the way.

I changed directions, walking through Harry's sage-green door. I hadn't given her home much thought. Based on the exterior, I guess I expected it to be clean and tidy. It was clean. It was tidy. But holy shit, Harry had a lot of clutter.

The walls were so busy I wasn't sure what to look at first. Hung over the pink floral-print wallpaper in the entryway were at least fifty framed photos. Most were landscapes with a few faces mixed in between. Before I could lean in for a closer inspection, Harry waved me to follow her down the narrow hallway.

"Laundry room is this way," she said.

We weaved through a living room. The space would have been a comfortable size but with four couches, each upholstered in a different shade of mustard, I felt like I'd just stepped into a dollhouse. The furniture clashed beautifully with the green striped wallpaper, not that you could see much past the bookshelves, TV cabinet and piano.

Knickknacks. Pictures. Trinkets. Harry was a collector.

"This is not what I expected," I said as we passed through the kitchen. Again, it would have been spacious if not for the six-chair dining room table in the center.

"What did you expect?" she asked.

"Less . . . stuff."

158

"If you've lived as long as I've lived and don't have *stuff* to show for it, then you haven't been living right."

I chuckled. "Maybe you're right."

Mom and Dad's house was open and airy. I'd always thought it was Mom's minimalist style. But maybe she simply didn't have enough photos or souvenirs to display.

Harry passed through one more doorway to the laundry room—which was surprisingly empty with only a washer, dryer and a metal drying rack. "Did your mother teach you how to use these?"

"My mother hasn't done a load of laundry since she married my father. But if you're wondering if I know how to wash clothes, yes. I won't ruin your appliances or flood your house."

Laundry was about the only household chore I'd done in years. In Nashville, I'd employed a weekly housekeeping service and a gardener to care for my property. My dry cleaning had been sent out under an alias to ensure it all came back. But when it came to washing my T-shirts, underwear, socks and jeans, I'd always worried about delegating it to an assistant. The last thing I wanted was to find out that my dirty boxers had been sold online.

There were some weird people in this world.

"I'll leave you to it," Harry said, tapping her dryer. "I'm helping Marcy with rooms today."

"All right." I nodded and flipped open the top of the washer, fitting the sheets around the agitator.

Harry walked out of the laundry room. "Don't lock the door."

"Okay."

The front door closed as I dumped a scoop of laundry

detergent into the machine. I turned it on, then retraced my steps through the kitchen. When I hit the living room, the sheer abundance of *stuff* snared me. And since Harry hadn't told me not to snoop, I snooped.

The books on the shelves ranged from non-fiction to cozy mysteries to historical romance novels with shirtless men on the covers. There was a shelf dedicated to tattered copies of the Bible. The piano was an upright, the top protected by a lace doily. Framed photos were bunched together by family. I recognized Marcy's face from what must have been her senior portrait. Beside it were pictures of kids and grandkids.

I picked up a photo of a boy wearing a green football uniform. His helmet dangled from the hand at his side. His shoulder pads were too big and his white pants sagged at the waist. But the kid's smile stretched ear to ear.

That was how it should be. Kids should smile when they played football.

Had I ever smiled like that in youth sports? Maybe before my talent had taken hold. Before fun had been replaced with pressure.

If there was a photo of me like this one, it would be in a storage tub at Mom and Dad's place. They didn't hang framed pictures on the walls because Dad preferred art from a local gallery.

A gallery I'd been to once, and only once, because as soon as I'd seen the curator—a woman with sleek red hair and bedroom eyes for my father—I'd known exactly why Dad liked the gallery.

A rush of envy hit as I returned the kid's frame to the piano's top.

Lucky guy.

The moment I stepped through the Winnebago's door, Nellie's scent filled my nose. I cracked the windows, leaving it to air out the smell of oranges and orchids, while I pulled a hat over my hair and put on a pair of sunglasses.

Risky as it was to brave downtown on a Saturday morning, staying here would only make me think of sex. How Nellie had moaned my name last night while I'd sucked on her clit. How her pussy had pulsed around my cock as I'd plunged myself into her tight body. How beautiful she'd looked beneath the moonlight, with her hair tousled and her clothes askew, as we'd walked to her car.

"Get her out of your head." I dragged a hand over my mouth, then set off across the gravel path that ran the length of the motel. I was five feet away from the sidewalk that led to First when a man's voice carried my way.

"Maybe we could come back in September. Before it gets too cold."

"I'd like that," a woman said. "I can keep my eye out for plane ticket deals. Or we could let Nellie buy them like she offered."

"Not happening."

Nellie? *Oh, shit.* My feet ground to a stop on the concrete but it was too late for me to escape. I glanced left just as Nellie's parents rounded the corner of the motel.

Darius Rivera spotted me and his face turned to stone.

I swallowed hard, my shoes like cement blocks. It took effort to pick up my feet and approach, hand extended. "Mr. Rivera."

Kylie's eyes narrowed.

Darius stared at me for a long moment, and I was sure he'd dismiss me, but then he fit his palm against mine. The fact that he'd shake my hand proved he was a good man. The better man. "Cal Stark."

"Nice to see you, sir." I nodded to Kylie. "Mrs. Rivera."

She glared and damn if it didn't make her look just like Nellie. I would have teased her about it if I didn't think she'd rip off my balls.

"I was just heading into town," I said. "I'll get out of your way."

"We were going that direction too," Darius said.

I expected them to put some distance between us. But as I started down the sidewalk, they fell into step beside me.

Every second was torture. I realized after a block that I wasn't breathing. Sweat beaded at my temples.

"Well, this is awkward," Kylie muttered.

I huffed a dry laugh. "Pretty much."

Yet even after admitting it, we didn't talk about anything. Not a single word. Not that there was anything to say. So we walked, step after step, until the bustle of downtown forced me to shift behind them.

My gaze flew over their heads to Nellie, standing outside the White Oak.

Her eyes were on her phone. She smiled at the screen, her fingers flying, then she tucked it into her shorts pocket. She was killing me with those shorts. Bare, smooth skin all the way to her sandals. Her loose tee draped off one shoulder.

A shoulder I'd kissed last night.

She turned our direction, spotting her parents first. Her smile was breathtaking. It fell flat when she looked over her father's head and found my face. Her eyes widened as she rushed our way, like she was coming to their rescue. "Hi. What's, um . . ."

"We bumped into Cal at the motel," her mom said, looping her arm with Darius's. "We're going to grab a table for breakfast."

Before they could walk away, I stopped them. "Mr. Rivera."

Darius turned. "Yes?"

I pulled off my shades so he could see my eyes. "For what it's worth, I'm sorry."

Kylie's eyebrows rose. Nellie's mouth parted.

We all knew why I was apologizing.

Darius gave me a single nod before he escorted his wife into the restaurant.

Nellie waited until her parents were inside, then her hands went to her hips. "This town isn't big enough. You have to move."

"This again? Not happening. Besides, I figured you'd be out exploring the area today."

"We're meeting for a late breakfast."

"Then the next time you come over for a fuck, mention your schedule. I'll do my best to accommodate."

Her nostrils flared. *Beautifully furious.* "Please tell me you didn't make that sort of comment to my parents."

"No. But it's good to know that I'm your dirty little secret."

"Oh, and I suppose you tell people about us." When I didn't respond, she rolled her eyes. "That's what I thought. Don't want the world to know you're screwing the scholarship kid, right?"

No, that wasn't why I hadn't told anyone. I hadn't spoken about it because I wasn't sure what to say.

"Whatever," she muttered. "What was that about? The apology to Dad?"

I shrugged and put on my sunglasses. "It was overdue."

She gave me a sideways glance. "We're going to wander around downtown today."

"I'm just grabbing some food. Then I'll stick close to the RV."

"Thank you."

"It'll cost you." That remark earned me another eye roll.

"Of course, it will." She raised her chin. "What do you want?"

"Tell me what you hate about me."

She frowned, looking past me to the windows of the café.

I followed her gaze, seeing her parents in a booth beside the glass. Darius was watching us as he pretended to read his menu.

"I hate that you're a liar," she said.

Ouch. It stung because she was right. "Can't argue with that."

"Bye, Stark."

"Bye, Rivera."

She hurried into the café while I continued down the sidewalk. Whatever appetite I'd had was gone, replaced by rocks in my gut, so I turned around and retraced my path to the motel.

She was right about more than me being a liar. This town wasn't big enough.

Did I really want to bump into her at random? Last night she'd been beautiful and naked in my bed. Then this morning, she was back to the woman who'd learned long ago to keep up her guard where I was concerned.

Maybe sex was just part of that barrier. Maybe it was a way for her to keep me in a box. Casual. Physical. Shallow.

And one day, when she was tired of that box, when she wanted more and met a man who could give it to her, she'd cut me off. It was destined to end.

When I arrived at the Winnebago, I went straight for the closet.

And while I waited for my laundry, I filled my suitcase.

CHAPTER TWELVE

NELLIE

FOR THE TENTH time since I'd unrolled my yoga mat at The Refinery, I glanced out the windows toward the street. Besides the instructor pacing the sidewalk while talking on her phone, there was no sign of Cal.

There'd been no sign of Cal for a week.

Not since last Saturday when he'd walked downtown with my parents.

I'd assumed he'd simply been avoiding public spaces while my family had been in town visiting. The apology he'd given Dad had been . . . nice? And totally out of character for Cal. He rarely admitted his mistakes. I'd figured his absence was another anomaly, and for once, he'd been heeding my wishes.

But since he'd moved here, Cal had been a constant irritation. Going a week without seeing him was unsettling. Where was he?

Neither Mom nor Dad had mentioned Cal during the rest of their short vacation weekend, though Dad had been quieter than normal as we'd wandered up and down First. Maybe one day we'd talk about Cal. Probably not. After all this time, there just wasn't much to say. What was done was done, and Dad had moved on.

My parents and I'd had a bittersweet farewell at the airport last Sunday with tight hugs goodbye. I'd already booked a trip to see them at Thanksgiving, and they were hoping to return to Calamity this fall.

Other than missing them a bit more than normal, my week had been fairly mundane. Without Cal popping up at random times, life had been almost boring.

I'd been sure he'd come to yoga today to torment me.

The door opened and my eyes flew to the glass. I hated that I hoped to see his broad frame cross the threshold.

But it was Larke who breezed inside the studio with a yoga mat tucked under an arm. She waved at me, stowed her shoes, then took the space beside mine. "Hey. Phew. I thought for sure I was going to be late."

"You made it just in time." Class started in two minutes. And still, no sign of Stark.

Larke relaxed onto her mat, sitting in an easy pose. "Have you ever been to Hawaii?"

"Yes." Hawaii always made me think of Cal. "Why?"

"I was thinking about booking a quick vacation over the school's winter break. Escape the snow. Maybe make it a girls' trip since the chances of me finding an actual man to take to the beach are dwindling daily. Would you want to go?"

"Definitely." Whenever it was, I'd make it happen.

"Yay." She smiled, unaware to how much that invitation meant.

I'd never been invited on a girls' trip.

In college, I'd watched girls leave in packs for their spring break vacations to Florida. Meanwhile, I'd stayed behind and worked extra hours. My most exciting winter break had been junior year when I'd flown home to Denver and had helped Mom deep clean and organize her kitchen cabinets on Christmas Eve. The years after I'd graduated from UNC had been just as uneventful.

A few years ago, I'd rented a tiny cabin in the Colorado mountains to get away from the city for a weekend, but I'd gone alone. Any other vacations I'd taken were usually working vacations when I'd accompanied Pierce to wherever he was traveling.

That was why I'd traveled to Hawaii.

Pierce had been going through a lot in his personal life. He'd wanted to get out of Denver for a week and clear his head, except he hadn't wanted to go alone, so he'd invited me along to hang out.

Cal also decided to play the role of supportive friend, and as a surprise, he showed up just hours after we'd arrived.

To this day, I wondered if his shock at seeing me answer the door was genuine. Knowing Cal, he'd shown up just to irritate me.

My plan had been to avoid him. The house Pierce owned on Maui was enormous, and we could easily have kept thousands of square feet between us. Which was exactly what we'd done during the first day on the island.

But that night, I had trouble sleeping. Cal found me in the theater room. One kiss led to two, then he carried me to his bedroom. After an hour of sex, I went to the kitchen for a snack.

Instead of giving me space, Cal followed in his boxers.

I was standing at the fridge, wearing only my robe and planning to make myself an omelet, when his bare feet came to a stop beside mine. But before I could take out the carton of eggs, he made a snide comment about cooking for him too since I had more practice at the stove. Not just because I was a woman but because I was too poor to have a personal chef like His Majesty King Stark.

Pierce broke up our screaming match at three in the morning.

Cal flew out the next day as soon as his pilot was awake and ready.

And I told Pierce that if he ever put Cal and me under the same roof again, even accidentally, I'd quit and never speak to him again.

A Hawaii redo sounded like magic.

Especially with a friend.

The instructor came inside and greeted the class before taking her position by the mirrors. Then silence fell over the room as we all began to practice.

I guess Cal wasn't coming to yoga. That should have loosened the knot in my stomach. Why didn't it?

An hour later, Larke and I waved goodbye as she headed toward her car, and I began the lazy stroll to my house. I passed the White Oak, peering inside the windows to see if Cal was inside. I stopped by the coffee shop, ordering a latte before glancing at every table, wondering if I'd find his face.

But it was like he'd vanished and the only person who remembered his imprint was me.

Cal was okay, right? He was probably just holed up in his camper. Unless . . .

Had he left town? Had my plan to make his Calamity experience agony actually worked? No. No way. He was too stubborn to give up. He was too competitive to lose.

But what if he was really gone?

That knot in my stomach only got tighter. I left the coffee shop with an iced latte in hand and the beginning of a headache blooming behind my temples.

If Cal was gone, then Calamity was mine. All mine.

The sidewalks should have felt different as I walked home. Free. Every step should have felt like a victory.

So why did I feel this strange twang of guilt? Like I'd done Cal dirty?

By the time I got home, my stomach was roiling. I hadn't taken more than three sips of my drink, but the coffee was tossed down the drain before I swept up my car keys and drove to the motel.

I bypassed the parking lot and headed straight down the alley.

There were no lights on inside the Winnebago. Cal's camping chair wasn't outside, and his Land Rover was gone.

I reversed away, fumbling for my phone as I pulled onto the street again, destination home. Pierce's name was beneath my finger, ready to be dialed, but I stopped myself.

"Cal is not my problem." I threw the phone into the passenger seat, and it bounced to the floor, safely out of my reach.

Maybe if Stark was gone, I could actually relax. This was a good thing. I'd stop looking for him on First Street. I'd stop wondering if we'd bump into each other at Jane's. I'd stop worrying about bruising his feelings.

And I wouldn't have to see his Land Rover parked outside my house.

"Damn it." I groaned at the sight of his SUV, though my heart did a traitorous skip. "Freaking Cal."

The sense of relief as I pulled into my driveway and parked in the garage was as frustrating as the man who met me on the sidewalk.

"Hi." He jerked up his chin.

Without his usual baseball hat and sunglasses, he looked exposed. Vulnerable. Cal was standing in the sunshine, dressed in a simple T-shirt and a pair of faded jeans. His hair was finger-combed, still too long and sexy. Put a football in that man's hands and my ovaries would likely explode.

The bastard.

"Hi." I crossed my arms over my chest. "Where have you been?"

He smirked. "I figured you'd miss me, sugar."

"What was that?" I cupped a hand to my ear. "I couldn't hear you over your ego."

His smug grin flattened. "Thought you wanted me to move."

"I do." Didn't I? *Yes.* He had to leave. The reason I was relieved to see him wasn't because I wanted him to stay. It was because now I knew where he was. Now he couldn't sneak up on me.

But yes, Cal absolutely had to leave Montana. The sooner the better.

"I spent the week in Bozeman," he said. "Got out of town."

"But you came back," I muttered. "Lucky me. What do you want?"

He inhaled a long breath, like what he was about to ask was going to take some effort. His fingers snapped three times at his side. "I need a favor."

"Let me guess. 'Tell me what you hate about me.'" I dropped my voice in an attempt to imitate his. "No. How about we just leave the specifics out of it? I find you abhorrent, end of discussion."

"Abhorrent?"

"Is that too big of a word for you?" Okay, yeah. It was sort of a nasty word too.

"Just . . . extreme." His jaw clenched. "Can we save the banter for another Saturday? Like I said, I need a favor."

"What favor? Wait." I held up a finger. "It better not be sexual."

He chuckled. "I don't really need to ask you for sexual favors, do I?"

No, he didn't. I was a willing participant and an instigator. Because when it came to Cal, I was a weak, weak woman. Those hazel eyes and that stubbled jaw were irresistible.

"What's the favor?"

"My agent is coming to town," he said. "He wants to go to dinner."

"Okay," I drawled. "Do you need restaurant recommendations? Because I just ate at the Pizza Palace. Highly recommend."

"God, can you not be snarky?" He shook his head. "I need a date to dinner."

And he was asking me? "Really?"

"Yeah. Will you go with me?"

"As your date? Have you lost your mind? I'm sure you

can find someone else." Hell, he could just stroll down First looking like he did today and he'd have multiple candidates to choose from within minutes. Like my yoga instructor.

"I need a date who's not a date. Someone who's not going to think it's an actual date."

"To meet with your agent? Why?" Wasn't that the sort of meeting you'd take one-on-one?

He rubbed the back of his neck. "He wants me to take this job."

"With a team? Which one?" A jolt of excitement raced through my mind at the idea of Cal playing football again. If Cal took a position, he'd be gone from Calamity. I'd know exactly where he was during the season.

"Not with a team. With a media network. I'd be an NFL commentator with ESPN."

"Oh." Watching him on camera wouldn't be nearly as exciting if he was providing commentary about a game instead of playing it. Especially considering his onscreen persona was usually so . . . Cal. "You? Really?"

"Trust me, you're not the only one surprised. I guess they want an unlikable asshole to rile people up. Cause some controversy and boost ratings."

"Well, they've found the right man."

"I'm not doing it."

"Probably a smart decision."

"My agent has been persistent." Probably because he didn't get paid unless Cal was working.

"Just say no. To drugs and ESPN," I teased.

"I have. He still wants to meet."

"Why would you need me to pretend to be your date just to watch you tell your agent no?" What was I missing?

"I don't meet with him alone."

I blinked. "Huh?"

"I don't meet with my agent alone."

"Seriously?"

"Yes. I've never met with him alone. It's a lesson my father taught me."

The mention of his father made my body tense. "He's your agent. Doesn't he work on your behalf?"

"He negotiates on my behalf. So I always have a witness for our conversations."

"That's . . ." *Sad.*

Cal really didn't trust anyone, did he? Not even those who should be on his side. Or maybe he'd trusted them and he'd been betrayed one too many times. Either way, my heart twisted.

"When I lived in Nashville, my assistant would go with me," he said. "But I don't have an assistant here. I'd ask Pierce but—"

"No." *Shit.* Cal knew I wouldn't make Pierce go to a dinner that I was perfectly capable of attending myself.

"It's one dinner, Nellie."

"Say please."

"Please." He said it without a grumble or grimace, meaning he was desperate.

"Fine." I shot him a glare when he grinned. "When?"

"Tonight."

"Tonight? What if I had plans?"

"Do you?"

I wanted to say yes. I wanted to tell him I had a hot date, simply to see how he'd react. But he'd see through a lie. "What time?"

"I'll pick you up at quarter to six. We're meeting at a steakhouse out of town. It'll take fifteen minutes to get there."

"Quarter to six. Anything else?"

He scanned me up and down, his gaze lingering as it caressed my tank top and leggings. His hungry gaze devoured me whole.

A pulse drummed low in my belly. A wave of heat spread through my limbs.

This feeling and that look on his face usually landed me in trouble, so I took a step away before turning and striding for the house.

"Nellie?" he called.

I slowed, looking back, but I didn't stop moving. Not until we had a locked door between us. "What?"

"Thank you."

It was genuine. Cal was rarely genuine.

It made me want him that much more.

"Go away, Stark."

-

Dear Diary,

Not the best Friday. I missed two questions on my US history test today. That sucked. We had to run the mile in gym and I got the worst side ache ever. That sucked. Then I passed Cal in the hallway after seventh period. Triple suck. I went a whole four days without seeing him but I guess that's the limit. He wouldn't even look at me. Just walked by with his blank face. He acts like I'm so beneath him. Asshole. I'm so glad it's the weekend. Mom said if she got good tips, we could go out to dinner tomorrow. I hope she gets good tips because I really, really want Chinese food.

Nellie

CHAPTER THIRTEEN

CAL

I RANG Nellie's doorbell at exactly five forty-five. It took her four minutes to answer.

Four minutes, where I stood outside under the sun, knowing that she was probably sitting on the couch, watching the seconds tick by on a clock before she'd finally deemed my penance complete.

"It's about damn time," I clipped as she opened the door.

"You could have waited in the car." She met my scowl with her own.

Her body was encased in a little black dress. The fabric molded to her figure, wrapping around her hips as it tapered toward her knees. The square neckline showed a sliver of cleavage. She'd strapped sexy-as-fuck heels to her ankles, and her hair was twisted in a knot, showcasing the silver hoops in her ears. Her green eyes were lined with black, making her irises pop, and she had on that goddamn red lipstick.

She was a living, breathing fantasy.

"You're not wearing that."

She glanced at her outfit. "Excuse me?"

"Change. Now," I ordered as my cock twitched.

"You know what?" She shook her head. "Go to dinner alone. Good luck."

My hand shot out and stopped the door as she attempted to slam it in my face. "Just change. Please."

I'd hit my quota of *please*s for the day, but apparently, it worked because Nellie dropped her hand.

"What's wrong with what I'm wearing? I thought we were going to a steakhouse."

"You look . . ." Incredible. Alluring. Magnificent, as always. "If you wear that dress, my agent will hit on you. And he'll stare at your tits all night."

If it was any other woman, I'd let him ogle my date. But not her. I didn't love Wade, but I wasn't ready to fire him either. If he crossed a line with Nellie, I'd not only can his ass, but there was a chance I'd punch him in the face.

"Fine." She huffed and strode through the living room, her ass swaying with every angry step.

Yeah, she had to change. Not just for Wade. But because I needed to get through this dinner and if she stayed in that dress, I'd strip her down before we even made it to the restaurant.

I stepped inside, closed the door and went to the couch. There was a new television on the stand in front of me. "So much for not wanting a TV, huh?"

"Changed my mind," she said as her footsteps sounded on the stairs.

"This woman," I muttered, then paced the room as I waited for her to change. It took less time than I'd expected for her to return, except she hadn't really fixed the problem.

She'd traded the dress for a pair of black pants with a slim fit that stopped at her ankles. The damn heels were the same. Her top was a sleeveless black turtleneck, and yeah, there was no cleavage, but it begged to be torn from her torso.

"You're fucking killing me." I pinched the bridge of my nose and willed the swelling behind my zipper to stop.

"It's this outfit or you can forget my company." She planted her hands on her hips. "You have three seconds."

"Let's go." I strode out the door, not bothering to wait for her to lock up.

Didn't she have a garbage sack or a tent she could put on? Some shapeless, boring number that disguised her curves? But hell, this was Nellie. I knew exactly what she looked like beneath her clothes, so she could be wearing a burlap sack and I'd find it sexy.

I had the car running and the air-conditioning cranked by the time she slid into the passenger seat. Her perfume filled the cab instantly. With her hair up, I didn't dare roll down the windows—one of my mother's lessons about preserving an updo at all costs. So I was forced to breathe Nellie in as I steered us out of town.

Christ, she smelled good.

"You look nice." Understatement of the century.

She barked a dry laugh. "That sounded painful. Is it really so hard for you to give me a compliment?"

"No," I mumbled.

She had no idea how beautiful she was. How much I wanted her. Craved her. She had no clue that she'd ruined me for other women.

Before Nellie, there'd been women. Casual flings. Random hookups. My third year in the league, I'd attempted the girlfriend thing, but it had fizzled in weeks thanks to my demanding travel and practice schedule.

Then there'd been that night in Charlotte and Nellie had fucked up my life. Every other woman paled in comparison.

No one was as beautiful. No one had that fire. No one made my pulse race, whether we were fighting or fucking.

Maybe I'd been comparing other women to Nellie since high school and hadn't even realized it.

There was an entry in her diary about how I hadn't looked at her in the hallways. Yeah, I'd never looked at Nellie back then. I'd done my best to pretend she hadn't existed.

It had been easier that way. The last thing I'd wanted was for one of the guys to catch me checking her out as she stood at her locker, loading up her arms with books. If any of the other girls had caught me watching Nellie, they would have made her life miserable, just because I'd failed to keep my eyes away.

I never should have looked at her. I never should have broken my focus.

But then . . . Charlotte. Fucking Charlotte.

Having her as my non-date tonight was a horrible idea. No question.

I'd asked Harry if she'd go with me, but they'd had some stupid family night planned. Pierce would have been the better choice, and even with the new baby, he would have tagged along. That would have been the smarter choice because there was no way I'd want to reach across the cab and squeeze his thigh.

My fingers tightened on the wheel as I drove. I stayed quiet. Nellie stayed quiet. What was there to say? We didn't share personal details, preferring to torment each other instead. Except at the moment, the silence felt . . . lonely.

God, I was sick of being lonely. "I miss football."

"Then take the sportscasting job."

I shook my head. "It's not for me."

"You could play."

"Nah. It was time to get out."

She hummed, and as the soothing sound faded, the silence returned.

I shifted, leaning an elbow on the console as I drove with one hand. "Tell me what you hate about me."

"You drive like an old man."

I chuckled. "No hesitation?"

"Not tonight." She smirked, then nodded to the speedometer. "You're going five miles under the speed limit."

"I don't like to drive fast."

She studied my profile, leaning her elbow on the console too. We were close. Too close. All I had to do was lean in and kiss that red off her lips. So I shifted in the opposite direction.

"Why don't you like to drive fast?" she asked. "It seems . . . I don't know. Shy?"

"I'm not shy."

"Exactly."

I sighed, not wanting to share this story, but talking was better than the silence. "When I was sixteen, my grandfather died in a car accident."

"Oh." She gasped. "I'm so sorry."

"He was my dad's father. We were close." Grandpa Stark had loved football, and whenever we'd play catch or goof around, it had always been a game. When I'd played with Dad, it had always been practice.

"It was a three-car collision," I told her. "Grandpa's fault. The insurance companies did an extensive investigation. They found that he was speeding, going at least twenty miles per hour over the limit. He must not have been paying attention. Maybe he swerved to avoid an animal or something. But he overcorrected and flew into the oncoming lane."

"Cal, I had no idea."

Not many knew. It wasn't something I'd wanted to talk about, especially at school. "One of the cars was totaled, but the driver walked away with a few scrapes and bruises. But the other car . . . the guy was a father of four. He died on impact. So did Grandpa."

Nellie reached across the cab, her hand almost settling on my shoulder before she pulled it back in exchange for a sad smile. "I'm sorry. I shouldn't have hassled you about it."

"You're not the first person to razz me about my driving. It doesn't bother me." Most people who knew the story would drive slower too, at least when I was in the car.

"I'm still sorry."

"Thanks."

The remainder of the drive was quiet, though the silence wasn't as unsettling. The tension was gone. Sad stories had their way of sobering the mood. But as the restaurant neared, a different emotion made my hands strangle the wheel —annoyance.

This visit of Wade's was pointless. I'd told him as much the last time we'd talked, but he seemed certain that if we sat down and *talked it through*, I'd change my mind. He was about to be disappointed.

I pulled into the steakhouse's parking lot, taking the last spot available. Then we both climbed out and made our way to the door. Together. Like a couple. Like we'd done this a hundred times.

Was that strange? There weren't many people I felt comfortable with but Nellie was one. When it came to her, I knew exactly what to expect. She had no hidden agendas. She didn't fake her way through life. She was the real deal.

Not many people would tell you to your face what they hated about you.

Which was why I'd only ask her.

"Hey." I slowed my steps as we approached the door. "Thanks for doing this."

She nodded. "I'm not doing this to help you. It's because you're buying dinner and a steak sounded better than left-over pizza."

I chuckled. "It's always brutal honesty with you, isn't it?"

"It's kind of my style."

"Yes, it is." I held the door open for her to step inside the darkened space. Then I followed, giving my eyes a moment to adjust. When they did, the first face I spotted was Wade's.

"Cal! There's my guy." He clapped his hands together, the crack too loud for the small space beside the hostess station. But that was Wade. He was unapologetically bois-terous and crass.

I'd opted for a pair of dark jeans and a button-down white shirt. But Wade, as always, was decked out in a tailored three-piece suit. This one navy and likely from Italy, paid for by the commission he'd earned from my contracts.

"Wade." I shook his hand, not adding a *good to see you* or *thanks for coming all this way*. It would only be bullshit.

"Looking good, buddy."

God, I hated it when he called me buddy. "Thanks."

"And who is this?" His gaze raked up and down Nellie like she was a lollipop and he was licking her head to toe.

I shot him a warning glare, putting my hand on the small of her back. "Nellie Rivera."

Wade held out his hand for a shake.

Nellie raised her chin and extended her hand. But instead of shaking it like a normal fucking person, Wade tried to lift her knuckles to his lips.

She ripped her hand away. "I don't think so, *Wade*."

I grinned.

"A fiery one." Wade laughed it off. "I like that."

Idiot. I really should fire him. But he'd scored me a huge contract to play with the Titans. He'd been with me from the beginning, and loyalty was a bitch.

"So should we sit?" he asked. "Talk about this incredible opportunity with ESPN?"

"We can sit. But I'm not taking the job. I've had enough cameras and reporters to last two lifetimes."

"Come on, Cal. I came all this way. Let's at least discuss it."

"There's nothing to discuss. I'm going to tell you exactly what I told you over the phone. I'm not interested."

My reputation was bad enough. The last thing I needed was to rip a team to shreds during a halftime report only to be ridiculed for my opinion later. No matter what I said, it would be twisted to make me look like a dick.

Granted, in my career there had been plenty of on-camera moments when I *had* been a dick. But the media had searched for it. They trimmed clips and made sound bites to suit their needs. To make me the Cal Stark everyone wanted me to be.

The asshole.

"Cal." Wade gave me a flat look. "Come on. This is huge. Only the greats get these chances. You'll make millions per season as a color commentator."

"I already made millions."

"Then make more." He meant make him more.

"It's a no, Wade. A fuck no."

His smile dropped and his jaw clenched.

"Now that we've got that out of the way," I said. "Would you like to sit down and eat? Catch up? But if you'd rather hit the road . . ."

"Yeah." His nostrils flared. "Think I'll bump up my flight. We'll talk later."

"Not about this."

"Fine." He strode past me, his irritation as fragrant as the scents escaping the kitchen.

Wade would pout for a week or two, then he'd call me like this incident had never happened. I'd be his buddy again, especially if he found another opportunity to cash in on my career while I was still relevant.

But for tonight, I didn't give a shit if he was pissed. He could have saved himself a trip if he would have just listened to me from the start.

"That went well," Nellie muttered as the door closed behind him. "He's a peach."

"Isn't he?" I dropped my hand from her back. "Well, that didn't take long. Should we go?"

"Oh, hell no." She frowned and took a step toward the hostess station. "You owe me dinner."

How could I forget? I lingered behind her, keeping a few feet between us, as she told the hostess my name. Then the hostess led us through the restaurant to a tall-backed booth against a shaded window. The steakhouse was rustic and dim, the atmosphere perfect for an intimate date.

I slid into my side of the booth as Nellie did the same, taking a menu and flipping straight to the wine list. Neither of us spoke as we made our selections and ordered from our waiter.

It wasn't until the wine was delivered that Nellie leaned her elbows on the table, assessing me with her sharp gaze. "So you really don't want more money?"

"What for?" I shrugged.

"Rich people love to get richer."

"I'm rich enough."

There was plenty in my bank account that continued to grow thanks to a steady income stream from my investments. I had my ranch. I'd build a house. If my father ever failed to support my mother, she would want for nothing.

I liked money. But I wasn't my dad, constantly needing more and more.

Nellie lifted her wineglass to her lips, taking a long sip. Her gaze never wavered from my own.

"Don't believe me?" I asked.

Nellie set the glass down. "I believe you. But I'm having a hard time reconciling the Cal who doesn't want to make millions of dollars a year by appearing on a few TV shows to the Cal who told me our senior year in high school that if I couldn't get a car with a decent muffler and fewer rust spots, then I needed to find a parking spot farther away from his Mercedes."

I cringed. Not my finest day. Had that day made her diary from senior year?

She'd had a piece-of-shit car in those days. Something she could afford. Probably her mother's hand-me-down. And I'd struck a low blow.

There were no excuses to make. It had just been me, a spoiled shit of a teenager, acting like a spoiled shit of a teenager.

"I'm both of those people, Nellie."

"Are you?"

I sighed. "I don't know."

She studied me for another long moment, and this time, I didn't have the courage to hold her gaze. So I plucked up the small booklet tucked between the salt and pepper shakers and flipped open the first page.

"A history of Calamity," I read, quickly scanning the article. Then, because I didn't want to talk about the past or about football or about ESPN or about anything that might make Nellie hate me more, I gave her the short version of the story.

"The town of Calamity was originally called Panner City."

"I didn't know that," she said. "I assumed it was named after Calamity Jane."

"Nope. The town was a settlement during the Montana gold rush. By 1864, three thousand miners lived here."

"That's a lot of people." More than lived in Calamity today according to the article.

I twisted the booklet to show her the old, sepia photo of what had to be the mining camp. Huts and tents were cramped together. On the next page, there was a photo of one man panning next to a stream. Beside it was a black-and-white sketch of a handmade sluice box.

"It was renamed to Calamity after a series of disasters struck in a period of just five months," I said, continuing to read. "The mine collapsed in Anders Gulch. A dozen men were killed. Then they had a spring flood that washed out the smaller sites. Next came a fire that burned nearly everything to the ground. It's speculated to have started in the saloon."

"Drunken bar fight?"

"Probably." I flipped the page, seeing more photos. "The last disaster happened in late summer. A lightning storm caused a herd of cattle to stampede through the camps. Flattened tents and people too."

"Eww."

I chuckled and handed her the booklet. While she read, I sipped my wine, grateful to whoever had come up with the idea to include Calamity history with the meal. It saved us from personal conversation.

Any conversation with Nellie was dangerous, not just because of her brutal honesty, but because she knew me too well. And for tonight, I just wanted to eat a meal across from a beautiful woman and not delve into anything deeper than this glass of cabernet.

Nellie put the booklet away and leaned back into her seat, giving me a smug grin. "Let's talk about football."

"Football?" Why was it so sexy that she knew football?

She shrugged. "Seems like a safe topic."

"Agreed." I mirrored her posture, relaxing into the booth. "What do you want to know?"

"The juicy gossip. And I mean the goods. The stuff you'd only know about because you were on the team."

I laughed. It was a laugh so easy and natural it took me by surprise.

It had been a long time since I'd just . . . laughed.

Maybe it caught Nellie off guard too because she stared at me with this strange expression on her face. Like when a receiver made a catch that he shouldn't have made. Like it was a miracle play that would land him on the highlight reel.

We spent the rest of our evening talking about football. I told her about fights in the locker room. About scandals that had never made the press. About the assistant coach who'd been fired for sleeping with the owner's daughter.

By the time we left the steakhouse, I'd laughed more times than I had in years. And when I parked against the sidewalk at her house, I wished for a few more minutes. For one more laugh. For another glimpse of her breathtaking smile.

"Thanks for coming with me tonight," I said.

"You didn't really need me there."

"Yes, I did." Wade would have kept pushing. And even if he'd left, exactly as he had tonight, I wouldn't have stayed to eat alone.

Nellie touched the door handle, but paused, her fingers poised to pull. She looked across the cab, her gaze tracing the line of my nose down to my lips.

For a moment, I thought she'd lean over. That she'd close this gap, and I'd spend the night in her bed, not the Winnebago.

God, how I wanted her. To savor her body. To strip off

that top. To kiss her lips until the red was on my skin, not hers.

Except she gave her head a tiny shake, then pulled the handle, the door popping open. She was three strides up her walkway before she slowed. The passenger door was still gaping open.

"Are you going to close the door?" I called.

She spun around, taking a step backward. Then she stopped. Her shoulders fell. "No."

"No, you're not going to close it?"

"Come inside, Cal."

I closed the car door on my way to hers.

CHAPTER FOURTEEN

NELLIE

AS WE STEPPED inside my house, Cal's hands came to my shoulders while he kicked the door shut. The sound was as loud as my thundering heartbeat.

A night with Cal was a horrible idea, and for a split second, I'd almost walked away. Why couldn't I walk away?

From the moment I'd stepped out of his car, my body had been trembling with this insatiable need for more. These days, I always wanted more.

Was it my turn to initiate sex? For the life of me, I couldn't remember who'd made the move last time. Did it matter? All I knew was that I burned for his touch.

I sagged against his chest as his hands skimmed up and down my arms, his fingertips leaving tingles in their wake. He pulled at the neck of my top, exposing my skin. Then his lips were there, barely a whisper as they traced the line of my jaw. "Fuck, I want you, Nell."

My eyes drifted closed as his breath caressed the shell of my ear. "Then take me."

On the floor. The couch. Against the wall again. I just wanted him inside me. I needed him to satisfy this ache.

The heat from his chest vanished as he stepped away.

I stood frozen, my heart in my throat, waiting for what he'd do next. Strip off my shirt. Loosen the waistband on my pants. Take down my hair. Cal was a master of anticipation.

His hand slipped into mine and as he tugged me forward, I opened my eyes and followed as he walked us to the stairs.

"Wait," I whispered.

He ignored me and took the first step.

No. I didn't want him in my bedroom. Any other room, but that one.

Cal had already ruined one of my bedrooms. Once he fucked me on my bed, I'd see him there. Always. I'd picture him naked between my sheets. I'd search for the scent of his cologne on my pillows.

But as he climbed the staircase, any other objection lodged in my throat.

I didn't want Cal in my bed, but I didn't want him to leave. The truth would lead to questions and the answers would only chase him away. So I let him tow me upstairs, and when we stepped through the threshold of my bedroom, I realized I should have pushed harder for a romp on the couch.

Cal looked like a dream in the muted light as he stood next to my bed. Handsome. Sexy. His laugh from dinner echoed in my ears.

That laughter had been magical. Unique. Tonight, he'd laughed his real laugh. A sound that came from deep in his chest because it was honest. And he'd given it to me.

"Turn around," he ordered.

I obeyed, facing him with my back to the bed.

Cal's hazel eyes darkened as he stepped away, his eyes never leaving mine as he started unbuttoning his shirt. One painful button at a time, it seemed to take hours. As each was loosened, I was granted a glimpse of his skin, until finally, he yanked the hem from his jeans and stripped it from his muscled shoulders.

My mouth went dry, taking in his abs and arms. The pulse in my core bloomed as I stared at the strength of his chest.

"Take your clothes off."

Again, I obeyed. Outside the bedroom, I fought him tooth and nail for control. But the rules were different when our clothes began hitting the floor.

My heels landed with a thud on the carpet as I unbuckled the straps at my ankles and kicked them aside. The cool air raised bumps on my skin as my shirt plopped to the floor. When I unzipped my slacks, they slid from my legs as I shimmied them down my hips until the sleek material puddled at my feet.

Cal stood unmoving, towering over me as his eyes feasted on every inch of my flesh. His breath shortened as I freed my breasts from the black lace bra. His mouth parted when I hooked my thumbs in the band of my panties and eased them down my thighs.

"Christ." His Adam's apple bobbed before he jerked his chin to the mattress. "On your back."

I arched an eyebrow. "Say please, Cal."

"You want me to say please?" He crossed the space

between us in a flash. "Then I won't be saying it alone. You want me to make you beg, sugar?"

Oh, God, yes. "Say. Please."

He leaned in, his lips touching mine as he growled, "Please."

I reveled in my victory.

"Now get on the bed. Legs spread wide."

I sat on the edge of the bed, slowly inching deeper onto the mattress until I could lie down. The touch from the quilt seemed to increase the buzz beneath my skin.

Cal's hand came to one ankle, placing it wide. Then he did the same with the other until I was bared to him, vulnerable and dripping wet. "Your pussy is so fucking perfect, Nell."

A lot of people called me Nell. But it was always different with Cal. It was that shortening of my name that had been my undoing from the start.

The night at his hotel in Charlotte, both of us a little raw, and he'd asked one question.

Why can't I get you out of my head, Nell?

"Fuck me, Cal." I'd said the same that night too.

"Patience." He planted his elbows on the bed, his shoulders spanning the space between my knees, and without any teasing, dove for my clit.

I cried out, arching my back as he sucked and licked. He was a man who knew how to please, and at the moment, I didn't want foreplay.

I wanted a toe-curling, blinding orgasm. A score.

Cal always scored.

His tongue worked magic through my folds, eating me

like I was his last meal. A finger plunged deep, followed by another, stroking the spot inside that made my limbs quake.

My hands threaded through his hair, gripping it tightly as I tilted my hips into his mouth, chasing that glorious release.

"Cal." My head thrashed. My chest heaved. Then everything tightened as the orgasm broke, wracking my body while my heart soared to the stars.

Our moans filled the bedroom. I'd hear them echo for months, just like I had in Denver. But as my orgasm rolled hard and long, I didn't care. For this, I'd cope with the memories.

He lapped at my wetness until the aftershocks subsided.

My legs and arms fell limp at my sides, my head spinning. No man on earth had such a wickedly talented tongue.

Cal kissed the inside of my thigh, then stood.

The sound of his zipper unlatching filled the room. Then came the ripping of a condom's wrapper, followed by the drop of his jeans as they joined the clutter on the floor. The mattress dipped with Cal's weight before he settled into the cradle of my hips.

His hands came to my face, pushing away the hair that had fallen out of the bobby pins I'd used earlier. "Open your eyes."

"Say—"

"Please."

I obeyed.

His face hovered inches from mine, and there was an intensity to his expression. A furrow between his eyebrows.

"What's wrong?"

"You're beautiful."

I stilled.

Cal had called me beautiful before. Usually with an undercurrent of irritation, like it pained him to admit I was pretty. Other times he'd said it as we'd been clawing at each other's naked bodies. Those compliments had been driven by unfiltered lust. But this was different. This was . . .

Intimate.

That word rang so loudly through my mind that I sucked in a short breath.

Cal caught my gasp with a kiss. My taste lingered on his lips. His tongue tangled with mine and any fear vanished, replaced with an all-consuming need to have him inside me. I wrapped a leg around his, molding us together. His arms bracketed beside my head, his fingers diving into my hair and pulling it loose.

"More," I whimpered.

But he didn't thrust inside. He tortured me with another kiss and his incredible weight pressing me deeper into the bed.

His kiss was languid and slow. His lips were soft and supple. He teased and toyed like he wanted me to remember this one. Like this was our first kiss.

Maybe it was.

Tonight was different, this path we were walking unfamiliar, but I stayed with him, lost in his arms.

We kissed like lovers. And instead of pushing for more, instead of urging him on, I let him sweep me away. I blocked out the past, the fights and angry words, and kissed the man who'd laughed with me at dinner. Who'd given me the best date I'd had in well . . . a long, long time.

His cock was hard against my core. He rubbed against

me and the throb in my lower belly became impossible to ignore. But I held on to him, wanting the kiss to last just another moment. Another second. Just in case it didn't happen again.

A first kiss.

And a last.

He groaned against my mouth, finally unthreading his fingers from my hair to reach between us. Then he fitted himself at my entrance, finding no resistance, as my body stretched around his length.

"Open your eyes," he said, his cock pushing deep inside my body, and when I obeyed, his gaze was waiting.

Desire and emotion swirled in his hazel irises.

My heart lurched. *Look away, Nellie. Block it out.*

This was Cal. Trusting him was as foolish as it was dangerous.

"Keep your eyes open as I fuck you." He spoke like he could read my mind.

Did I object? No. I wanted to watch. I wanted to see him come undone.

Stroke after stroke, he pushed us higher and higher, until the edge was as close for me as it showed on his face. He barely blinked. Neither did I. We stayed locked together until we came together, our bodies shuddering in a simultaneous rhythm.

Cal collapsed on top of me, our bodies slick with sweat as we regained our breaths. His heart thundered against my own, and before I was ready, he slid free, shoved off the bed and disappeared to the bathroom.

With the condom dealt with, I expected him to get dressed and make a hasty exit.

Instead he returned to my side, yanking back the covers of the bed and forcing me to move. Then he flopped onto the sheets, burying his face in a pillow as he lay on his stomach and sighed. An arm snagged out, wrapping around my waist to haul me closer.

"Are you . . . cuddling?" I liked cuddling. But with Cal? We'd never cuddled.

"Sleeping." He closed his eyes, pulling me closer. "I'm tired. I'll leave in a bit."

There was a *hell no* on the tip of my tongue, but I couldn't work it free. Because I really, *really* liked cuddling. And it had also been a long, long time. What was the harm in a quick nap? I closed my eyes and relaxed too, snuggling into my pillow as Cal dragged the quilt over our naked bodies.

Fifteen minutes. We'd sleep for fifteen, maybe thirty minutes, then I'd take a shower and he could go to his camper.

Fifteen minutes.

Then I'd put my guard back up.

And kick Cal out of my house.

———

NIGHT HAD FALLEN when I jerked awake. The heat from Cal's body had turned my bed into a sauna.

I pushed up on an elbow, the covers falling to reveal my breasts.

Cal was sound asleep beside me.

Lifting a hand, I reached to touch his shoulder and shake him awake, but stopped short. He looked at peace, his face relaxed and his hair mussed. He looked like a man who'd needed to sleep for a decade but had been waiting to find the right place to rest and had finally found it in my bed.

He looked like he belonged here.

That notion had me slipping free of his arm draped across my hips. My bare feet hit the floor, and I tiptoed to the closet, not daring to turn on a light as I felt around for a pair of sweats and a hoodie. Then I clutched them to my naked chest, easing the bedroom door closed and willing it, for once, not to squeak.

It squeaked. *Damn.*

I held my breath, listening for Cal to stir. But the room stayed silent and there was no rustling on the bed. I hurried to my office, still not bothering with a light as I pulled on my clothes, then snuck downstairs, filling my lungs once I stood in the safety of my kitchen.

Oh, God, what was I doing? In all the years of this strange back-and-forth with Cal, there hadn't been a single hookup where he'd spent the night. Any time I'd gone to him, I'd made sure to leave the minute my orgasm haze had cleared.

I paced the length of the kitchen, shoving hair out of my face and pulling out the few pins that hadn't worked themselves free. They clattered as I dropped them on the island.

The clock on the microwave glowed green at three fifty in the morning. Beyond the windows, the porch lights from the neighborhood homes brightened stoops, but otherwise, the street was dark.

Sleep would be impossible with Cal upstairs, so I went to the kettle on the stove, filling it with water and setting it to boil. I took the teapot off before the spout could whistle and filled a mug with my favorite green tea. Then I carried it to the living room couch where I curled into a corner and flipped on the TV.

With the volume at the setting just above mute, I didn't hear much of the movie playing, but the lights kept me company. The dull murmur helped keep the worries in my head from screaming too loud.

This meant nothing. It *had* to mean nothing. Cal was just tired. The bed in the Winnebago wasn't large enough for a man his size. He'd been in Bozeman and maybe he hadn't slept well wherever he'd been staying.

It means nothing.

I repeated it to myself over and over and over, until the sunrise filtered into the room.

The creak of the lowest stair stole my attention. I looked up to see Cal walk into the living room with his shoes in one hand. He'd pulled on his shirt but hadn't closed the buttons. The waistband of his jeans was undone and the denim draped down his long legs.

Of course he'd have the gall to look sexy. The bastard.

"I meant to leave." He yawned. "Didn't realize how tired I was."

"It's fine," I lied.

He raked a hand through his hair and sat on the opposite end of the couch, leaning forward to pull on his shoes. "You didn't run me out of your house. And you haven't tried to run me out of town in a while. What gives?"

I shrugged. My make-Cal's-life-agony plan had fizzled early on. "I don't like doing mean things. I don't like feeling guilty."

"Because you're not an asshole."

"You drew that straw in high school, remember? You're the asshole. I'm the smart one."

He chuckled. "True."

"What about you?" I asked. "You haven't tried to make my life miserable. Don't you want me to leave Calamity?"

He stared at the TV, his shoulders falling. "I don't know what I want, Nell."

This man was killing me. I had to fight myself to stay on my end of the couch and not hug the jerk.

His phone rang and he shifted to dig it out of his pocket. He took in the screen, then blew out a long breath before answering. "Hi, Mom."

There was a cheerful voice on the other end of the call, though I couldn't make out her words.

"No, it's fine. I was awake." There was a softness to his voice, a tone I'd only heard him use with Elias. And now his mother. "Yeah, getting ready for a workout. What's up?"

He frowned as she spoke, shaking his head. "I already told him no."

Told who? Wade? Was this about the commentator job with ESPN?

"Yeah, I get that it's important to Dad. But like I told you yesterday, Benton is going to have to find someone else."

Benton. What was happening at Benton?

"Look, Mom. I'd better let you go. Talk soon, okay? Love you." He ended the call and glanced over. "They're having some fundraiser shit at the school. They wanted someone to speak to the donors. I haven't talked to my father directly in years, but without asking, he pitched my name to the dean. Had Mom tell me. Guess he thought she'd be able to convince me to do it."

"Oh." I wouldn't want to talk to those stuffy alums either, but that was Cal's crowd. At least, it had been. Apparently, it was still his father's. "You haven't talked to your dad in years?"

"No." He shook his head. "The piece of shit talks about me. Brags to his friends. But he doesn't contact me, and I sure as hell don't contact him."

Wait. Piece of shit? In high school, Cal had told me the problems he had with his dad. But I'd assumed those had passed as he'd gotten older. That they'd eventually bonded over extreme wealth and arrogance.

"This will sound strange," I said. "But I like you more if you dislike your father."

He huffed a laugh. "Figured you would."

"And your mom? Are you close?"

"As close as we can be. I love her. I'll do whatever I can for her. But she's chosen him. And until he's out of the picture, we'll always have that strain between us."

I couldn't imagine not having a loving relationship with both my mother and father. I couldn't imagine how it would feel to take sides. If I was having a bad day, Dad was my first phone call. If he didn't answer, I went straight to Mom. And the older I got, the closer we became.

They weren't just my family, they were my friends too. I genuinely enjoyed every minute we spent together.

What had Cal done on his trips home to Denver? Where did he go for the holidays? Granted, during the football season, he'd usually had games. But what about now that he was retired?

"I'm sorry," I said. "That must be sort of lonely."

"It's not as lonely in Calamity."

Because he had Pierce, Kerrigan and their kids. He was as much a part of their extended family as I was.

And for weeks, I'd been ordering him to leave.

Except where else did he have to go?

That familiar guilt began creeping through my limbs, making me squirm in my seat. There were feelings here, besides the guilt. Besides the lust. And they churned my insides into a tornado.

If I wasn't careful, he'd destroy me. And I'd vowed a long time ago to never let Cal Stark win.

"I'd better get out of here." He stood from the couch and walked to the door. "Thanks for the good time. I'll see you soon."

"Cal," I called as he twisted the knob. "Not soon. I, um . . . I need some time. Some distance."

The guard he'd dropped last night came slamming down over his face. His jaw clenched. "You got it, Blondie."

I flinched as he slammed the door behind him. It didn't matter if he was mad. It had to be this way. I'd learned a long time ago not to trust Cal.

That was never going to change.

—

Hey Diary,

Cal was nice to me today. For like five minutes, he was not
Satan's spawn. I was walking to biology from English and the
bottom of my backpack broke open. It wasn't even the strap I
had duct-taped. Seriously the thing is a piece of crap. I knew I
should have bought a new bag instead of spending my extra
money on this padded bra. But hey, the nipple comments
aren't coming as often. Winner. (That's sarcasm, in case you
couldn't tell.) So anyway, my bag broke and all of my books
flew out in the middle of the hallway. No one stopped to help
me pick them up. Shocker. (More sarcasm for you.) Someone
kicked my history book and sent it flying down the hall. The
spine is broken now. If it would have happened at any other
break, I would have at least had Sareena there to help. We've
been trying to stick together more. Power in numbers, you
know? They pick on her when she's alone just like they tease
me. Anyway, Cal stopped. He actually stopped. I thought I

was going to die of shock for a minute when he handed me my bio book and didn't like, throw it at my face or something. He sort of smiled at me too. Cue me almost falling on my butt. I totally froze. I just stared at him as he stacked my books. For a split second, he was that guy who'd kissed me. And stupid, stupid me, I fell for it. He even walked with me to English, like I was this real person, not some random who sits in the front row and actually reads our Shakespeare assignments. He could have just walked in and sat down. He could have just left me to pick up my books alone and continued pretending like I was a nobody. Instead he walked through the door and told Mr. Robinson, loud enough that everyone could hear, that he had to help the scholarship kid because she can't afford a decent backpack. The whole class laughed. Because that's all I am to them. Poor. Have I mentioned that I hate Cal Stark? Yeah. Still do. He's such an asshole.

N.R.

CHAPTER FIFTEEN

CAL

NELLIE'S DIARY had snuck its way out of my car's backseat and into my daily routine. Somehow I needed to take it back to her house. But considering she'd asked for *distance* after our night together two weeks ago, there hadn't been the chance to return it. That, and I'd skipped town again.

I'd spent the past two weeks in California simply to avoid Nellie. Though considering her diary had come along on the trip, there'd been no escaping her.

The entry about her backpack was open on my lap as I sat in my chair outside the camper.

Did Nellie still talk to Sareena? She'd been another scholarship kid at Benton. I'd forgotten about her until reading Nellie's diary.

Sareena had styled her black hair with these choppy layers. It used to hang in her face, and I'd always wondered how the hell she could see as she'd walked. Or maybe she'd purposefully styled it that way in an attempt to hide.

She and Nellie had stuck together like glue our senior year, but I hadn't realized they'd been so close as freshmen. Mostly, I remembered seeing Nellie alone that year.

That's how she'd been that day her backpack had broken. She'd been on her hands and knees, scrambling to pick up her things. The hallway had been crowded with people but she'd been alone.

It was the reason I'd stopped to help. Because I'd been able to relate. I probably should have just kept walking. I really should have kept my mouth shut when we'd walked into class.

Some of the shit that used to come out of my mouth had been grade-A jackass. I'd sounded a lot like my father. And damn, I wished I could say it had stopped decades ago.

I wished our similarities ended in the mirror.

But I'd said rude shit for years and doubted that would ever change. If it popped into my head, it often came spewing out of my mouth. Hence the reason I wouldn't be doing that fundraiser speech at Benton. And why I wouldn't be commenting on football games.

If a player fucked up, I'd say they fucked up. If a coach made a bad play call, I'd be the first to point out his mistake. If a referee made a judgment error, I'd go for the kill.

I had enough enemies. I didn't need to add others to that list.

The crunch of shoes on gravel caught my ear, and I slammed Nellie's journal closed, stuffing it behind my back.

Harry rounded the corner of the motel, and instead of heading to her house, she changed directions when she spotted me. "Well, look who's come out of hiding."

"Not hiding. Just back in town."

"Another trip? I wondered if you were gone." She came to her chair, sitting with a slight grimace.

"Knees or back?" I asked.

"Knees."

"It's my back that hurts." I shifted and stretched out my legs. This morning I'd woken up and dressed in a pair of shorts and a T-shirt for a workout, but instead I'd putzed around the RV, cleaning up and unpacking the bag from my trip.

Then when I'd finally come outside, I'd decided to read Nellie's diary while there was shade in this spot. I'd run in the heat later and work up a decent sweat.

"Supposed to be hot today," I said, gesturing to her cuffed Wranglers and long-sleeved tee.

"What did I tell you about discussing the weather?"

I chuckled. "Sorry."

"Where'd you go this time?" Harry asked. "Bozeman again?"

"Big Sur. Rented a house and spent a couple weeks beside the ocean."

"California," she said. "I went to LA once when I was in my twenties. Decided then and there I didn't need to go back."

"I'm not much for LA myself. Too many people. But I do love the ocean. I probably would have stayed another week or two, but I've got a meeting with my architect tomorrow to go over some details about my house."

The initial plans had been drafted and sent to the county for a building permit. With any luck, they'd be approved soon and my contractor could break ground at the ranch.

If I decided to stay.

I was done fooling myself that living this close to Nellie wasn't hazardous for my health.

Pierce and Kerrigan had invited me to their place for Independence Day last week. They were returning to a more normal routine now that Constance was out of the newborn phase—whatever that meant. They'd wanted to host a barbeque and invite some friends.

Rather than show up and risk a fight with Nellie, I'd lied and extended my vacation plans.

A month ago, a year ago, I would have gone *because* of Nellie. I would have picked a fight just to rile her up before we snuck off for a quickie. But God, I was tired of fighting with her. Maybe because after that dinner two weeks ago, I knew what it was like to laugh with her instead.

I'd been missing out.

"Did you visit friends in Big Sur?" Harry asked.

"No."

"So you went alone?"

I shrugged. "Yeah."

"That's depressing."

She wasn't wrong. Still, I shot her a frown. "I'm going through a transition right now. Needed to escape."

"A transition." She scoffed. "To what?"

"Retirement."

Harry blinked, then threw her head back and laughed to the cloudless blue sky.

"Hey. I'm mourning the loss of my career."

"By taking vacations alone and becoming a recluse in my daughter's Winnebago?"

"I'm not a recluse," I muttered. "I went to the grocery store yesterday after I got back."

"And I'm guessing you were the last customer, shopping a minute before they closed just to avoid other people."

It hadn't taken her long to get a read on me, had it? "Is there a point to this harassment?"

"Yep."

I waited for her to deliver said point, but she simply stared at me. Harry's scrutiny went on so long that I started to squirm, finally caving and dropping my eyes to my tennis shoes. That withering stare of hers reminded me a lot of Nellie.

Nellie, who I had thought of constantly for two weeks. Nellie, who'd kept me company with this old diary. Nellie, who had no idea how much it had hurt when she'd asked me to stay away.

"Who are you, Cal?"

"Good question, Harry."

"What do people say about you?"

Easy answer. "That I'm an asshole."

"Are you?"

"Some days." I had the diary to prove it.

"Why are you an asshole?"

I huffed. "We don't have time to get into that question. Sun's rising. Like I said, it's gonna be a hot one." And this was not a conversation I wanted to have.

Harry stood and motioned for me to follow. "Come on."

I debated telling her no, but I suspected that wouldn't be an option. So I let her take a few steps to get a head start, far enough away that she wouldn't notice the journal when I stood. Then I walked behind her as she led the way to her house.

It was cool as we stepped indoors. The shades were

drawn and she must have opened the windows last night to let in the breeze. I'd done the same in the camper.

She flipped on the lights as she walked into the living room. Even though I'd seen the clutter, it still took me by surprise. It looked busier than it had the first time. Had she bought more stuff?

Hovering beside the walls, she leaned in close to inspect the hung frames. It was like she'd forgotten which photos she'd placed on the various spaces. To be fair, I could have walked by them each and every day and forgotten them all too.

The faces, some in color while others were in black and white, blended together.

She passed a row, about to move to the next, when she swayed backward and touched one with a gold-trimmed frame. It was more at my eye level than hers, but she stretched and unhooked it from the nail. Then she handed it over.

The picture's colors were muted from age. The photo was of a man standing with his arms crossed over his chest and a scowl on his face.

He wore a pair of dusty jeans and a plaid shirt with snaps instead of buttons. Its pockets had that Western-style point. His cowboy boots were scuffed and his dark hair was creased, like he'd been wearing a hat and someone—probably Harry—had insisted he take it off for the photo.

"This is my husband. He was probably about your age when this was taken. You remind me of him."

"It's the scowl, right?"

She nodded. "Yes, but his was better than yours. My Jake

was a hand at a local ranch. Preferred cattle to people nine out of ten times. Hated pictures, as you can tell. He was rude on a good day and indifferent about almost everything. He had this eye roll that made me want to punch him in the face."

I laughed. "Did you? Punch him?"

"Thought about it." She smiled, her eyes locked on the photo. There was a longing in her expression, like she'd move heaven and earth to see that scowl again. "We lost him eight years ago. Heart attack."

"I'm sorry."

"He lived a full life. That's all he ever wanted."

"I'm glad."

"Me too." She gave me a sad smile. "My parents thought I was crazy for marrying him. My mother told me to find a nice young man who wasn't afraid to smile. But what she didn't realize was that Jake smiled for me. He loved me. He loved our Marcy. He was a good man with a guarded heart. And because of it, he was generally a pain in the ass."

"Are you saying I'm a pain in the ass?"

"Yep. And I think most people would agree." She faced me and raised her chin. "But life's not about what most people think. Life's about finding the right people. The ones who will take you at your worst, so you can give them your best."

I rocked on my heels as her words drove straight through my heart. Her perspective wasn't one I'd considered, maybe because my father was a pain in the ass and he didn't have a good side. Was it possible to have both?

Harry took the photo from my hands and rehung it on

the wall. Then she pointed toward the entryway. "Now get out of my house. I have a hair appointment."

I chuckled. "Maybe do something about the gray."

The corners of her mouth turned up. "You are a pain in the ass."

"Thanks, Harry."

"You're welcome, Cal."

I glanced over my shoulder before I left the living room.

Harry stood on her toes, her gaze on the photo once more.

So I left her alone to share a quiet moment with her husband while I eased the door closed behind me.

The sun was blinding as I headed for the Winnebago and put Nellie's diary in a kitchen drawer. Then, having procrastinated long enough, I went for my run.

Sweat dripped down my spine after the first three miles but I kept running, weaving up and down the side streets of Calamity to avoid the bustle on First. Even beneath the shade of the trees, the air was thick and hot. Not a breath of wind graced the sky.

Children played in backyards, their laughter and squeals carefree and untethered. Beyond the fences of a few homes, dogs barked wildly as I passed. On every block, at least one man was out mowing his lawn.

A woman with a stroller crossed my path as I lapped a community park. Her eyes widened slightly as I jogged by, either because I was drenched or because she recognized me.

Opposite a jungle gym was a baseball diamond, and a few kids were running the bases while another hit pop flies at home plate. The boy at home plate spotted me and froze, the bat dropping from his grip.

Maybe if they saw me enough, my novelty would wear off. Maybe they'd just wave next time. Hell, maybe I'd stop and hit a few grounders for them next time. But for today, I ran, mile after mile.

I blamed the heat for turning down Nellie's street. It had zapped my restraint. I'd avoided it as I'd made my trail, but as my lungs began to burn and the strength in my legs waned, my resolve weakened.

This *distance* had lasted two weeks.

And damn it, two weeks was long enough.

Her brick house came into view as I crossed the road, my shoes slapping on the pavement. Then there she was, her hair pulled into a knot at the top of her head while she pushed a lawnmower over her grass.

My feet came to an abrupt halt when I reached her sidewalk. I stood, chest heaving for breath, as she cut a swath in the lawn. Her back was to me, and the racerback cut of her tank left her shoulders bare. Her denim shorts were frayed at the hem and molded to the curve of her ass.

Fuck, but she was gorgeous.

I'd thought the same thing years ago when I'd watched her mow a lawn—the yard at Mom and Dad's. Not a damn thing had changed. Watching her was better than any football game on television or any halftime show.

Just Nellie beneath the sun.

She slowed at the corner, pressing the handle to turn the mower. She walked my direction and glanced at me. Then she did a double take, dropping the bar. The sound of the mower's engine died instantly.

Not that I could hear much over my roaring pulse. My heart felt like it was about to beat out of my chest.

She left the mower and crossed the lawn, stopping on the sidewalk in front of me. "You're back."

"Miss me, sugar?"

She dropped her chin to the grass-stained toes of her tennis shoes. "Pierce said you went to California."

"Yeah. Thought I'd get out of town for a bit."

"Okay. Well, um . . . I'd better get the yard finished."

"That's it?"

She met my gaze and lifted a shoulder. "What else is there?"

"Tell me what you hate about me." *Tell me anything, just so I don't have to leave.*

"I hate that you've been on my mind more than I'd like."

"For the record, I hate that about you too."

A smile graced her pink lips as she wiped at the sweat on her brow with the back of her hand. Her cheeks were flushed. Her face shiny. We could have a blast in the shower, rinsing each other clean. But I feared that if I took a single step, she'd retreat. She'd leave me standing here alone.

"Why did you watch my games?"

"I told you already." She tossed out a hand. "In the hopes I'd see you lose."

"Liar." That telltale twitch of her nose gave it away.

Her eyes flared, the fire kindling behind those beautiful green pools. "Why do people stare at a car crash? It's hard to look away from a disaster."

I planted my hands on my hips. "Can you just be real with me? For one damn minute?"

"You first."

Well, fuck. I didn't have anything to say to that. How could I be real with her when I wasn't even real with myself?

So I stayed quiet.

And she retreated, shaking her head and stepping to the lawn. "That's what I thought. Go away, Stark."

She didn't have to tell me twice.

CHAPTER SIXTEEN

NELLIE

"IT'S weird to be in the office." Pierce spun his chair toward the windows behind his desk, rubbing a hand over his bearded face. "It's so quiet. I keep waiting to hear the baby cry."

"What are Kerrigan and the kids doing today?" I asked, closing my laptop that I'd brought in for our meeting.

"She took them to the park this morning before it got too hot." He swiped his phone from the desk and pulled up a photo, handing it over.

Constance was in her stroller, a sun hat shielding her precious face. Elias, also in a hat, stood proudly beside his sister wearing a huge, big-brother smile.

My emotions swirled like the fresh cream I poured into my morning coffee. Happiness. Envy. Pride. Desire. And a pinch of loss. Because as the years passed, I wondered more and more if I'd missed my chance for a family of my own. That story might not be in the cards I'd been dealt.

There'd be no smiling photos of children on my phone.

"I've been thinking about getting a cat." I handed Pierce his phone. "Maybe two."

He gave me a sideways glance. "You don't like cats."

"I don't like *your* cat. She's a demon."

"This is true." He kicked an ankle over his knee. "What else is going on?"

"Not much." I shrugged. "I think we're pretty well caught up."

"How's Kathryn working out?"

"So far so good." I'd hired a twenty-two-year-old recent college grad as my assistant. "She's smart. Hardworking. I think she'll be a good fit."

Kathryn had grown up in Calamity, and after graduating this past spring, she'd moved home to be close to her family. She was as eager as she was smiley. Every task I'd given her she'd tackled with enthusiasm and a litany of questions. But her best trait? She wasn't a football fan.

During her interview, when I'd mentioned that Pierce had a few famous friends, like Cal Stark, and she'd need to be discreet, she'd been clueless about who he was. Kathryn preferred sewing to sports. She'd already promised me a quilt for Christmas.

It had been three days since Cal had jogged by my house, dripping with sweat. His shirt had clung to his pecs and abs, and it had taken every ounce of willpower not to invite him inside for a shower.

But I'd asked him for distance and firmly believed it had been the right choice. The less time we spent together, the less time I'd crave him. The less time I'd wonder what he was doing, where he was spending his days, and who he was spending them with.

Like I'd told him this past weekend, I hated that he was constantly on my mind.

This *tell me what you hate about me* gimmick needed to stop because each time I confessed, I gave away too much.

Why did he care? Why was he so worried about my opinion? Was it his retirement? Was there something happening personally? There was only one person who Cal would confide in willingly. Lucky for me, he was sitting four feet away.

"Can I ask you something, off topic?" I asked Pierce.

He nodded. "Of course."

"Have you noticed anything strange with Cal? Or stranger than his usual brand of strange?"

"No. Why?"

Because I was worried about him. "I've bumped into him a few times lately. He's been acting . . . off."

"What do you mean?" Pierce sat straighter, the concern for his friend etched on his face.

"Well, he's living in a camper, for one."

"Yeah, but that's just until he gets his house built on the ranch he bought."

A ranch Cal hadn't mentioned to me, not even at our non-date dinner date. No, I'd heard about his *ranch* at my last girls' night out at the brewery. Cal's builder had stopped by our table to say hello to Larke, and she'd asked him about his project lineup. The moment he'd dropped Cal's name, I'd perked up and shamelessly eavesdropped.

"Personally, I think the Winnebago is hilarious." Pierce laughed. "Leave it to Cal to decide that buying or renting was too much of a hassle, so he rents someone *else's* RV. Yes, it's strange considering he could afford any property in Calamity. But if you think about it . . . it makes sense."

"It does?" Because it really didn't.

"Cal likes to give everyone the impression that he's not into commitment, but look at his life. It's been solely focused on football. His career has been his one and only priority. And he just walked away. Cal commits. When he does, it's for the long haul. So he chooses his commitments carefully."

Like his friendship with Pierce. And in the absence of wanting to commit to a house, he'd rented a Winnebago.

"Those poor people will lose their camper when he burns it to the ground," I muttered. "Then he'll probably blame it on the owners and slap them with a lawsuit."

Did I actually believe those statements? No. But Pierce was giving me an odd look, like maybe he'd heard the genuine concern for Cal in my voice. Like he saw the feelings I was trying my hardest to hide and ignore.

A sassy comment seemed necessary. And for good measure, I tacked on another. "If he can't even be nice to kids in wheelchairs, there's no hope that he treats those motel owners the right way."

"Huh?" Pierce's forehead furrowed. "What kid in a wheelchair?"

"His last game. The Super Bowl. Remember there was that kid in the wheelchair from the Make-A-Wish Foundation. He was next to Cal during a post-game interview, and Cal had the game ball. He should have given it to the kid instead of keeping it for his own trophy case."

"He did give him that ball."

"No, he didn't." I remembered watching him walk away from the cameras, the ball firmly tucked under an arm.

Pierce shook his head. "He took the ball to the locker room and had the entire team sign it along with a team jersey. And no one knows this but Cal let it slip one day. I guess the kid's parents were struggling financially, so Cal paid for them to take a vacation to Disney World right before the boy died. Trip-of-a-lifetime sort of deal. Then he covered their medical bills. He even went to the kid's funeral."

"What?" The boy had died? My heart cracked and my eyes flooded. That poor family. Why hadn't Cal told me the day I'd mentioned that boy? Why would he do all of that for a family of strangers? My soul ached for that boy's parents. And it ached for Cal.

"I heard an announcer say once that no quarterback was as good at the fake handoff as Cal," Pierce said. "I thought that was fitting because he's a pro at faking his life too. He shows the parts that he wants the world to see."

"They're not the good parts." I dabbed the corners of my eyes dry. "Why does he do that?"

Pierce gave me a sad smile. "You'll have to ask him."

"Yeah." I nodded and stood. "I'll let you get back to work."

The weight in my heart made my footsteps heavy as I returned to my office. Concentrating on anything was almost impossible because my head was stuck on Cal. After an hour of struggling through a few emails, I blew off my inbox and pulled up Google.

It took a little research but I found the boy's obituary. Hollis York. The photo of him smiling, wearing a Tennessee Titans jersey broke my heart. A few more clicks and I landed on his mother's Facebook page. Her profile picture was of

Hollis in his wheelchair, smiling from ear to ear, as Cal knelt by his side.

That signed game ball was in the boy's lap.

The media should have picked up on this. Cal's agent or his manager should have shared this with the press. Or maybe they had. Maybe it hadn't fit the image the networks wanted for Cal and that was the reason no one had seen this photo.

How many other examples of this Cal—a good, decent Cal—had been missed by the masses because they'd been too busy watching reruns of him get ejected from a game for flipping off a referee after a missed call?

Pierce swung into my office around four before he left for the day. Five minutes after he walked out the door, I did the same, saying goodnight to Kathryn who was stationed at the front desk.

I drove into town, but as my turnoff neared, I kept going straight, the downtown buildings streaking past my window as I headed to the motel. Cal's SUV was parked in the alley next to the Winnebago.

He was sitting in that camp chair outside the RV's door, wearing a pair of athletic shorts. His torso was tan and bare, his abs on display for no one but me. He had on a baseball hat and sunglasses. Somewhere he'd scrounged up a standing umbrella, and it cast an oval of shade over his makeshift patio.

I parked and climbed out of my car, leaving my phone and purse behind as I walked his way.

There was a beer can in the mesh cupholder of his chair. Cal lifted it as I approached. "Beer's in the fridge."

"No, thanks." A beer would lower my inhibitions and

today, like any day, I needed them when Cal was within touching distance. I took the empty seat beside his. "Why, when you have this nice chair, do you sit in that one?"

"Because this one's mine. That's Harry's."

The older woman wasn't here, yet he left her seat open in case she'd stop by.

"What do I owe for the pleasure of this visit?" he asked.

"The truth." It was my turn to make demands, and since neither of us cared for small talk, I didn't hesitate. "Tell me why you hide yourself from the world."

"I don't know what you're talking about, Blondie. I was a pro quarterback in the NFL. As you know, I spent some time on Monday Night Football. Wouldn't exactly say I was hiding."

I sighed, so damn tired of the façade and snark. "You know what I mean."

He snapped his fingers three times before lifting his beer to his lips. Trickles of condensation fell down the silver aluminum, two landing on his knee as he gulped. When the can was empty, he crushed it. Then we sat in silence, until the shade of the umbrella had shifted and the sun skimmed our toes.

Cal finally cleared his throat. "My dad is an asshole. You know that."

"I do."

"He cares about his image. Not his reputation, his image. The house. The cars. The money. The status. The trophy wife. The young girlfriends."

Did it surprise me that Cal's father cheated on his wife? Not in the slightest.

"And I'm the football-star son," he said. "I am just a part

of his image. I decided a long time ago that I wasn't going to look the same as Colter Stark."

"So you're an asshole of a different breed?"

He shrugged. "It's what I know."

The show. He'd learned from his father to put on a show. "But you're not really an asshole, are you?"

"Nellie." He shot me a flat look.

"You were kind to that boy in the wheelchair. You paid for his medical bills. You helped his family. Why didn't you tell me that?"

Cal snapped his fingers again, which meant I was unsettling him with this topic. *Good.* "People have their mind made up about me. You included."

"You didn't give me a lot of choice." I sat straighter. "You have been awful to me more often than not. In high school, you used me. Tormented me. Belittled me."

"Yeah, because you decided I wasn't good enough."

"Me?" I pointed to my chest. "What are you talking about?"

He sat taller too, twisting in his chair as he leaned in closer. "That day by the pool. Our freshman year. You remember it, right?"

Of course, I remembered that day. Girls didn't forget their first kiss.

"You told your dad I was a dumb jock. That you hated me. Right after I confided in you. Right after I trusted you. Right after I let you in."

Wait. He'd heard me talking to Dad? My mind raced, trying to recall the details of that day. They were fuzzy, blurred from time and hate.

Mostly I remembered thinking he was so cute. Sitting

beside him, talking to him, had been such a rush. My heart had been in my throat the whole time. Then he'd leaned in, and I remembered the kiss being over so fast that my brain hadn't had a chance to catch up.

Maybe I'd called him a dumb jock. Dad had warned me away from him, but Dad had warned me away from all boys.

"I was fourteen," I said. "Talking to my dad about boys. Do you actually think I would have told him the truth? That the son of his client had just kissed me? Of course I lied."

"I didn't take it as a lie."

Because we'd been fourteen. And I'd probably bruised his ego. Was that the reason he'd been so horrible to me afterward?

Nearly twenty years was a long time to rewind and replay in a new light. But God, it made sense. Cal had reacted like most boys at that age would have. He'd taken his revenge.

Part of me wanted to rage at him. To smack him upside the head for being so incredibly stubborn. But we'd been kids. Miscommunication was our specialty. And since high school . . .

The years of arguments, bitterness and resentment seemed like such a waste. And for the second time today, Cal Stark made me want to cry.

That fourteen-year-old bully had let me in. And I'd thrown it in his face.

"I hurt your feelings and you pushed me away," I whispered.

He lifted his empty, crushed can, shaking it like he wished it was still full. "What would you have done in my shoes?"

"Probably the same thing," I admitted. "That still doesn't explain why you push everyone else away. Why you put up this front."

He lifted a shoulder. "It's easier that way."

"Why?"

"Why not?" A bullshit answer, but before I could call him on it, he stood from his chair. The RV rocked slightly as he took the stairs, slamming the door behind him.

A flock of small birds flew overhead, disappearing with a swoop and sway into the sky.

And I sat frozen, staring at Cal's empty chair.

These feelings for Cal—the guilt, the affection, the yearning, the fear—weren't going to go away, were they? No matter if he lived in Calamity or Calgary or Calabasas, they all had one thing in common.

Cal.

He was tangled in my heart.

And it was only a matter of time before he'd break it.

–

Diary,

Cal got my dad fired today. That jerk ruined Daddy's business. And it was all a lie. Dad had to pick me up from school
again because Mom took a double shift for some extra money.
I offered to help Dad mow. We did one house first, then went
to the Stark place last. I hate going there and I could tell that
Dad didn't want me there either, but it would have been too
late if he'd driven me all the way home and then gone back to
the job. So we just went and he did the edging while I mowed.
Cal was there this time. I was finishing up in the front yard
when he came home with his dad. He didn't even look at me
as he got out of the car, but whatever. That's nothing new.
They went inside the house and like ten minutes later, Cal's
dad came storming out and got in Dad's face. He said that I
wasn't allowed to come here anymore and that I've been
stalking Cal. Can you freaking believe that? Why would I
want to stalk Cal? I hate Cal. Dad stood up for me. He didn't

even have to ask if it was true because he knows I'd never do that. He said Cal had to be mistaken. Well, that sent Cal's dad over the edge. He got red in the face and screamed that his son wasn't a liar. Oh, wait. It gets better. He accused me of sneaking into their house the last time I was there and stealing one of Cal's football jerseys. What?! I said that was a lie and called Cal a liar. Cal's dad told me to shut up. My dad said he couldn't speak to me like that. So Cal's dad fired Daddy and told us to get the "f" off his property. I cried the whole way home. Dad promised it would be okay and that it was just one client. I was like almost feeling better. Except then we got home and the phone started ringing. All of Dad's other clients called and fired him. Yep. Worst. Day. Ever. Cal's dad told all his rich friends about what happened and they believed it. Of course they'd believe it. Mom got home fifteen minutes ago. They sent me upstairs to do my home-work so they could talk. I don't know what they'll do if Dad's not getting paid. Maybe he can pick up new clients? It just makes me so flipping mad. We shouldn't even have to worry about this. All I want to do is punch that liar Cal Stark in the face tomorrow when I see him at school. But then I'd get kicked out of Benton and Mom would really be angry and Dad would have gotten fired for nothing. This is so not fair. None of this is fair. It's all Cal's fault. I hate him ten times more than I did yesterday.

Nellie

CHAPTER SEVENTEEN

CAL

THE SCRIPT on the diary entry was harsh and thick, the words scratched into the paper rather than scribbled.

Yeah, I'd lied. And I'd do it again.

It had been five days since Nellie's visit to the Winnebago, and as I had all summer, I'd spent those days rereading her diary. This particular entry was one I'd revisited often. Each time I read it, I wanted to shake her. To scream in her face that I'd lied for a good reason.

The book was open in front of me on the RV's dining table, resting beside a glass of water. My hands were balled into fists as I scanned the entry about the day Dad had fired Darius. Her words took up three full pages.

A different man might have felt sorry for the hardship he'd caused. Not me.

Sure, I'd apologized to Darius, but not because I'd lied. My apology had been for the harm it had caused his family. The financial stress I'd put on a man's shoulders.

Each time I replayed that day, I couldn't see another

option. Put in that situation again, at that age, a lie had been the only choice.

Though maybe I should have expected my father's over-reaction. He'd taken it upon himself to ruin Darius by calling a handful of friends, asking them to fire Darius. Word had spread like the plague and my lie had snowballed.

All I'd wanted was to get Nellie away from my house. Away from my puke of a father.

He'd picked me up from school that day. The entire drive home he'd bitched about having to chauffeur me around. Normally, it was Mom's responsibility but she'd had a conflicting dentist appointment. He'd promised that the day I had my license, he'd get me a car so he'd never have to shuttle me again.

Fine by me. I'd wanted a car to have some independence. What teenager didn't want freedom?

We'd just pulled into the driveway when he'd spotted Nellie mowing the lawn. He leered at her, long enough that I'd felt sick. Then he'd made a comment that had made my skin crawl. Something like *she's gonna be a hot one*. I couldn't remember his exact words.

He'd nudged his elbow to mine like I hadn't noticed Nellie before. Like he'd be proud if his son scored a hot girl-friend. Like had she been twenty-four, not fourteen, he would have chased her himself.

What the actual fuck was wrong with him?

In a way, I'd overcompensated for his views on women. While he was in multiple relationships, I'd avoided them almost entirely. I'd preferred hookups through college and my early years in the league. And I'd always made sure the women knew the score. I'd double wrapped with the condoms. Once I'd been drafted, unless a woman could show me her ID that proved she was over twenty-one, I'd steered clear.

Then had come that night in Charlotte.

The only woman who'd stirred my blood since had been Nellie.

Then again, she'd stirred it for years. Even when I hadn't been willing to admit that she was special.

That maybe I'd fallen for her.

That maybe I was in love with her.

Was that the reason I'd gone to extreme measures to keep her away? Getting Darius fired had definitely been severe.

After Dad's nasty comment, we'd gone inside. He'd walked to the window to stare at Nellie again, and I'd lost my mind. I'd spewed a load of bullshit about Nellie stalking me and stealing things from my bedroom.

Dad had flown off the handle and stalked outside. Then I'd listened from an open window as he'd confronted Darius.

Darius had instantly defended Nellie. No question. He'd stood up for his daughter automatically. What would it have been like to have that type of man as a father?

The reason Dad had taken the matter so far was because Darius hadn't backed down. He hadn't bowed down and kissed the great Colter Stark's ass.

I respected the hell out of Darius for that.

Because had Nellie's and my positions been reversed, no way my dad would have gone to bat for me without a lengthy interrogation first.

No, I wasn't sorry for my lies.

But I hadn't forgiven myself for them either.

What had happened with Darius's business? Had he found new clients? Or a new job? I hadn't had the guts to ask Pierce. I sure as fuck hadn't dared ask Nellie.

I thumbed to the next page, starting one more entry before I made myself some dinner.

"That's mine."

My eyes flew from the diary to the voice outside the Winnebago. These hot July afternoons meant I had to leave the windows and door open to keep the RV from becoming too warm and stuffy. I should have closed the goddamn door.

Nellie stood at the base of the stairs, her eyes glued to the journal on the table.

"I can explain."

"Go to hell." She stormed up the stairs as I slid from my seat. She reached for the book, but I picked it up before her fingertips could brush the leather cover. "That's my diary. Why do you have that?"

"Because I took it."

"So you can add thief to your résumé?" She grabbed for it again, but I yanked it away. "Give it back. Now."

"No."

"That's private. Hand it over."

I shook my head, turning sideways to keep her from getting the diary. "What happened to your dad? After that day when my dad confronted him and—"

"Fired him?"

"Yeah." I nodded. "What happened to his business?"

"There was no business. He gave it up. He decided that it wasn't worth dealing with asshole customers like the Starks." She sneered. "So he sold all of his equipment and went to work for a competitor. He finally had to quit a few years ago. It was too hard on his knees, doing work meant for younger men."

"He's retired?"

"He's fifty-three, Cal." She scoffed. "Retirement at that age requires money. No, he's not retired. He works for a printing company in Arizona, operating one of their presses."

I studied her face and the flush of her cheeks. "I'm sorry. About that day."

"No, you're not."

"Okay, you're right. I'm not sorry. I'd do it again."

"Because you're a liar."

"No, because my father is a sick bastard. He stared at you, and I didn't like the gleam in his eyes. I lied to protect you. I lied because you're—"

Mine.

She'd always been mine.

"I'm what?" She planted her hands on her hips, waiting for me to finish my sentence. When I didn't, she made another snatch for the diary but I wasn't giving it up.

"Why did you sleep with me? In Charlotte?"

Nellie ignored the questions, swiping for the journal again. "Give that back."

"Tell me."

"Give me that diary." She stepped closer, reaching for it as I shifted it from one hand to the other. Her fingertips brushed the spine so I raised it high, pressing it against the camper's ceiling. "You asshole! Knock it off."

"No." I kept it high and out of her reach, even as she tried to jump for it. "Why did you come to my room in Charlotte?"

"That diary is none of your fucking business." She leapt

for it again, and when she didn't even come close, she smacked me in the stomach. "Damn it, Cal."

"Answer the question and I'll give it back." Maybe. "Why did you fuck me in Charlotte?"

"How could you steal that from me? It was never intended for you." She stared up at me, and the hurt on her face almost made me cave. But I needed to know the truth about Charlotte.

"Nell." I dropped my arm. "Please."

She heard the desperation in my voice and didn't reach for the diary. Her chest heaved. "Because you fucked me over. Because you fucked my family over. And I was so fucking tired of you always winning. I wanted to win. I wanted to show you I wasn't that insecure girl anymore. And I figured if there was a time for revenge, it was that night."

My team—*I*—had just lost the AFC Championship. Pierce had flown to Charlotte to watch the game. Nellie had tagged along too since she'd lived there once and wanted to visit for nostalgia's sake. They'd used the tickets I'd gotten for Pierce, and when she'd showed up in my seats, she'd been wearing the other team's jersey.

After the loss, the coaches and my teammates had flown home to Tennessee. But I'd requested an exception from policy to stay and spend time with Pierce. We'd been at the same hotel. Nellie had been too. I hadn't been good company, so after Pierce and I'd had a room service dinner in my suite and a couple of drinks from the mini bar, he'd given me some space.

I'd been wallowing when a knock had come at the door.

Nellie had stood in the hallway, still wearing that fucking jersey.

"So you came to my room to gloat?" When she looked to her feet, I took her chin, tilting her face until our eyes locked.

"Yes," she said. "I knew you were at a low point. And I wanted to be mean like you were mean."

I'd opened the door and let her into the room, fully expecting her to rub salt on my gaping wounds. To revel in my failures. To remind me that the reason we'd lost the game was because I'd thrown an interception in the first quarter and the team hadn't gained the momentum needed to recover from my fuckup.

"But . . . you weren't mean."

She swallowed hard. "Because you looked sad. You looked heartbroken. You looked like the boy who'd kissed me once. The one who'd put so much pressure on himself. The one who took responsibility for a loss that should have been shared with a team, not carried alone."

My heart squeezed.

God, she was a good woman. So fucking good. Too damn good for me.

I'd kissed her that night. When she'd told me she was sorry for the loss, I'd been so surprised that I'd just . . . kissed her. Then she'd let me tear that jersey from her body.

We'd spent the night in a tangle of desperation, until the next morning when I'd woken up and she'd already been gone, back to her hotel room, and we'd pretended it had never happened.

"After we started fucking, were you with anyone?" It was the question I'd refused to let myself ask for four years.

"That's none of your business." She frowned. "It's not like we're in a committed relationship."

"I haven't," I confessed. "Been with anyone."

In four years, the only woman in my bed had been Nellie. Why would I need or want anyone else?

"W-what?" Her mouth parted. "Charlotte was four years ago."

"Yeah. I'm aware." I tossed the diary onto the table, framing her face with my hands before she could take it and disappear. Then I dropped my lips to hers, kissing the shock from her expression.

She molded to me, her hands sliding up my chest as she stood on her toes.

I banded an arm around her back and held her close, trapping her to me so she couldn't escape. My other hand roamed up and down her spine, my fingers finding the silky strands of her hair. My tongue plundered her mouth, exploring every corner like I had that first time.

She held nothing back, her lips as desperate as my own.

I swept her off her feet and carried her down the hallway, dropping her on the mattress. A breeze carried through the bedroom, a caress on my skin as I yanked off my shirt.

Nellie must have come to the camper from work. Her green blouse was tucked into a black pencil skirt. Thank fuck that skirt had some stretch because I shoved it up her thighs, bunching it at her hips as she spread her legs.

My shorts were off in a flash, dropping beside her heels onto the floor. Then one quick tug and her panties were history.

I fisted my shaft, holding her gaze as I stood at the foot of the bed, naked and hard and desperate for this woman.

Her hair was spread on my pillow. Her eyes hooded and wanting.

"Have you? Been with anyone?" *Say no. Please, say no.*

"No," she whispered.

"Thank fuck." I dropped a knee to the bed, hovering at her entrance to drag the tip of my cock through her folds. "Are you on the pill?"

A single nod was all I needed before I thrust forward.

"Cal." She gasped, her back arching as she stretched around me.

I groaned and dropped my forehead to hers. "God, you feel so good, sugar."

For once, there was nothing between us but the sins of my past.

"Move." She held on to my shoulders, a leg curling around my hip. "Hurry."

I pulled out and slammed inside once more, studying her pretty face as ecstasy spread across her features. The blush of her cheeks and throat. The perfect *o* of her mouth. Her eyes squeezed shut as her inner walls fluttered.

Sunlight streamed through the windows, illuminating her sheer beauty.

I ran a fingertip across the bridge of her nose, rubbing away her makeup to see her freckles. My freckles.

Then I braced myself on an elbow and showed her the strength of my body, the control and the restraint. I worked her up, higher and higher, as her hands flowed like water over the muscles of my arms, chest and back.

Her nails dug into my shoulders as her breath hitched.

"Come, Nell." I bent and took a nipple into my mouth, sucking so hard that she unraveled.

She came on a cry that echoed through the room and carried beyond the windows. She pulsed around my length, her orgasm triggering my own.

I poured myself into her body, marking her as mine, then collapsed beside her, my breaths ragged as we stared at the ceiling.

Birds chirped as they flew outside. The sound of traffic carried from beyond the motel. Nellie's panting was as heavy as my own.

"Why do we always end up here?" she asked.

I propped up on an elbow, staring down into her emerald eyes. In bed, we were fire. We could block out the rest of the world. It was easier here.

"Why did you come here today?" I twirled my finger around a lock of her hair before tucking it behind her ear.

Neither of us answered the other's questions. We simply let them hang in the air until I brushed my lips to hers.

The kiss was too tender. I realized my mistake as my lips moved lazily and my tongue swirled with hers. But I didn't push to give it an edge. I didn't quicken the pace or touch her anywhere else. I simply savored the woman who'd consumed my damn life.

And I crossed a line with that kiss.

When I broke away, there was genuine fear on her face. Like I'd shattered an unspoken rule. There'd been feelings beyond hate and resentment in that kiss. Shame on me.

"Be back." I stood from the bed, giving her a minute as I strode to the cramped bathroom.

I heard her footsteps on the stairs before the water in the sink had turned hot.

"Damn," I muttered.

No surprise, when I came out, she was gone.

And so was her diary.

CHAPTER EIGHTEEN

NELLIE

DON'T STARE AT CAL. *Don't stare at Cal.*

My gaze found him instantly. He was pushing Elias on the swing set in Pierce and Kerrigan's yard, and my traitorous heart melted as they shared a smile.

Damn it, Nellie.

"Here you go." Larke appeared at my side with two cold White Claws.

I took mine, popped the top and chugged.

She gave me a sideways look. "Are you okay?"

"Great! Just hot," I lied as the smell of smoke and burgers wafted from the grill.

Pierce and Kerrigan were hosting a summer barbeque at their house today, and their sprawling deck was crowded with happy people.

I'd showed up, expecting not to know many, but I'd made quite a few acquaintances during my time in Calamity. Nearly all the faces were familiar. Kerrigan was sitting on a lounge chair beneath a patio umbrella with the baby in her arms. Constance's sleeping face was shaded by her floppy pink hat.

Pierce stood with a spatula in his hand at the barbeque, talking with the huddle of men who'd joined him.

Two Grays Peak families had arrived last week and this was doubling as a *Welcome to Calamity* party. There'd be more festivities as more of our team moved. It would be nice to go to work on Monday morning with familiar coworkers in the office.

Everyone wore a smile and sunscreen.

Meanwhile, I felt like I was about to come out of my skin. Because of course Cal was here. I'd had days to brace for this afternoon, but I still wasn't ready to face him.

It had been five days since the Winnebago. Since I'd made the idiotic decision to swing by and hit him up for sex.

Loneliness had steered me to the motel that day. Work had been hectic, and on my drive home, I'd called my parents but neither had answered. Somehow, I'd convinced myself that if Cal was set on staying in Calamity, why not get some orgasms out of the deal? Why not benefit from his hot body?

Then I'd found him with my diary. I'd known from a single glance that it was one of my old journals.

I wasn't even that mad. It irritated me that he'd stolen it from my house, but it hadn't enraged me like it would have years ago. What did that mean?

Ironically, he'd chosen the worst of all my diaries. As the school years had progressed, Cal had become less and less of a headache. An annoying crumb on an otherwise clean countertop, but my studies had taken the bulk of my attention while his focus had stayed on football. Our interactions had been in the random shared classroom and the silent occasional passing in Benton's hallways.

Cal could have read all of my diaries, and I wouldn't have really cared. There wasn't anything in those journals that he didn't already know.

Maybe I should be angrier. Maybe I should have resisted the temptation. But he'd kissed me and everything had changed.

Or maybe that kiss had made me realize things had changed four years ago. It had changed the night I'd left my hotel room in Charlotte and walked to his.

The end of this fling was inevitable. But as usual, we'd avoid that uncomfortable conversation by avoiding each other.

Was that why he'd brought a date to this barbeque? To have a buffer?

Cal had walked in twenty minutes ago with Harry on his arm. The older woman was standing next to Kerrigan's parents, and when she glanced my way, I smiled, having officially met her earlier.

She'd waltzed onto the deck and had ordered him to fetch her a drink, which he'd done without argument. Then she'd introduced herself, rubbing her elbow to mine, before pulling Larke into a hug.

What had she meant with that elbow rub? Had she heard us together in the Winnebago? Or had Cal talked about me?

I found him again, helping Elias off the swing. The boy raced through the yard toward a football on the grass. He swept it up and gave it his hardest throw. It went about three feet, but Cal cheered and clapped like Elias had thrown it seventeen yards.

It had been so much easier to keep Cal at a distance when I'd thought he was awful to children. Why couldn't he be mean to kids? And the elderly? Why couldn't he have stayed on the opposite end of the country?

But when he was this close, when he looked so good in a pair of faded jeans and a simple white T-shirt, when I knew there was a softness he refused to show the world, how was I supposed to resist? Cal wasn't wearing a hat or sunglasses today. He had no reason to hide because this was a safe place.

I was glad he'd found a safe place. I only wished it wasn't mine too.

"Nellie." Larke nudged my elbow, drawing my attention.

"Huh?" I tore my gaze from Cal.

"Okay, what is going on? You've been staring at him since you got here."

"Ugh." My shoulders slumped, and I turned my back to the yard so my gaze couldn't wander. "Things are a little bit complicated at the moment."

Larke inched closer. "You and Cal?"

I nodded, staring past her to Pierce. As far as I knew, he didn't have a clue that I'd been sleeping with Cal for years. And this barbeque was not the time to divulge our secret relationship.

"I hate him." There was no conviction in my words, so I gulped the rest of my drink. "I'm having one more."

"Have two. If you need a ride home, I'll be your designated driver. Then you can tell me everything."

"Okay." I smiled at her and disappeared into the house, going for the beverage fridge.

Pierce didn't need coolers for his summer barbeque. No, he'd just stocked the industrial-sized fridge in their pantry with every kind of beverage imaginable. The pantry that was the size of my bedroom and not only had a spare fridge but also a wine cooler and freezer. Their kitchen was equally as impressive as was the rest of the massive home.

The money Pierce made was staggering. This was a level of wealth I struggled to comprehend, even after years of working for his company. I definitely hadn't understood the enormity of it when I'd been in high school.

I'd always known the other kids were rich. Cal and Pierce and Phoebe McAdams. But it hadn't been until I'd started with Grays Peak that I'd realized just what millions—billions—could buy.

Sure, I'd helped Dad mow the lawns of extremely wealthy people, the Starks included. But I'd never set foot in Cal's home. From the exterior, it had simply been massive. There'd been pools and saunas and tennis courts and guest-houses bigger than my actual home.

But when you stepped inside, it was like stepping into another world.

I gave Kerrigan the credit for giving this house its homey feel. She grounded Pierce. He could buy her every star in the heavens but all she really needed were the people who lived inside these walls. All she wanted was a normal life. It was why he stood outside flipping burgers. Elias's artwork deco-rated the fridge. A few stray toys were scattered across the island. Beside the fridge was a baby bottle drying rack.

This was a home. A family.

Being happy yet envious of your friends was hard.

"Hey." Kerrigan came inside with Constance in the crook of her arm. "Thanks for coming today."

"Of course." I smiled as she went to the actual fridge in the kitchen, pulling out a bowl of salad with one hand. "What can I do to help?"

"Would you hold her?" she asked, walking over with the baby.

"Yes, please."

Constance stirred for a second as Kerrigan transferred her to my arms, but after pursing her tiny, pink lips, she went right back to sleep as I traced my finger over her smooth, precious cheek.

Aunt Nellie. I could live with that job. Pierce was an only child, and I could be his honorary sister.

"Want to go get pedicures tomorrow?" Kerrigan asked. "I feel like we haven't had much time to visit since you moved here. I miss you, and Larke keeps bragging about the time you're spending together, and I've been getting jealous."

I laughed. "Yes, pedicures sound wonderful. I have zero plans tomorrow except mowing my lawn."

Maybe Cal would run by again.

Maybe not.

"Okay, I think this is everything," Kerrigan said as she surveyed the island covered with bowls and plates and platters. "Do you think we'll have enough food?"

"You could feed all of Calamity," I teased.

"I was so excited to have everyone here I went overboard." She shrugged. "You'll take leftovers, right?"

"Sure." I snuggled Constance closer. "Why don't you eat first? I'll keep her."

"I'm starving, so I won't argue."

As she waved everyone inside to start filling plates, I shuffled to the deck, my gaze glued to the yard.

Elias was racing across the grass, his legs pumping as he looked over his shoulder, giggling as Cal chased him. Their laughter filled the air.

"Gotcha!" Cal swept Elias off his feet and tossed him in the air.

"Unka Cal!" Elias squealed as Cal threw him again.

Unka Cal. Elias didn't call me Aunt Nellie. But that boy loved Cal. Wholeheartedly.

Tears flooded my eyes, and I blinked furiously to keep them from falling.

I loved Cal too.

Somewhere along the way, I'd fallen for Cal Stark.

Except it wasn't a love that came with smiles and laughter and promises of happily ever after. One-sided affection was the worst kind of heartache. A deep, black hole formed in my chest, and if I didn't have this baby girl in my arms, I might have let the pain take me to my knees.

But I stayed on my feet, my eyes on the yard.

Cal set Elias down, then glanced toward the house. Our eyes locked.

Elias raced up to the deck's stairs, barreling past me for the kitchen and chaos.

I stayed locked on the man in the lawn.

The man who hadn't been with another woman in four years. What did that mean?

Finding him reading my diary had been a shock, but his confession? Cal was a puzzle and no matter how many times

I shifted the pieces, turning and testing, I couldn't make them fit together.

He was a superstar with sex at his disposal. Sure, we'd hooked up on occasion, but it hadn't been a regular fling. How many women had thrown themselves at Cal's feet since our first hookup in Charlotte? Had he really turned them away? For what? Me?

Unless his abstinence between our encounters had been for another reason. Superstition maybe? Football players were strange about their habits, and after Charlotte, the Titans had gone on a winning streak that had led them to the Super Bowl.

I'd gone to that game too, wearing the opposing team's jersey once more. And once more, after the game, I'd knocked on his hotel room's door.

Cal was a different lover after a win.

He was more playful. More demanding. More experimental.

A shiver raced down my spine, and I tore my eyes away, retreating to the house. I felt him enter the kitchen, his presence impossible to ignore.

His shoulder skimmed mine as he passed me for the pantry, disappearing for a moment before returning with a bottle of water.

"Cal, will you bring me one of those?" Harry asked, taking her plate heaped with food toward the deck where people were finding seats on chairs and the patio tables.

"Sure." He ducked into the pantry once more, and again, brushed his shoulder against mine as he passed by.

I swallowed hard, forcing air into my lungs.

How could he touch me like everything was normal?

Like I didn't want him, only him? Like this wasn't going to end in a bloody mess?

The lump in my throat was choking me but I was smiling, the picture of contentment. Cal wasn't the only one good at a fake.

Why him?

Pierce's gaze darted my way as he scooped a spoonful of potato salad onto the plate he was making for Elias. The spoon froze midair. "What's wrong?"

"Nothing." I smiled wider.

"Nellie."

I shook my head, tucking my chin to watch the baby so he wouldn't see the tears in my eyes. Two fortifying breaths and I raised my face, shoulders back, chin held high.

Never let them see you hurting.

It had taken a couple of years to grow a thick skin, but that had been my motto junior and senior year at Benton. I hadn't really shed the layers since.

"I'm good." I turned my attention through the windows.

Cal was smiling down at Harry as she lifted her water to him, asking for him to twist open the top. One fast swoop and it was off. Then he patted her shoulder with a teasing grin stretched across his mouth.

She elbowed him in the thigh, making the whole table laugh.

Cal tried to disguise it with a glower but he adored Harry. He treasured Elias. He'd die for Pierce.

Why did he let these other people in? Why did he show them his heart? Yet I was just the woman warming his bed?

I was just the woman who hated him.

Like he could sense my stare, he glanced up, staring at

me through the window. Was that how it would always be between us? Always a barrier? Always a distance?

"Why don't you put her in the swing in the living room?" Pierce asked, nodding that direction. "We'll hear her if she cries. Then you can eat while the burgers are hot."

"Okay." The strength to keep myself together was beginning to fail, so I retreated to the swing, strapping Constance into the cradle and setting it to a gentle sway. But instead of eating, I disappeared down the hallway for the closest bathroom.

The moment the door clicked shut behind me, the tears burst past the dam. One burned hot down my cheek before I could squeeze my eyes shut. I wiped my cheek dry, dragging in a burning breath, then another before facing myself in the mirror.

"Why him?" I asked my reflection.

The sad woman on the other side of the glass had no answer.

A sob escaped, and I slapped a hand over my mouth. The door's knob turned and then there he was, the subject of my heartache.

"Ever heard of knocking?" I asked, my voice shaky.

Cal eased his large body into the bathroom while I turned on the faucet, letting my hair fall forward to shield my face.

"What's wrong?" he asked.

"Nothing."

He reached around me, touching the tip of my nose. "Your nose twitches when you lie."

"No, it doesn't." Yes, it did. My mother's did the same.

Cal shut off the water, then took my shoulders and turned me away from the mirror, studying my face. "Nell."

"Don't." The concern in his voice and in his sparkling eyes would snap the thread I was desperately trying to hold.

His hands shifted to my face, cupping my jaw.

"Don't." I glared up at him. Where was the man who'd fight me at every turn? The man who'd make fun of my hair or clothes. The man who'd call me a secretary. That was the Cal I needed in this bathroom.

"Stop." He sighed, then dropped his lips to mine.

Damn him for kissing me.

Damn me for kissing him back.

Rising on my toes, I stroked my tongue along his lower lip, hoping to spur him on. Hoping that if I pushed him enough, we'd strip each other down and he'd fuck me in this bathroom. Then I could use sex to put up a barrier.

Except he wasn't playing, not today. Normally I could count on him to take the lead, but he pulled away, his lips wet. The concern still etched on his face. "What's wrong?"

"Nothing." I waved him off, spinning out of his hold for the sink. I gave myself a moment to stare at the handcrafted bar of soap on a stone dish. When I looked up, Cal's gaze was waiting through the mirror.

It begged for the truth.

And I didn't have the energy to hide it. Not anymore.

"Why do you let them in and not me?" I whispered.

"Because you hate me."

"Do I?"

He swallowed hard. "You need to hate me. It's better that way."

Better. Because then he could use me when he needed to

get laid. Because if I hated him, he could stay behind his walls where it was safe. Where he'd open the door to certain people, but I was not one of the chosen few.

It was high school all over again, and I was still the outcast.

"I hate that you're a coward." I stood straighter, watching through the mirror as my words hit their mark.

"Yep." He nodded and put on that impassive face I'd seen for years.

"I hate that you're a fraud."

He nodded again.

"I hate that you made me not hate you." My nose began to sting as angry tears warned. I needed to get the hell out of this bathroom. "Get out of my way."

He dropped his chin, shuffling backward two steps, giving me enough space to escape.

I slipped through the house and snuck out the front door, rushing to my car parked in the driveway. A row of vehicles bordered the private lane as I sped away from the house. Sheer disappointment—in Cal, in myself—kept the tears at bay.

How could I have been so stupid?

I pounded my fist on the steering wheel at the turn onto the highway. I'd let myself cry when I got home. I'd ugly cry my makeup off. No one was there to hear. No one was there to care.

I'd go home to a quiet, empty house and be . . . alone.

This was not the life I'd hoped for when I'd packed my belongings for Calamity. How could I live here if he stayed? Could I really see Cal at Saturday afternoon barbeques? Or pass him on the street?

Maybe this had been his plan all along. Maybe he'd wanted me to fall in love with him because he knew if he broke my heart, I'd give up.

"He wins."

Two words I'd promised myself I'd never say.

CHAPTER NINETEEN

CAL

NELLIE'S sweet scent lingered in the bathroom, even after I'd heard the front door close.

My hands were braced beside the sink, my eyes closed. I couldn't bring myself to look in the mirror. To confront the coward.

What the fuck were we doing? What the fuck was *I* doing?

I'd watched Nellie's face crumple as she'd stared at me earlier. We hadn't talked since she'd been to the camper and found me with her diary.

When I'd followed her to the bathroom, I'd expected to find her pissed. I'd expected her to ream on me for stealing her journal. Instead, she'd been sad. And she'd slapped me with a question I wasn't prepared to answer.

Why do you let them in and not me?

Why? Because she terrified me. Because she had a power unlike any other person on earth. If Nellie deemed me unworthy, it would destroy me. And I already knew she was too good for an asshole like me.

Was that why I'd kept asking her to tell me why she hated me? To make sure that it stayed in the forefront of her mind?

Christ. I was not a man who lacked self-confidence, both on and off the field. But when it came to Nellie, I was different. Soft. Weak. I didn't stand a chance.

Shoving away from the sink, I strode out of the bathroom, nearly colliding with Harry in the hallway. How long had she been standing there? What had she heard?

Probably too much judging by the scowl on her face.

I scowled right back. "What?"

"You're in love with that girl."

Yes. Yes, I was.

I'd loved Nellie since she'd dumped coffee in my pants on First Street. Maybe I'd loved her since Charlotte and she'd consoled me after a loss. Maybe I'd loved her since the day she'd let me kiss her at fourteen.

But could I admit it out loud? No. I'd shoved Nellie away because I'd had twenty years of perfecting that game. Of pushing her away so I wouldn't get hurt.

"You're not denying it," Harry said.

I shrugged.

"What are you doing here when she just sped away like her tires were on fire?"

"Can we not talk about this?" I raked a hand through my hair and took a step forward, but before I could flee this hallway, Harry arched her eyebrows and silently dared me to walk away. "Come on. Let's just go back to the party."

"What are you afraid of?" she asked.

"I'll ruin her." The confession came freely.

Harry's gaze softened. For a split second, I thought she'd let this go. Then her hand whipped through the air and connected with the side of my head.

"Hey." I rubbed the spot where she'd smacked me. "What was that for?"

"You're a coward."

"And you're not the first woman to call me that today."

Her expression flattened. "My Jake was an ass, like you. But the man wasn't a coward. I expected more from you, Cal. I thought you were the champion."

"I'm not." My shoulders sagged. "Football, yes. But not for Nellie."

She rolled her eyes, then she spun around and marched away.

I followed, stopping when she took the wrong turn. "Where are you going?"

"Home." She snapped her fingers. "And you're my ride. Let's go."

"We haven't eaten yet."

"Maybe you haven't." She lifted a shoulder. "But my plate's empty. I'm a fast eater."

"I'm not leaving the party." Hell, we hadn't even been here for an hour yet.

"Keys are in that fancy rig of yours, right? I'll just drive myself. You can hitchhike home."

"Harry." I planted my hands on my hips. "No."

She narrowed her gaze. "I'm leaving, Cal. With or without you."

For fuck's sake. These damn women were exhausting. "Fine."

"Meet you in the car." She smiled, then strode down the entryway for the door.

She'd sit out there, roasting in the late-July heat, simply to spite me. If she were younger, I might let her sweat. But I wasn't about to have an old lady die on my watch.

"Fuck." I passed the living room, glancing at Constance asleep in her swing.

She was the cutest baby I'd ever seen, and it had been hard not to stare when Nellie had been holding her earlier. Watching them together had given me this twinge. A pinch I hadn't felt since Elias was born and I'd gone to Denver for a visit.

The day I'd arrived, Nellie had been there too. She'd looked so beautiful that I'd told her she should look into Botox to do something about the wrinkles on her forehead.

That had pissed her off enough that she'd left.

What was wrong with me? Why was I such a damn mess? I could blame it on the shit role model that was my father, but really, it was me. *The coward.*

"Hey." I jerked my chin to Pierce as I stepped onto the deck.

"What's up?" He walked over, glancing over my shoulder to the house. "Where did Nellie go?"

"She left. And Harry and I are taking off too. Harry's not feeling great."

"Oh. Damn." He clapped me on my shoulder. "Are you coming back?"

"Yeah." There was nothing for me at the Winnebago. Nellie had stolen the book I'd been reading. "I'll see you in a bit."

I lifted a hand to wave at Kerrigan, then hustled for the driveway.

Harry was in the passenger seat of the Land Rover with the door open to let in some air. Next time, I'd have to remember to take my keys with me and lock the door.

I slid behind the wheel and hit the ignition button, then plucked my sunglasses from the console. Even with the shades on, I sent her a glare. "I'm never inviting you to another party."

"Newsflash, Cal. There isn't a party in Calamity I can't attend without your invitation."

I growled, knowing she was right, and put the SUV into reverse. Of all the people for me to make friends with in Calamity, why had I picked this salty woman? Damn Harry for being so popular.

When we'd arrived earlier, I'd assumed that I would need to make a few introductions. Nope. Harry knew everyone but the Grays Peak employees, who I hadn't met either. And Harry hadn't met Nellie.

My beautiful Nellie who'd left here on the verge of tears.

Was she okay? Maybe I should stop by her place to check in. At the very least, if she wanted to be at the barbeque, I could give her the all clear. She could return in my stead.

"You can drop me at the lobby," Harry said as we neared the motel.

"Okay." I eased into the parking lot, seeing Marcy through the office windows.

Harry waved at her, then opened her door, but stopped before stepping out. "Does she feel the same way about you?"

I blew out a long breath. Nellie didn't hate me. But love? "I don't know."

"Only one way to find out. And now that your afternoon is clear . . ." Her eyes darted toward First, like she could see to Nellie's front door. "Take a chance."

Maybe. Maybe I should.

Or maybe I should let Nellie go.

"Have a good afternoon, Harry."

"Why do I get the feeling I should smack some sense into you again?" She sighed and stepped outside, shaking her head as she walked to the office.

I eased onto the street, hating that Harry's disappointment hit so hard. *Whatever.* I drove along First, the sidewalks crowded with people exploring downtown. Calamity was just as busy as everyone had warned, the summer tourist traffic making it hard for me to spend much time downtown.

Yesterday, I'd stopped at the grocery store for some beer, my contribution to Pierce's barbeque, and had been asked for three autographs. The day before, I'd pulled into the gas station and the guy on the opposite end of the pump had not-so-conspicuously taken my picture.

Until the bustle died, I'd be sticking close to safe places. The Winnebago. Pierce and Kerrigan's.

The turnoff to Nellie's house approached.

I tightened my grip on the wheel.

Don't turn. Do not turn.

The green street marker inched closer.

Keep going straight.

My foot eased off the gas and pressed the brake.

Don't.

I turned and drove to her house, parking against the curb.

The tires were stopped. The engine was off. But I couldn't bring myself to open the door.

What was I going to say? What was I doing here? Granted it was broad daylight, but the lights inside were off. Was she even home? Maybe she'd gone for a drive. Maybe she'd stopped downtown.

I shouldn't be here. It was too soon. Nellie and I did better when we gave each other space. *Tomorrow*. I could come back tomorrow. Or the next day.

Before I could pull away, my phone rang through the car's speakers. I hit the button to answer my mother's call. "Hey, Mom."

"Hi. I was hoping to catch you."

"What's up?"

"Cal . . ." She sighed. Mom always sighed before a guilt trip. Son of a bitch. I was going to hate this phone call. "The fundraiser at Benton is next weekend. I just got off the phone with Dean Hendrickson."

"Mom—"

"Before you interrupt me and say no, just listen. Please."

I stifled a groan. "Okay."

"They already announced you'd be speaking."

"No."

That was my father's fuckup, not mine. He should never have volunteered me. What did he think? Now that I was retired, I had free time? The bastard hadn't even bothered to run it by me first. What if I'd been busy?

"Cal, this is important. Don't do it for your father. Don't even do it for me. Do it for one of the kids who will be there. Dean Hendrickson just told me her story and it is heartbreaking."

Dean Hendrickson knew how to play my mother, didn't he? Like she knew how to play me.

"What kid?"

"They've invited some of the top students from each class to attend the gala. There will be a student at each table, a chance for them to meet some alumni. That sort of thing."

"Okay," I drawled.

"Well, I guess there's a young sophomore girl attending. She's one of those scholarship kids we all pitch in for."

The pity in my mother's voice made my skin crawl. The image of Nellie in her Benton uniform popped into my mind, and there was nothing about her to pity. Only admire. And if she would have been in this car, she would have cringed.

Hell, I cringed.

"This girl is apparently quite the gifted student and athlete. She's playing on the lacrosse team and is going to be the star. But, oh, Cal." Mom sniffled. "Her father just died this past spring. It was a freak accident at his work. This poor girl has been having a hard time. Dean Hendrickson thought it might mean a lot to her if she could hear from a fellow athlete. Maybe boost her spirits."

I dragged a hand over my face. "I'm a football player, Mom. Not lacrosse."

"Does it matter? Please. You won't have to speak long. But maybe you could just give a hopeful message about endurance and hard work. Anything. And I've requested she be seated at our table so we can meet her. You're so good with kids, Cal."

And there it was. The guilt. It was so thick and heavy that not even the air-conditioning could chase it away.

"Mom—"

"Please." There was a tremor in her voice. "I know you value your privacy. And I understand why you don't do speaking engagements like this."

Because I wasn't some mentor for kids. I wasn't a hero or man they should aspire to be. The only good advice I could give was to work your ass off. Give your life to a game.

What kind of guidance was that? *Shit.* It was all shit. Because once the game was gone, you'd find yourself living in an RV in a small Montana town with nothing to show for your life but a plush bank account and an addiction to an old diary.

"I don't even know what I'd talk about," I muttered.

"You've got a week to come up with something. If you wanted to come home early, I'd help you with your speech." Mom must be desperate. She hadn't even helped me with my speeches when I'd attended Benton as a student.

I let out a frustrated groan. *No. Just say no.*

"This is important to me," she added.

No, it was important to Dad.

And if I recalled correctly, Dean Hendrickson and my parents were members of the same country club. I was merely a puppet on their twisted strings.

"Please?" I could hear her hands clasp together, shaking them like she'd dropped to her knees to beg. Regina Stark rarely begged.

Fuck my life. "Fine."

"Oh, thank you. I'll call the dean right now and tell him you've agreed. He'll be so excited."

"Uh-huh," I muttered. "Five minutes. I'll talk for five minutes."

"I'm sure that will be wonderful."

"I gotta go, Mom."

"Of course. Text me your travel plans."

"Yeah," I mumbled, then ended the call.

My finger went to the ignition, ready to turn on the car, but I hesitated, my gaze turning to Nellie's brick house.

What did she want from me? What did I want from myself?

I blew out a long breath and started the car, abandoning the curb as I flipped around and returned to First. I sat at the stop sign, looking right, then left. There was no sign of Nellie mixed in with the nameless faces. Yet she was on every corner, at every stop.

I pictured her at The Refinery, wearing her sexy leggings and cropped tank with her hair pulled into a high ponytail. She was at Jane's, dressed in jeans and a tank for a night at the bar with her girl posse. She was leaving the coffee shop, an iced latte in hand, as she spent her weekend strolling downtown.

A honk from behind me had my eyes shooting to the rearview. I held up a hand in apology, checked for traffic, then pulled onto the street, driving to the motel.

I parked in the alley, in my usual spot, and looked at the Winnebago.

Nellie had left her mark here too.

She was everywhere.

Because this was her home. This was her town.

And I couldn't take that from her. She'd come to Calamity to build a life. If I could give her nothing else, at least I could let her find peace.

So I shut off the car and rushed inside, once more pulling

my suitcase from the closet. But this time, I didn't pack for a vacation. I emptied every drawer. I filled every pocket of my backpack. I stuffed toiletries into their case.

Before I climbed in my car to drive to Colorado, I stopped by the motel's office.

And handed Marcy the keys to her Winnebago.

Dear Diary,

Today was the last day of school and now I'm officially a sophomore. Only three more years to go at Benton. Then I swear on my heart and soul, I will never set foot in that school again. And I'll never have to see these assholes again either. No more John Flickerman. No more Phoebe McAdams. No more Pierce Sullivan. And no more Cal Stark. Three years to go. Is it too soon to start a countdown? (JK. But not really.)

Nellie

CHAPTER TWENTY

NELLIE

"PIERCE, DO—OH, SORRY." I held up a hand as I stepped into his office and realized he was on the phone.

"Come in," he mouthed, waving me toward his desk. "Good luck tomorrow."

What was happening tomorrow? Who was he talking to? I walked close enough to hear a deep voice speak on the other end of the call.

A deep voice I hadn't heard in a week.

Cal.

"Talk to you later." Pierce ended the call and set his phone aside.

"Was that Cal?"

He nodded. "Yeah."

"Where is he?" Somehow, I knew he wasn't in Calamity. I hadn't driven past the motel to seek him out. I hadn't stopped by the Winnebago. But since the barbeque last weekend, I'd just had this sense that he was gone.

"Denver."

"Ah. Why?" A month ago, a week ago, I would have pretended not to care. But what was the point in faking it anymore? Wrestling with my feelings for Cal had zapped my energy, and I just didn't have the strength to hide my curiosity. The unknown was killing me, and either Pierce told me what was going on, or I'd crack and call Cal myself.

"There's a fundraiser at Benton tomorrow. A dinner for the alumni. My parents go every year. It's something the school has done for a while now to raise money, mostly for building improvements. Some is allocated to the scholarship programs."

Cal had told me about the fundraiser, the one his father had volunteered him to attend. But he'd told his mom on the phone that day he wasn't going. He'd been adamant.

"They asked him to speak," Pierce said.

"And he agreed?" When had he changed his mind? And why?

"His mother guilted him into it." Pierce sighed. "And I get the impression he was in a rush to leave Calamity."

Because of me.

Had he been as miserable as I'd been? Had he spent a week of sleepless nights trying to figure out what to do? Trying to decide just how far he'd let myself bleed before wrapping the wounds and walking away?

"Want to talk about what's been going on with you two?" Pierce asked.

I shrugged. "I don't even know where to start."

"How long has it been going on?"

"Since the AFC Championship game we went to in Charlotte."

Pierce's eyes widened. "That was years ago."

"Four. So yeah, it's been going on for a while." I pulled out the chair opposite his desk and plopped into the seat, sagging beneath the weight on my heart. "It was nothing."

"Then it was everything," Pierce said.

I nodded. "Yes."

As the years had passed, Cal had become this constant. Mostly an annoyance, but he'd been my refuge too. Our casual, sex-only relationship had blossomed so slowly I hadn't even realized how entangled we'd become. No surprise the few men I'd dated in Denver had barely lasted a week. It was hard to date someone when you cringed as they moved in to kiss you. When you looked at their face and saw someone else.

And the fucking worst part was, I hadn't even realized it. I'd been a blind fool.

No one compared to Cal.

Four years of lying to myself. Four years of brushing him aside. Four years of hate that hadn't really been hate.

God, I loved him.

"Why won't he let me in?" I whispered.

"Because he's scared."

"H-he told you that?" Had they talked about me?

"He didn't have to." Pierce gave me a sad smile. "I know Cal. He might give that tough show, but inside, he's just the man who wants to be loved for something other than his talent on the football field."

"He doesn't make it easy."

Pierce laughed. "You don't exactly make it easy either, Nellie."

Well . . . damn. He wasn't wrong. "Fair point. Is he coming back?"

"I don't know. He hasn't told me much. But if I had to guess, I'd say no. He moved out of the Winnebago."

"He did? What about his ranch?"

Pierce shrugged. "No idea. He might sell the land."

So that was it. Cal was gone. Wasn't that what I'd wanted? To claim Calamity as my own? My stomach twisted and churned. I hadn't been able to eat much this week because my insides had raged like a hurricane.

He was gone.

Just when I finally realized that I loved him, he'd left. *Damn that man.*

Maybe it was for the best. We would never work. Our communication skills were abysmal at best. We'd fight daily. We'd drive each other mad.

Besides, he'd had his chance to tell me how he felt. Instead, he'd let me do all the talking. He'd let me walk away and told me to hate him.

"Nellie?"

My gaze whipped to Pierce as a tear streaked down my face. "I'd better get back to work."

I shot out of the chair and rushed from his office, practically jogging down the hallway for the restroom. Darkness blocked out the world as the door closed behind me.

Cal was gone.

The smart, self-preserving thing to do would be to let him go. We might burn as hot and bright as a blue flame, but eventually, we'd turn to ash. There'd be nothing left but the charred remains of two hearts.

My hand came to my chest, pressing against the ache. This pain would dull. The hurt would pass. In time, I'd forget all about Cal Stark.

We had to let each other go.

And he'd already done his part, hadn't he? He'd walked away.

The door jarred open, slamming into my back. I'd forgotten to flip the lock.

"Oh. Shoot. Nellie?" Kathryn held up both hands. "I'm so sorry. I didn't realize anyone was in here."

"It's fine," I said as she pulled the door closed. "I'll be out in a minute."

I gave myself three aching heartbeats in the darkness before flipping on the lights and wiping the mascara smudges from beneath my eyes.

"Why am I crying?" I asked myself in the mirror. It was done. Over.

He'd walked away from Calamity. He'd walked away from me.

More tears welled, so I swiped for a paper towel to blot them dry. But they wouldn't stop. No matter how many deep breaths I took, no matter how fast I blinked, the tears kept coming. *Damn it.*

We had a staff meeting in thirty minutes. The whole office would know I'd been crying.

Was this what heartbreak felt like? I'd never had my heart broken before. I'd never let anyone in who'd had that kind of power.

Until Cal.

And I hadn't really let him in, had I? I'd told him he was a coward. But so was I. All those times he'd asked me what I hated about him, I'd ignored the obvious. It had been right there in front of my face.

Tell me what you hate about me.

Cal hadn't been asking why I hated him. He'd been asking if I wanted him anyway. If I could let go of the past, the mistakes and the hurt, and just . . . love him.

"Shit." I sniffled and let out a dry laugh as I buried my face in my hands. "I'm an idiot."

How was I supposed to fix this if he wasn't coming back to Calamity?

"Ugh." My groan echoed through the bathroom.

Maybe he'd reject me. Maybe we'd kill each other. But if I didn't try, I'd never forgive myself. I'd spend the rest of my life wondering *what if*.

So I hurried from the bathroom, marching down the hallway to Pierce's office.

His eyes snapped up from his monitor as I burst through the doorway. "What's wrong?"

"I need a favor. It's a big one."

A slow grin spread across his mouth. "I'll call my pilot."

CHAPTER TWENTY-ONE

NELLIE

THE BENTON ACADEMY hadn't changed in fifteen years. The two-story, red brick building was just as intimidating now as it had been the day I'd walked away after graduation.

Women dripping in jewels, wearing expensive gowns, laughed and smiled as they passed by the columns at the grand entrance. Men dressed in tuxes climbed the wide staircase to the front double doors.

Every window was illuminated, the rectangles casting a golden glow into the dimming evening light. Lanterns lined the sidewalk. The lawns were freshly mowed and the scent of cut grass clung to the air.

That smell was normally a comfort because it reminded me of Dad. But tonight, it did nothing to curb the anxiety rattling in my bones. My nerves were frayed, not only in anticipation of seeing Cal, but just being at Benton again.

I'd vowed never to set foot on these grounds again. Yet

here I was, frozen on a sidewalk that I hadn't crossed since I was eighteen.

"Coming, Nellie?" Pierce's mother asked, glancing back when she realized I'd fallen behind.

"Be right there," I said, forcing a tight smile. "I'm going to look around a bit. For old times' sake."

"Of course." She nodded, taking her husband's arm. "We'll meet you inside."

Pierce's father escorted his wife past the bronze statue of Albert Benton, the school's namesake.

My senior year, a group of students had vandalized the statue as a prank. The two students who'd been caught on camera, wrapping dear old Alfred in toilet paper, had nearly been denied graduation. Their parents had probably made some calls—and written checks—to get their kids out of trouble.

I doubted that courtesy would have been extended to the scholarship kids.

God, I hated this place. The opulence. The arrogance. What if I just stayed outside and waited for Cal to come out after the dinner?

Don't be a coward, Nellie. I squared my shoulders and walked past the statue, my nerves spiking with every click of my stiletto heels on the cement. I scanned the crowd gathering at the staircase, looking for the man who'd stand head and shoulders above the rest.

But there was no sign of Cal.

Which was probably a good thing. In the past twenty-eight hours since I'd burst into Pierce's office and asked for his help to score me an invite to this fiasco, I still hadn't figured out exactly what to say.

Maybe I just needed to see him and it would come to me. Maybe I'd be able to admit that we were better together than we were apart. Even if that meant constant bickering. Even if that meant disagreeing about almost everything.

I'd rather spend a lifetime arguing with Cal Stark, than laughing with anyone else.

My stomach was in a knot as I walked, my heels teetering on the bottom step. My heart hammered, and my skin felt too hot beneath this gown.

With the short notice, I hadn't had time to shop for anything new. Luckily, I kept a few dresses in my closet for these fancy occasions. It wasn't uncommon for me to attend functions on behalf of Grays Peak.

I'd opted for a black gown, adorned with columns of sequins that added a dainty shimmer to the fabric. The skirt was full with a slit that ran up my thigh. The top had two thin straps and a deep V that exposed my sternum.

It felt fitting for tonight.

If Cal was going to break my heart, there might as well not be anything in his way.

Oh God, I hope he hadn't brought a date.

The skirt swished as I climbed the stairs with a fake smile fixed firmly on my face. Pierce's parents, who I'd grown to adore during my time working for their son, had made a call—and promised a hefty donation—to get me a seat at their table.

I hadn't explained why I'd needed to come tonight, and because they were amazing, they hadn't asked why. They'd simply swung by my hotel in their town car on their way to Benton and picked me up for the event.

"Good evening," the man stationed beside the door greeted as I approached. "Your name, madam?"

"Nellie Rivera." My voice shook. If he noticed, he didn't let on as he scanned the guest list.

"Welcome, Ms. Rivera. On behalf of the faculty and staff at Benton, we hope you enjoy your evening. The festivities are taking place in the dining hall. Down the hallway on your left."

"Thank you." I swept past him, breezing into the entry-way, standing at the mouth of hallways I'd walked hundreds of times.

Guests milled around the space, making conversation. Their voices echoed in the open space, carrying toward the tall ceilings. The smell of floor wax and lemon wood polish filled my nose and transported me into the past.

I wasn't a woman in a fancy gown but a teenager again, wearing a red and black plaid skirt with yellow pinstripes. My starched white button-down shirt was tucked tight and covered with a black cardigan embroidered with the Benton crest on a breast pocket.

My legs felt wobbly. My palms clammy. But I refused to study the floor as I walked like I would have when I'd been a student. I held my chin high, my eyes aimed forward, and followed the crowd toward the dining hall.

We passed a row of lockers and I instantly found number 197. My locker from freshman year. Memories from those years whipped around me like a gust of wind.

My first day of school, when I'd realized that everyone already knew everyone, and I'd been the outcast. The days when I'd wanted to scream. The others when I'd cried. The few where I'd laughed.

So much had changed from the first day I'd loaded my books into that locker to the last day when I'd hauled them away. I'd ended my freshman year jaded and bitter. Separate from the others, not only by their choice but mine too.

It had been easier to erect barriers so they couldn't hurt me.

Especially where Cal was concerned.

But it was time for the walls to come down, especially where Cal was concerned.

The noise grew louder as I approached the dining hall. People filled the space, visiting and laughing. Old friends, rich friends, reunited.

A server with a tray of champagne flutes stood at the doors, offering a glass.

"Thank you." The bubbles burst on my tongue as I took a sip, then scanned the room. Where was he? My hand trembled as I searched, and a splash of champagne escaped the flute and coated my hand.

"Damn it," I muttered. That was going to be sticky.

With a quick chug, I drained the glass, handing the empty to a waitress as she passed, then turned and weaved through people as I retreated to the hallway and the ladies' room. It was empty as I pushed inside, moving to a sink to wash my hands. Then I took a calming breath, examining my face in the mirror.

My eyes were lined with coal, the shadow making the green pop. I'd opted for a pale pink lipstick tonight, a subtler shade than the red I typically wore to special functions. My ice-blond hair cascaded down my back in loose waves. I looked pretty. And terrified. No amount of makeup could hide the nerves.

The door opened and I glanced over as a woman in a silver gown strutted inside. I dismissed her, then did a double take. *Oh, hell.* Phoebe McAdams.

"Hi," she said, setting her clutch on the counter to dig out a lip gloss. Like most of the other women in attendance, she was decked out in jewelry. Diamonds glittered at her neck, ears and wrists. Her wedding ring was so large it probably weighed her hand down like she was toting a baseball against her knuckles.

I blinked, waiting for her to tell me I didn't belong. To ask what I was doing here in *her* school.

But she leaned closer to the mirror and reapplied lip gloss.

This bitch. She didn't even remember me.

Funny how people didn't remember those they tormented, but the one on the receiving end never forgot.

Phoebe looked beautiful, just like she had as a teenager. But as I snuck one more look through the mirror, I saw my beauty too. We could each shine. And maybe I always had. Maybe that was the reason she'd been so awful to me as an adolescent.

Good, old-fashioned jealousy.

I stood a little taller and walked by. "Have a nice night."

"You too." She did her own double take as I passed behind her for the door.

"Nellie?"

I kept moving, the door closing on Phoebe as I returned to the party and snagged another glass of champagne.

The dining hall had been transformed for the event. Round tables draped with crisp white linens filled the space.

White curtains had been hung to hide the food buffet line and vending machines.

A small stage and podium had been erected at the head of the room. Bouquets of red roses adorned each table. The evening light was waning beyond the rows of windows that overlooked the courtyard. The lawn and flower beds were perfectly manicured, just like they had been in the years when I'd spent my lunches in this room.

So much was unchanged. Yet it was entirely different.

Or maybe that was simply me. I was different.

Pierce's parents stood beside a table in the center of the room, and when they spotted me, waved me over.

I joined them and made introductions with the other members of our table as the waitstaff began bustling around, replacing empty champagne flutes with glasses of wine as they encouraged us to take our seats.

The champagne helped calm a few nerves, but until I saw Cal, my heart would be in my throat. He was here, right? Maybe he was running late? As the conversation continued at our table, I searched the room, looking toward the stage.

A familiar profile and a pair of broad shoulders caught my eye. My heart did a cartwheel.

Cal sat at one of the front tables, wearing a tailored black tux. His spine was stiff, his posture rigid. One hand dangled at his side and his fingers were snapping.

Snap. Snap. Snap.

He was nervous.

I wanted nothing more than to cross the room and wrap him in my arms, but with everyone taking their seats, it would be too conspicuous. For this, I didn't need an audience. I'd have to wait until the dinner was over.

Cal's mother sat at his side, her dark hair twisted in a tight chignon. Beside her was Colter Stark, reclined in his seat with an arm draped casually over the back of her chair.

Colter laughed at something, and even from a distance, I saw Cal's jaw clench.

They looked alike, something I'd forgotten or maybe hadn't noticed as a teen. Colter was a handsome older man, his hair the same color as Cal's except for the gray threaded at his temples. But there was no kindness in Colter's eyes. His expression was the epitome of superiority.

Dickhead.

I tore my eyes away as the chair beside mine was dragged away from the table. A boy wearing a pair of black slacks and a pressed blue shirt took the seat. On the pocket, he had pinned a name tag.

Franklin O'Connell
Junior

A mop of red hair hung in his face as he touched the edge of his plate. His shoulders curled in so deeply that if he could have disappeared beneath the tablecloth, he would have tried.

Pierce's parents had told me on the ride over that there'd be some students attending tonight. Kids who excelled, either academically, artistically or athletically. Sitting at the table to our left was a girl with a violin charm on her bracelet. The boy at the table to our right was so tall that I assumed he was on the basketball team.

"Hi." I shifted, holding out my hand to the kid beside me. "I'm Nellie."

"Frankie." He shook my hand, his grip too tight. "I mean Franklin."

"Nice to meet you." I leaned in close and dropped my voice. "Is this your first fundraiser dinner?"

He nodded. "There are a lot of forks."

I laughed, taking in the three beside each of our empty plates. "At least we don't have to do the dishes."

A small smile graced his mouth.

"How do you like Benton?"

He shrugged. "It's all right."

"You're a junior?"

"Yeah. I will be in the fall."

Our conversation was cut short when a man took the stage and leaned into the microphone at the podium. "Good evening, ladies and gentlemen. Thank you for coming tonight. We are so honored to have you in our school."

He introduced himself as the dean of students, then proceeded to lay it on thick as to why we were all here. A chance to improve the lives of the next generation. The opportunity to sculpt young minds and provide them with an unparalleled education.

Dean Hendrickson finished his welcome message, then the waitstaff began delivering the first course. As the clink of forks on plates mingled with conversation, I split my attention. Every few bites, I'd glance toward Cal, whose back was mostly to me.

He spoke to his mother here and there, but he mostly talked with the student at their table.

I did the same.

Franklin was shy but incredibly bright. It took through the main course for him to open up and speak freely.

"So you love math," I said. "What do you think you'll do for college?"

"I don't know. Maybe MIT. Depends on if I can get financial aid. I'm, uh . . . one of the scholarship kids here."

I hated the way he dropped his gaze as he finished his sentence. I hated the way he poked at his steak.

"I was a scholarship kid here."

"For real?" He looked me up and down. "Did the rich kids suck back then too?"

"Pretty much."

"What did you do about it?"

I grinned and held up my knuckles for a fist bump. "I beat them at whatever I could."

"Nice."

"They won't always be jerks. Well, some of them might." Like Phoebe McAdams who'd been sneaking looks in my direction. "But some of them grow out of it."

"I don't really talk to them. I just do my own thing, you know?" Franklin nodded toward Cal's table. "That's Maria. She's on scholarship too. She gets pretty good grades but she's killer at lacrosse. We kind of hang out a lot."

His cheeks flushed as he stared at her, a crush written all over his face.

We finished our meal discussing more about his favorite hobbies, and as the dessert was served Dean Hendrickson took the podium once more.

"I hope you enjoyed this lovely meal, and I hope you've had a chance to get to know the students at your tables."

No one at ours but Pierce's parents and me had spoken to Franklin. Maybe that was because we were seated closest to him. Or maybe because, like I'd told Frankie, some people would always be jerks.

"We're so lucky to have a guest with us tonight who's

agreed to speak a few words," Dean Hendrickson continued. "I don't think he needs much of an introduction. Not only is he a Benton alum, but he's one of the most successful and well-known quarterbacks to have played in the NFL. Ladies and gentlemen, please welcome Mr. Cal Stark."

Cal stood from his chair, looking devilishly handsome. His face was clean-shaven and his hair combed. His jacket accentuated the width of his shoulders. The slacks couldn't hide the strength in his thighs.

No man had ever looked so fine in a tux.

If all went well tonight, maybe I'd get to undo his tie with my teeth.

My gaze tracked his every step as he walked to the podium and shook Dean Hendrickson's hand. Then he stood at the microphone, glancing out over the crowd.

My breath lodged in my throat, wondering if he'd spot me, but his gaze swept the opposite direction before it landed on his table.

"Thanks for having me tonight," he said, tugging the microphone higher so he wouldn't have to bend over. "I don't give a lot of speeches. It's not really my thing."

The crowd stilled and the room went quiet at the obvious discomfort in his voice.

Part of me wanted to raise my hand, to wave so he knew he had at least one supporter in the room, but I sat like a statue while my heart raced.

"I was going to talk about football. Go figure." That earned him a few laughs. "But then I sat next to this special young lady at dinner tonight. And while I appreciate the rest of you being here, I'm going to toss out the speech I'd planned, and just share some thoughts for her."

Dean Hendrickson, who stood off to the side of the room, shared a worried look with Cal's father.

"Maria." Cal gave her a nod. "I knew a girl like you once, back when I was just a student at Benton. She's a lot like you. Strong. Tenacious. Smart. Talented. And she hated me with a passion."

Another laugh trickled through the hall.

The room began to blur at the edges. My vision tunneled to Cal, like it had whenever I'd watched him on the football field.

"I wish I had great advice for you tonight, Maria," Cal said into the microphone. Every person here had to see the softness in his eyes as he spoke to the girl. If they didn't, they were blind. "But I'm a dumb jock who made his fortune throwing a football. My experiences won't help you much. But Nellie—that's the girl who hated me—here's what I think she would tell you if she were at this microphone in my place."

At my name, Franklin nudged my elbow, but I didn't dare take my eyes away from Cal. Why was he talking about me? Where was he going with this?

"Be honest," Cal said. "Be kind. Nellie is both and it has always set her apart."

The lump in my throat was beginning to choke me, so I reached for my water glass, the goblet shaking as I brought it to my lips.

"Work hard." Cal's deep voice filled the room, corner to corner. No one dared to whisper. "Hard work can often level an otherwise unequal playing field. See, here's where I throw in the football metaphors."

Once more, laughter trickled through the room.

"Never lose heart." Cal gave the girl a sad smile. "When the world tries to steal your joy, steal it right back. Wealth will never determine your worth. And don't give up on what you want. Fight for it. Every day. If what you want is a job or an award or a town to call your own, fight for it. There isn't a person on earth who fights the way my Nellie fights. I see her spirit in you."

My Nellie.

That had to be a slip. Did he know I was here? *No.* There was no way. He'd just said *my Nellie* to this room of strangers. His parents were in the audience, and he'd claimed me as his.

I dragged in a breath through my nose, willing myself not to cry as Pierce's mom reached over and squeezed my hand.

"People come and go from our lives," Cal said. "It's not fair. It's never easy. Hold the people you love close. Cherish their memory when they're gone. Know that they are watching, so make them proud."

Maria reached up and wiped at her face, like she was catching a tear.

"I promised you this would be short," he told her. "You have a very bright future, and I, for one, am grateful that I've been able to share this meal with you tonight. That I've met you. Thank you for being here."

Cal stood a little taller, his gaze sweeping the crowd again. "It's because of donations that kids like Maria and Nellie and so many others can attend Benton. At some point, probably after I give up the mic, Dean Hendrickson is going to ask you to make a donation. But I'm going to ask you too. I'll be giving one million dollars to the school tonight, to be used exclusively for scholarships."

The gasps and murmurs were deafening. *Oh my God.* My jaw dropped.

"My parents will be matching that donation as well," Cal said. From the look that Colter shot his son, this was news. "How about a show of hands from all those who will also be contributing tonight?"

Women and men raised their arms. A couple of people laughed as they joined the fray, knowing that Cal was publicly shaming them into a donation.

He smirked as he bent low to the microphone, casting a glance toward Dean Hendrickson. "Hope you're taking note of those raised hands."

The dean smiled and nodded wildly, starting a round of applause.

Without another word, Cal strode from the stage. But before he could resume his seat, Maria stood and wrapped her arms around his waist.

He hugged her back, patting her shoulder. Then he held out her chair so she could sit. Except first, she turned and found Frankie for a wave.

He waved back.

Cal followed Maria's gaze, straight to my table. Our eyes locked. The applause continued.

Since I was seconds away from a full-fledged anxiety attack and unsure what else to do, I panicked. I did what high school Nellie had always wanted to do but hadn't had the guts.

I flipped off Cal Stark.

CHAPTER TWENTY-TWO

CAL

"THANKS, CAL." Dean Hendrickson shook my hand for the third time. "Think about the sign on the football field."

"It's not necessary. Really." I didn't want or need the Benton practice field to be renamed in my honor. Hell, I didn't even need the *thank you*s. Just a receipt for the donation I could give my accountant, and for the dean to let me go so I could chase after Nellie.

"Are you—"

"Yes, I'm sure." I forced a tight smile. "Would you excuse me?"

"Oh, of course."

After the event had concluded, Hendrickson had rushed to our table and trapped me. There was a line of people waiting to take his place—either to kiss my ass or chastise me for guilting them into donating money. I had zero fucks to give. All I wanted was to find out why Nellie was here. That was, if I could actually find her.

I stood taller than most people in the room, but I'd still lost her in the crush.

"Hey, Cal." A man thrust his hand into mine as I turned away from my table, trying to shuffle past people toward the doors.

"Hi," I clipped, shook my hand free and kept on moving. I ignored him and every other person who approached, my eyes sweeping and searching.

Damn it, where was she?

After she'd flipped me her middle finger, I'd laughed until the applause had died. All was right with the world when Nellie was giving me the bird. While the dean had given his closing remarks, I'd looked over my shoulder a hundred times to make sure she hadn't snuck out. The minutes had dragged on as I'd waited for this bullshit party to finish.

Then I'd lost her. She better not have left Benton.

If she was in Colorado, that had to be a good thing, right? My heart was beating out of my chest, pushing me to move faster, but there were people everywhere.

"Cal!" Maria appeared at my side with a redheaded boy in tow.

"Hi." For her, I stopped. Actually, it was for the boy. "Hey, you were sitting next to Nellie. Do you know where she went?"

"Wait." Maria's eyes bugged out. "That blond lady was Nellie? Like the Nellie from your speech?"

"Yeah. Where'd she go?"

"Oh, uh, she left." The boy—Franklin, according to his name tag—pointed to the door.

Fuck. "Got your phone handy?" I asked Maria.

She nodded, digging it out of the pocket in her dress.

I rattled off my phone number, waiting until she'd keyed it in. "Call me. Text me. Whatever. But keep in touch."

"Okay." She beamed. She was the opposite of Nellie in appearance with her dark eyes and hair, but like I'd stated at the podium, they shared a spirit. And this kid was going places.

"I gotta go." I patted her on the shoulder, then brushed past them, darting toward the row of windows. The center aisle was blocked and the only way I'd catch Nellie was if I could avoid being stopped every three steps.

I was able to avoid the masses but then got stopped by the bottleneck at the door. My feet inched forward until finally, I was able to slide past a couple and break free into the hallway.

My polished shoes clicked on the tile as I lengthened my strides, breaking into a jog. I didn't have to run far before I spotted a head of blond hair.

Nellie leaned against a locker in the hallway, her shoulder resting on the gray metal while her arms were crossed.

Waiting.

I slapped a hand to my chest, the adrenaline coursing through my veins, as I slowed. Then I sidestepped a couple walking arm in arm, moving toward the opposite side of the hall.

Nellie's gaze raked me from head to toe when I stopped at her side. "Looking sharp tonight, Stark."

"You're beautiful." So stunning it hurt.

That dress should be criminal, and if she'd let me, I'd happily strip it away. I'd bury my hands in her hair and

THE BULLY

myself in her body to show her just how fucking glad I was to see her tonight.

"What are you doing here, sugar?"

"Taking a walk down memory lane." She pushed off the locker, her fingertips gliding over the numbered plaque. "Feels a little bit like returning to the scene of a crime."

Number 197. Her locker from freshman year.

"I saw you first," I blurted.

"Huh?"

"Freshman year orientation. I saw you first. Before you saw me. You were right here, turning the combination into the lock and it wasn't working."

"The office wrote it down wrong."

I inched closer as a stream of people passed us for the exit. "You were wearing jeans and this rainbow tie-dyed T-shirt."

"I think I remember that shirt." She cringed. "The girls always bitched about the uniforms, but I never minded."

I stepped closer, towering over her, and tugged at a strand of her hair as I stared into those green eyes. "I wanted you before you wanted me."

"God, you are competitive. Setting the record straight that you win?"

"Fuck yeah." I grinned. "What are you really doing here, Nell?"

"I'm—" Before she could finish her sentence, a figure appeared at our side.

"Cal. A word." My father's nostrils flared. "Privately."

"Busy right now." I reached for Nellie's hand, threading our fingers together. It was the first time I'd ever taken her hand in public. But if I had my way, it wouldn't be the last.

Dad dropped his gaze to our interlocked hands just as my mother joined the conversation.

"Colter, this is not the time or place for"—she spotted Nellie and how closely we stood together—"oh. Hello."

"Hi, Mrs. Stark." Though this had to be uncomfortable for Nellie, I loved her more for the warm smile she gave my mother.

"Mom, this is Nellie. Nellie, my mother, Regina."

"So lovely to meet you, Nellie." The hope in Mom's eyes as she held out a hand was a gut punch.

The first woman I'd introduced to her would be the last if Nellie broke my heart. Or if she didn't.

Nellie untangled her fingers from mine to greet my mother. "Nice to see you again."

"Oh, we've met?" Mom studied Nellie's face, trying to place her but came up short. "I'm so terribly sorry. I must have forgotten."

Dad's lip curled. "Remember that gardener I fired because his daughter was stealing and stalking Cal? This is that daughter."

Nellie stiffened.

Mom drew her hand back, which pissed me right the fuck off. We'd be having words about that later.

"About that stealing and stalking." I stood taller as I faced him. "It was all bullshit. Dad, you kept gawking at Nellie like she was your next meal, so I lied to keep you away from a fourteen-year-old girl. Sorry, not sorry."

Dad's face turned to granite as Nellie snorted a laugh.

A woman walking by gave him an assessing look, leaning in to whisper to her companion.

Mom's mouth pursed in a thin line as she did her best to

blank her expression. Maybe the reason I hid my feelings was because I'd learned it from watching her.

"I don't know what you're talking about." Dad adjusted his bow tie. "We need to talk about that stunt you just pulled."

"No, we don't. You can put up, or shut up. Next time, don't volunteer me to give a speech."

"You committed money that wasn't yours to promise."

"Don't worry, Dad. If you can't cover it, I'll pay it for you."

"I can afford it," he gritted out.

"Great." I leaned past him to pull Mom into a quick, sideways hug. "You look lovely tonight. I'll call you tomorrow."

We'd have things to discuss. But exactly what, depended on Nellie.

"Thank you for coming." Mom's smile was strained with the obvious tension cloaking our huddle, but her manners were impeccable as always. "A pleasure seeing you again, Nellie."

"Have a good night."

The words were barely out of Nellie's mouth before I clasped her hand in mine and dragged her down the hallway.

The people ahead of us all turned to leave through the main foyer, but I glanced over my shoulder, making sure there wasn't a staff member close, then pulled Nellie straight. We passed another bank of lockers heading toward a corner that would take us to the senior wing.

Our strides ate up the hallways, our shoes clapping against the tile floor as we breezed through the school.

A glass case cramped with trophies sat outside the

double doors to the gym. I'd helped win Benton a handful of those awards. We passed the library and a row of classrooms, places where I hadn't treated Nellie the way she'd deserved to be treated.

"I don't like being here," I said.

"Neither do I."

Reading her diary had been hard enough. Being here was like having every mistake, every wrong, thrown in my face. Like she'd teased . . . we'd returned to the scene of a crime.

Nellie matched my pace as I strode for the exit, hoping like hell there wasn't an alarm that would sound.

"Did you drive?" I asked.

"No, I came with Pierce's parents. After dinner, I told them they could leave, and I'd get a ride to the hotel."

"Which hotel? You know what, never mind." It didn't matter. Either she'd be staying in mine or I'd be moving into hers.

"Where are we going?" she asked as I pushed open the door, letting her step outside first.

"Somewhere that isn't tainted."

A place where I hadn't acted like a shithead to Nellie. Or where she hadn't overheard me acting like a shithead.

We passed a tall, chain-link fence that bordered the football field. Once upon a time, there'd been a side entrance that looked like it was chained shut but the staff had never actually closed the padlock. With any luck, that habit hadn't changed.

I stopped at the gate.

"This dress isn't made for climbing, Cal."

"Want me to help you take it off?" I smirked and tested

the lock. It popped open, so I loosened the chain enough to create a gap where we could slip through.

Nellie and I both gathered up the skirt of her gown, careful to keep it from ripping as she ducked beneath the chain.

When she was through, I followed, then took her hand once more and pulled her across the grass.

"Ah. Hold on." Her spiked heels dug into the ground, so she kicked off her shoes, carrying them as we walked toward the fifty-yard line.

The light from the school building cast a glow onto the field, highlighting the white yard lines and numbers. The chalk was fresh. It was the end of July and the kids would be starting practice soon, if they hadn't already.

I slowed my steps, my heart still racing, but now that we were outside, I felt like I could breathe. Now that I was on the field, a place where I'd spent countless hours, maybe I'd be able to do this. To be real with her. To be honest.

"I used to see you out here with your friends," she said, dropping her shoes before spinning around. Her hair whirled like the skirt of her dress. "I always wondered what it would be like to be one of you."

"You would have hated us even more. The girls especially."

"Probably." She laughed. "I saw Phoebe McAdams tonight. We crossed paths in the ladies' room. She didn't recognize me at first."

"She came up to me and said hello." She'd also thrust her wedding ring in my face like she'd expected me to be jealous. Phoebe had been self-absorbed in high school, and clearly, she hadn't grown out of it.

I stopped in the center of the field, watching Nellie as she looked around the field. Besides a new scoreboard, not much had changed since I'd played here as a kid. No doubt Dad would insist his million went to the athletics program. He could have his name on the field for all I cared.

I breathed in the fresh air and tilted my head to the sky.

With the city lights, there were no stars. Not like there was in Calamity.

"Why did you steal my diary?" Nellie came closer, then picked up her skirt to sit on the ground, leaning back on her arms.

I dropped to a seat, stretching out my legs beside hers. "An impulse."

"Let me rephrase. Why did you *keep* my diary?"

"Because it was yours." I lifted a hand and traced the line of her pretty nose. "Because I wanted that connection to you."

She hummed, turning to the sky. The waves of her hair draped behind her, the tips brushing the lawn.

"I love your hair." That seemed safe enough to admit. "I don't have a thing for blondes, but I really love your hair."

"Is that why you call me Blondie?"

"Yes. And I call you sugar because you're sweet to everyone but me."

She sat straight, drawing her knees to her chest. "Two compliments in a row. How much champagne have you had to drink tonight?"

"Not enough." I chuckled. "You're so smart, Nell. The smartest person I've ever met. I tease you about being a secretary, but you know it's only a joke, right?"

"Yeah." She nodded. "I didn't at first. But I do now."

"I'm . . ." Christ, this was hard. Baring your truths to another person—*the* person—was more intimidating than facing any opponent on any field. More terrifying than any loss. "I'm better at having people hate me than love me."

"I know."

Harry had told me that life was about finding the right people. The ones who'd take you at your worst, so you could give them your best. That was my Nellie.

I tucked a lock of hair behind her ear. "I don't want you to hate me."

"I don't."

That was something, but it wasn't enough. Like marching down the field but being short of the end zone by inches.

"I need you to say the words because I'm scared. Because I don't even know where to start. Show me where to start. Show me how to do this."

"You're not the only one who's scared, Cal. This is risky for me too."

"I get that." I swallowed hard. "Tell me what you *don't* hate about me."

Her eyes softened. "I love that you have a big heart hidden in that massive chest, even though you keep it a secret. I love that you love Pierce and his family. I love that you fight with me and you fight to win."

"More." I needed her to keep saying that one four-letter word.

"I love that you did things to protect me that I didn't understand at the time. Like that day with your dad."

And the day I'd thrown water on her. There were endless examples that I'd explain if she gave me the chance.

"I didn't know it would spiral," I said. "I didn't know he'd ruin your dad's business. For that, I'm sorry."

"I think when my dad learns the truth, he'll agree that you did the right thing."

"He's still my father." I sighed. "I've done my best, but there's no erasing the bastard."

"Lucky for you, he lives in Colorado, not Montana."

"Do I live in Montana?"

She lifted a shoulder. "Guess that's up to you."

"No, it's up to you."

"Then I say you live in Montana."

The air rushed from my lungs. "Thank fuck."

"But we can't keep doing this to each other. The secrets. The pretending we don't care. We have to stop hiding from each other. Cal, I lo—"

"Shut up." I pressed a finger to her lips.

That earned me a frown.

"I changed my mind. I want to say it first."

"Of course you do," she muttered when I dropped my finger.

I leaned in close. "I love you."

"I love you too."

I'd had a lot of victories in my life. This one? By far the sweetest. "Tell me you love me."

"What?" She leaned away. "I just did. Were you not listening to me? Seriously?"

"I heard you." I grinned. "Do it again."

She cupped my face. "I love you."

The words had barely escaped before I sealed my mouth over hers, sweeping inside for some of that sugar.

Nellie clung to my shoulders, kissing me until we were

both breathless. Then I swept her up off the ground, spinning her in my arms.

"Fuck, but I love you, woman."

Nellie wrapped her legs around my waist, her fingers threading through the hair at my temples.

A bank of lights on the school's second floor shut off. They were closing up, and it wouldn't be long before the entire building was dark.

"We'd better get out of here," Nellie said. "We could fly home tomorrow."

"Can't yet."

"Why? Did you have plans with your mom?"

"No. Now we have to spend the weekend fucking in a hotel." We'd do Charlotte and all the other hookups again, but this time, we'd do them better.

She rolled her eyes. "Cal Stark, you are such a romantic."

I brushed my mouth to hers. "If you want romance, I'll show you romance."

"Nah." She smiled against my lips. "Tell me more about this hotel room."

EPILOGUE

NELLIE

THREE YEARS LATER...

"Cal's, um, a little extreme." Mom tried to hide her eye roll, but she failed. "He realizes this is T-ball, right?"

"He just gets excited for the kids." And this was an improvement over the last three weekends, not something I'd admit to my parents. When it came to my husband, they were overly critical, so I'd learned to be careful about what I shared.

Mom and Dad, each seated in a camp chair beside mine, shared a look.

"Let's go. Let's go." Cal clapped his hands as the kids on our team raced out of the dugout with their gloves in hand. "Be ready, boys. Three up. Three down."

"Oh, my." Dad pinched the bridge of his nose.

I blew out a soothing breath, hoping some calming vibes would carry across the baseball diamond to my husband who paced along the baseline.

I'd carefully mentioned to Cal last week that too much pressure on these kids might dull the fun. It had instantly sobered the seriousness, and he'd backed off substantially today.

But even a quiet Cal was intense when it came to sports.

He might be taking his role as coach a bit seriously, but he was living for Tuesday night T-ball practices and Saturday afternoon games. So I'd kept my commentary on his intensity to myself.

Besides, the parents on the team didn't seem to mind that Cal showed up with black under-eye paint before each game and insisted the kindergarteners do laps around the bases before a set of pushups.

While Pierce was technically the head coach of Elias's baseball team, Cal had been such a strong influence as the assistant that most of the kids went straight to him for instruction.

Pierce didn't care because he met Cal's intensity beat for beat. The other dads were just as dedicated. A line of them stood behind the dugout as the unofficial cheer squad with water bottles at the ready for the inning change.

Meanwhile, I watched the games next to Kerrigan, each of us enduring the muttered comments from the mothers who weren't as competitive as their male counterparts.

"It's just a game," Dad said. "They're so little. Oof."

"He's doing it for Elias," I reminded him. "And he's a good coach. It's good practice for when Tripp is old enough for a team."

Dad hummed.

Mom bit her lip.

Gah! These two were driving me crazy. I'd been defending Cal for years, and this attitude of theirs was getting old.

"Mommy, where is my choc-it milk?" Tripp hopped up from his seat on the grass, enunciating each word as he planted his fists on his hips.

Tripp had the clearest diction of any two-year-old I'd ever met. With his articulation and his size—he'd surpassed every growth chart since birth thanks to Cal's giant genes—most people didn't believe me when I told them he was only two.

"You've had enough chocolate milk." I bent down and picked up the water bottle I'd stashed in my oversized purse. "You can have water."

Tripp's hazel eyes widened. "No water. I want my choc-it milk."

"Sorry, baby. All I have is water."

His face crumpled before he flung himself onto his knees and started to wail.

Now he looked two.

"Tripp Stark, we are not having a tantrum today about your milk." I bent to pick him up, but before I could haul him to his feet, Mom was out of her chair and fussing over her grandson.

They might be uncomfortable around Cal, but our son was adored.

"Oh, my little Tripp." She picked him up with a grunt. "Boy, you're getting big. How about we go to the swings and the slide?"

He clung to his *Nana*, wrapping his arms around her neck. As she set off for the playground, he glanced over her shoulder and shot me a glare.

That glare he'd learned from his father. I laughed and blew him a kiss. "Have fun!"

"He's got her wrapped around his pinky finger, doesn't he?" Dad chuckled, taking the chair that Mom had vacated. It was the same green chair Cal had bought years ago to sit outside that Winnebago he'd rented for a summer while his house was being built.

Our house.

After we'd come home from the Benton fundraiser, Cal had moved into my home. He'd complained for months that the house was too small for a man his size, that the hallways were too narrow and the stairs too shallow.

Months and months of muttered comments that I'd addressed with eye rolls. You'd think the man would have been thrilled to finally move into the house on the ranch. But the night before the moving crew had been scheduled to arrive, he'd hemmed and hawed about leaving that tiny brick house. *Moving is a pain, Nell. We could just stay.*

That time, I'd rolled my eyes so hard I'd given myself a migraine.

It wasn't like we'd done any actual moving. Cal had hauled exactly two boxes from the car to the house because when I'd picked up one to carry it myself, he'd had a conniption since I'd been pregnant with Tripp.

I'd thrown out my birth control pills on our Vegas wedding-slash-honeymoon week. It hadn't taken long for his all-star swimmers to score a touchdown.

"How are you feeling?" Dad asked, putting his hand over mine.

"Good." I reclined in my camp chair, pressing my free hand to my belly.

At five months pregnant, I was already showing. Cal was sure we were having another giant baby boy like Tripp, but I was holding out hope for a girl. Since we were waiting to be surprised, we'd find out who was right this September.

"I'm glad you guys are here," I told Dad. Even if their relationship with Cal was awkward, I'd missed my parents.

"Me too." He smiled and the two of us turned our attention to the baseball diamond where a little boy from the opposing team carried a bat toward the tee at home plate.

Mom and Dad had flown in for the week, and at some point during their stay, I was hoping to have a serious conversation about their future plans. They'd both tossed around the idea of retiring, and even if they only spent the summers in Montana, it would give my children the opportunity to have a close relationship with their grandparents.

Cal's father was non-existent in our lives but his mother visited every few months. And though I'd grown to love Regina, we'd always have Colter between us.

I had no idea if my parents could afford retirement yet, and they wouldn't touch a penny of Cal's money.

Dad's pride was expensive.

Even after three years, they were hesitant around Cal. Especially Dad. So naturally, instead of acting like the buffer, I made sure to thrust the two of them together as often as possible. Eventually they'd find something to bond over, right?

It hadn't been me or Tripp. Maybe the baby?

"Well, it's a good thing they don't keep score," Dad said

as the batter was thrown out at first, ending the game. "That was a killing."

"Yeah." The volunteer umpires might not keep score, but Cal did.

Dad stood and folded up our chairs, stuffing them in their cases.

Cal finished with the team and walked over to join us with a smug grin. "Twenty-five to zero."

"Congratulations, Coach."

"Uh . . . good game," Dad muttered.

"Thanks, Darius." Cal nodded. "I know I get a little into the game."

"Just a smidge," I teased.

He brushed his lips to mine. "How are you feeling?"

"Hungry. I'm ready for lunch."

"Where's Tripp?"

I pointed to the playground where Mom was pushing him on a swing. "I'll go get them and meet you at the car."

"I'll come with you," Dad said, giving Cal a hesitant glance.

"How about you guys load up the chairs?" I handed mine over before he could argue, then gave my husband a reassuring smile.

He nodded and set off for the car, matching his strides to Dad's.

Cal was trying. God, how he was trying. But Mom and Dad didn't know him well enough. They hadn't spent enough time in Calamity to see Cal fully let down his guard. Their three weekend trips a year hadn't been enough. And whenever we'd gone to Arizona, the visits had been too quick.

Mom and Dad had accepted my choice, but they were still cautious, especially Dad. He was still protecting me. He just didn't realize that it wasn't his job anymore.

It was Cal's.

I set off across the park toward the swing set and collected my son and mother. Then we all piled into our Escalade and headed home. Even with every window rolled down, the air in the SUV was sticky and thick. I sat behind Cal, meeting his eyes in the rearview mirror.

He looked miserable, and my parents' vacation was only beginning.

Mom and Dad had agreed to stay in our guesthouse instead of the motel. It meant they could be closer for Tripp, but it also meant they couldn't escape Cal like they had in their past visits. There'd be no space, no downtime to regroup.

I was grateful that we'd invited a bunch of people over tonight. Hopefully a crowd would diffuse some tension.

Mom and Dad thought this casual party was so they could meet our friends. Really, it was to give Cal a break from their scrutiny.

By the time we turned onto our property at the ranch, Tripp was as hangry as his mother, so we all congregated in the kitchen and scarfed sandwiches. Then Mom and Dad excused themselves and disappeared to the guesthouse.

"They still hate me," Cal said as the door closed behind them.

"Hate is a strong word. They don't hate you." I walked to his side, wrapping my arms around his waist. "But yeah, it's awkward."

He frowned. "Gee. Thanks."

"They'll come around."

"You've been saying that for three years, sugar."

"And I still believe it's true. Look how long it took you to win me over?"

"So by the time Tripp graduates from high school, they might like me?"

"Give or take a few years."

"It's not fair." He sighed. "My mother loves you."

Regina did love me. Whatever standoffishness she'd had initially hadn't lasted long. The day Cal had called to tell her we were getting married, she'd sent me two dozen roses. And as soon as we'd made it back from Vegas, she'd flown to Calamity to spend a week in Montana, mostly to get to know her new daughter-in-law. She adored her son and loved mine entirely.

"This will be a good week," I told him. "I have a good feeling."

He shrugged, already putting up the wall so no one but me would see how deep my parents' aloof attitude cut.

If they didn't start lightening up by tomorrow, we were going to have a very long, very overdue chat about their feelings toward my husband.

"I'm going to put Tripp down for his nap." Cal kissed the top of my hair. "Maybe lie down with him."

"Okay. I'm going to get a few things ready for tonight."

His hand splayed across my stomach. "You'd better rest too."

"I will." I leaned my temple against his heart, taking a long inhale of his scent, then let him go so he could snuggle with Tripp.

They both fell asleep on our bed, the two of them curled

together while I walked around the house, picking up toys before settling on the couch to read for an hour. When the guys finally woke up, both of them with mussed hair in that same shade of chocolate brown, the caterer buzzed in from the gate at the driveway.

Our home at the ranch was a dream. The land itself was beautiful, nestled against the mountain foothills with sweeping meadows and a view worth millions. Cal had insisted on a state-of-the-art security system to keep out the *crazies*.

At eight thousand square feet, the house was larger and fancier than any home I'd ever had. And though I loved living here, it screamed wealth. And that scream was yet another thing driving a wedge between Cal and my parents.

They'd probably balk at the fact that we'd hired a caterer for the party instead of cooking ourselves, but Cal had insisted. He didn't want tonight to be stressful for anyone, especially his wife.

So as the caterer assumed control of my kitchen, my parents returned from the guesthouse, settling in the living room with their attention fixed on Tripp. They barely looked at Cal, so he turned on ESPN for some background noise.

Thankfully, Pierce and Kerrigan arrived with their kids. Larke showed up next, followed by the rest of our friends from town. Harry arrived last, and as usual, knew everyone but my parents.

Mom and Dad were the epitome of friendly. They laughed and joked with our friends, but they always chose the cluster that didn't include Cal.

Yeah, we were most definitely having a chat tomorrow.

"Ugh," I muttered, plucking a carrot from the vegetable tray on the kitchen island.

"What's wrong?" Larke asked.

"I'll tell you later. It's just more of the same crap with my parents and Cal. At our next girls' night, I'll give you the full scoop."

"Yeah, I've, uh . . . got a little scoop of my own."

"You do?" I studied her face, my gaze dropping to her water glass. Everyone in the house was drinking a beer or glass of sangria. Everyone but me. And Larke. "You're not drinking."

"I'm not drinking."

My jaw dropped. "Are you pre—"

"Shhh." She put a finger to her lips. "I haven't told anyone yet. Including Kerrigan."

"But you're telling me? Before your sister?"

"Duh. You're my best friend."

"Aww." I pulled her into my arms. "You're my best friend too."

I'd made a lot of best friends in Calamity. The absolute best? Cal. Not that I'd admit it. His ego still needed tending.

"Details later," I said, letting Larke go and lowering my voice. "I had no idea you've been sleeping with someone."

"I'm not. I mean, I did, but just as a fling." She checked over her shoulder to make sure no one was listening. "I met him in Hawaii."

"Oh."

Our girls-only trip had never happened. Larke, Kerrigan and I had gone to Hawaii, but both Cal and Pierce had tagged along. Larke hadn't said it, but I got the impression she'd felt like the fifth wheel, so this year for spring break, she'd taken a beach vacation alone.

And got knocked up.

"Who—"

Before I could finish my sentence, Pierce hollered, "Hey, Nellie! Get in here! Cal, you too."

I rushed to the living room, expecting to find something wrong with Tripp, but he was off playing somewhere with the other kids. "What?"

Every adult stared at the television.

Pierce snagged the remote from the end table and cranked the volume.

"What's going on?" Cal came in behind me, his hands going to my shoulders. Then he saw the screen. "Oh."

Before he could sneak out, I slapped my hand over his, holding him to me. "Don't you dare disappear."

Next to the ESPN announcer's face was a headshot of Cal. "This next story tonight is going to pull at your heart-strings. Many of you remember Cal Stark who was just inducted into the Pro Football Hall of Fame. The former star quarterback for the Tennessee Titans is making news again this spring after donating thirty million dollars to create a sports camp outside Bozeman, Montana for disabled children and kids with terminal illnesses."

I leaned against Cal's body, smiling as the announcer continued to explain how the camp was currently under construction and would open next summer.

We'd already started receiving online applications for kids interested in attending. Pierce was kicking in fifteen million too, and though he'd hated doing it, Cal had been calling former teammates and NFL colleagues, either to donate time or make celebrity appearances at the camp.

"The camp is named Camp Hollis York after a youth who met Stark through the Make-A-Wish Foundation," the announcer said. "Sadly, Hollis passed years ago, but not before making an impression on Stark. In the press release, Stark said, and I quote, 'Hollis York was a brave and kind soul. Knowing him was one of the greatest privileges in my life. This camp is to honor his memory and celebrate his love of sports.'"

My eyes flooded as I looked up to Cal.

He swallowed hard, wrapping an arm around my shoulders to pull me closer. Then before I could stop him, he let me go and escaped to the kitchen, hollering, "Let's eat."

Pierce handed me the remote and followed Cal. Then the rest of the party retreated, leaving only Mom, Dad and me with the television.

"Was it your idea for the camp?" Dad asked.

"No, it was his."

Dad shared a look with Mom, then stood, passing me for the kitchen. He walked right to Cal, clapped him on the shoulder and gave him a nod. "Proud of you, Cal. That camp is a great idea."

"Thanks, Darius."

"And good idea, catering this shindig. Save Nellie and you the hassle of cooking. Plus we'll have leftovers while we're here this week."

"Uh . . . yeah." Cal looked at Dad, then to me.

I smiled wider.

"He's a good man, isn't he?" Mom asked, coming to my side.

"The best."

She sighed. "We haven't taken enough time to get to know him."

"No, you haven't."

"I'm sorry. We'll do better."

"Thanks, Mom."

Tripp flew past us, racing toward the kitchen and Cal. "Daddy, can I have my choc-it milk?"

I laughed and went to the fridge, pouring my son some milk in his favorite cup. Then I retreated to the living room to shut off the TV.

A pair of strong arms banded around me as I tossed the remote on the couch.

"I'm proud of you too," I told Cal.

"Team effort."

He'd told me his idea for the camp not long after our wedding, and from the moment he'd voiced his dream, I'd been right at his side, encouraging him to see it through. Once football had consumed his life. Now, his focus was our family. But this camp was a wonderful purpose for him and a chance for him to stay connected to the game he loved so much.

I spun around, rising on my toes for a kiss. "I love you."

"Love you too."

"Mommy, I need more." Tripp came running my way, his already empty cup thrust into the air.

"Okay, baby." I took the cup, knowing I was in for a fight because it was getting refilled with water.

"Nell. Wait."

"Yeah?" I turned to see one of Cal's heart-stopping smiles.

"Tell me what you hate about me."

Years together and he'd never quit this little game. I'd had to get creative since, when it came to Cal, there was a lot more to love than to hate.

"I hate that you're going to snub our guests later and haul me to the bedroom for a quickie. It's rude, Cal."

"And I'm not even sorry."

I winked. "Neither am I."

BONUS EPILOGUE

CAL

"Nellie!" I bellowed from the bedroom, slamming the drawer to my nightstand closed.

Where the hell were my diaries?

I marched out of the bedroom and down the hallway to search for my infuriating thief of a wife.

"Nellie," I hollered again, getting no reply. "Damn it."

Tripp's room was empty as I poked my head inside. There was a pile of Hot Wheels on the carpet next to a labyrinth of orange racetracks.

Trinity's room was empty and trashed too. Instead of dolls or dress-up clothes strewn on the floor, my four-year-old daughter had set up a putting green this morning. Her plastic golf caddy was turned upside down and the balls were everywhere. My girl loved her sports.

Over the years, both Tripp and Trinity had spent weeks with me at Camp Hollis. Football. Baseball. Basketball. Soccer. Volleyball. They knew the rules of each sport better than most adults. My kids, like me, loved to play sports and they'd been blessed with natural athletic abilities.

Tripp preferred basketball, and at six, was almost able to shoot a full-sized ball into a ten-foot hoop. He swished them into the eight-foot height without much struggle. But my Trinity refused to choose a favorite game. She was constantly throwing balls, inside or outside the house. Her closet was stuffed with a collection of balls and clubs and bats.

The putting green, and Tripp's Hot Wheels, would need to be cleaned up before bed tonight, but not until I'd found my wife and my diaries.

I stalked down the hallway. "Nellie!"

Silence.

Fuck.

She was probably hiding because she knew I was pissed.

I walked faster, bypassing the empty living room and kitchen. I was about to head for the opposite end of the house to see if she was in her office when a flash of blond hair caught my eye.

Nellie stood on the deck with the mountain foothills and autumn trees in the backdrop beyond our sprawling yard.

I ripped open the door and stepped outside to find my wife sitting beside the gas firepit.

Was she warming her hands on this crisp fall day? No. She was tearing pages out of a book—my book—and setting them ablaze.

"What the fuck are you doing?"

"What's it look like?"

"Don't." I reached for the last bundle of pages in her hands, but I was too late. She dropped them into the flames.

"There." She swiped her hands. On the cushion beside her were the empty shells of her high school diaries. "Done."

I dragged a hand through my hair, my heart dropping. "You burned my books."

"No, I burned *my* books."

"Those diaries are mine." They'd been mine since I'd found the first one in her office. They'd been mine since I'd claimed the others not long after our wedding.

"Oh, really?" She arched her eyebrows. "Did you write them?"

"No, but damn it, woman." I loved those diaries. "Why would you do that?"

"Because I am sick of talking about high school." She shot off the couch. "I'm sick of you obsessing over the past."

"I don't obsess—"

"Yes, you do. Case in point, our fight last night."

I scoffed. "It wasn't a fight." Maybe a heated discussion, but there'd been no shouting or name-calling. And we'd had sex afterward. If it had been a real fight, Nellie wouldn't have let me touch her.

"Semantics." She flicked her wrist. "You got mad because I called you shallow our junior year."

"I wasn't mad." Okay, I'd been mad. "I just wanted to understand."

"I've told you that story a hundred times. I called you shallow because you were acting shallow."

"They were new shoes."

She looked to the clear, blue sky. "God, give me patience so I don't strangle the father of my children."

"They were new shoes," I repeated. "Any kid would have been pissed."

I'd been walking to chemistry and carrying a hot chocolate. Someone passing in the opposite direction had bumped me, and a blob of cocoa had escaped my cup and landed on my new Nikes. They'd been a birthday gift from Mom, and I'd been pissed, a fact I'd made sure the entire class had known. Nellie had been sitting in the front row and had heard my bitching.

That night, I'd made her diary.

"We were teenagers, Cal. None of it matters. How you acted. What I wrote. It's pointless. But every time you read one of my diaries, you take us back there. And I'm tired of going back there. So freaking tired. Can't you understand that?"

Well . . . fuck. "Yeah. I can. But I liked reading your journals."

"Why?"

"Because it's a connection to you." I shrugged. "And maybe because it's my way of atoning for those mistakes. I can at least explain some of them."

"First of all, you've explained them. Ad nauseam."

Technically, this was the third discussion about the shallow comment, but in my defense, the previous conversations had been years ago.

"And secondly, atonement isn't necessary." She stepped closer, fitting her hands to my waist as the last of the paper turned to ash beside us. "I love you. But the time of the diaries is over."

"I love you too." I sighed and pulled her into my arms, dropping my cheek to her head. "I can't believe you fucking burned them."

She laughed. "You'll get over it."

"Not likely," I grumbled.

"Daddy!" Trinity raced around the corner with a soccer ball in her hands. "Can you play with me?"

That was a question she asked me fifty times a day. And I did my best to always say yes.

"Sure, princess." I let Nellie go, but not before dropping a kiss to her lips.

"I'm going to make dinner," she said.

"Okay." I started for the stairs that dropped to the lawn. "Where's your brother?"

"I don't know." Trinity's eyes were as green as her mother's as she tipped her head to the sky and screamed, "Tripp!"

My girl had a pair of lungs.

"What?" Tripp called, pedaling his bike through the grass from where he must have been riding in the driveway.

"We're playing soccer, bud," I said.

"Okay." The bike was dropped and he raced over, stealing the ball from his sister's arms.

"Hey! No fair." She elbowed him and the two of them ran around, bickering, until I finally intervened and kicked off a game.

The full-sized goal I'd had installed next to the basketball court hadn't gone to waste.

An hour later, with red faces and big smiles, we rushed inside as Nellie summoned us to dinner. The normal nighttime routine consumed the rest of the night, and after the kids were bathed and dressed in their pajamas, we picked up their rooms and settled on the couch for a movie. Both Trinity and Tripp were asleep by the time the credits rolled.

We tucked them into bed, and as we eased their bedroom

doors closed, Nellie met me in the hallway and took my hand. "Close your eyes."

I obeyed and let her tug me down the hallway toward our own bedroom.

"One more step," she said, then pressed a hand to my heart. "Okay. Stop. Open your eyes."

"What am I looking at?" I scanned the room.

There was the same ridiculous number of decorative pillows on the bed. The bottle of peppermint foot cream on Nellie's nightstand was out, probably because she'd beg for a foot massage later. She had her Kindle plugged into its charger.

And where I'd had her diary, my nightly reading, there was a new leather-bound book in its place.

"What's that?"

She smirked and shut the door, flipping the lock. "Read it and find out."

I crossed the room, opened the journal and read the one and only written entry.

The entry where Nellie described exactly how she'd felt while I'd fucked her last night. An entry that used a lot of words I wouldn't have found in her high school journals. An entry that made me hard as a goddamn rock.

"What is this?"

She sauntered my way, unbuttoning her jeans. "I burned the old diaries. But I never said I wouldn't replace them."

"With this?" I held up the book, one I'd make sure my kids never found.

"There are a lot of pages in there, Cal. Think you've got enough moves to keep the content interesting?"

"Is that a challenge?"

She grinned and whipped off her shirt. "Yep."

"You're on." I surged, picking her up and tossing her on the bed.

Then I got to work, making sure she had plenty of material for my new diary.

ACKNOWLEDGMENTS

Thank you for reading *The Bully*! Nellie and Cal's book poured out of me, and I hope you enjoyed reading their story as much as I loved writing it.

Special thanks to the incredible team who contributed their talents to this book. My editor, Marion Archer. My proofreaders, Julie Deaton, Karen Lawson and Judy Zweifel. My cover designer, Sarah Hansen.

Thanks to Monica Murphy for being such an amazing friend, peer and author. To Jenn for being my football guru and wonderful friend. To Nina for all that you do. A huge thanks to the members of Perry & Nash for loving my books whether they are from Devney Perry or Willa Nash. To the fantastic bloggers who take the time to read and post about my stories, thank you! And lastly, thanks to my friends and family. I'm so thankful for you all.

ABOUT THE AUTHOR

Devney Perry is a *Wall Street Journal* and *USA Today* bestselling author of over forty romance novels. After working in the technology industry for a decade, she abandoned conference calls and project schedules to pursue her passion for writing. She was born and raised in Montana and now lives in Washington with her husband and two sons.

Don't miss out on the latest book news.
Subscribe to her newsletter!
www.devneyperry.com